I0764547

HIGH MOOR

MOONSTRUCK

GRAEME REYNOLDS

First Published by Horrific Tales Publishing 2013

This Edition Published by Horrific Tales Publishing 2021

http://www.horrifictales.com

A CIP catalogue record for this book is available from the British Library

ISBN: 978-1-910283-35-6

Cover Artwork by Ben Baldwin

HIGH MOOR: MOONSTRUCK

BY

GRAEME REYNOLDS

PROLOGUE

26th October 1996. Böhmerwald Forest, Germany. 18:06.

Megan leaned against the window and watched the sky darken above the silhouetted outline of the forest. She let out an exaggerated sigh and stomped back into the cabin's main living area with her arms folded, flopping down on the threadbare sofa. "It's not fair, Marie. Why couldn't I go with Connie, James and Isaac?"

Marie stood in the kitchen area, slicing vegetables for the evening meal. "You know why. Because your Mam and Dad said so. Now stop your moaning and get me the tinned tomatoes from the pantry."

Megan groaned, got up from the sofa, and shuffled towards the cupboard where the food was stored. "Well, can't I at least go outside and play before dinner? I won't go far."

"No, and you know the reason for that, as well."

A shadow passed across the young girl's face. "Because of the bad man?"

Marie put down the knife and turned to face her, then crouched so that their eyes were level. "Yes. Because of the bad man. It's dangerous out there, Megan, and I promised Connie that I'd take care of you while she and your Dad are out getting food."

The girl's brow creased. "The bad man will never find us all the way out here, though, will he? Not this far in the woods."

"I hope not, Megan. I really do."

"Marie, when can we go home? I don't like it here. My bedroom smells and I miss my friends."

Marie turned her head so that Megan wouldn't see the damp sparkle of tears in her eyes, but couldn't control the waver in her voice when she spoke. "We can't go home, sweetie. Not back to where we were. The others will find a new place for us to be safe, but until then we need to stay out of sight. Do you understand?"

Megan put on her most serious face. "I think so. Do you miss them? Michael and the others?"

She nodded and wiped the moisture from the corners of her eyes. "Yes. I miss them and I'm looking forward to seeing them all again. In the meantime, though, I'm supposed to be making dinner. Do you want to help?"

Megan shook her head and made a face. "No, those vegetables smell like sick. Do I have to eat them?"

"Yes, you have to eat them. If you're not going to help then go and play with your dolls or something. Your Mam won't be happy if the food's not ready when she gets back."

Megan considered her options for a moment, then turned and ran to her bedroom, slamming the door shut behind her.

Marie couldn't help but grin. Megan reminded her of herself at that age, and she was beginning to understand what her poor mother had had to put up with.

Half an hour later, Marie poured herself a large glass of wine and collapsed on the sofa. The evening meal bubbled away on the stove and she'd cleaned the kitchen area, although Megan was supposed to have helped with that. Now she thought about it, Megan had been very quiet since she'd gone to her room. "Megan, come and help set the table for dinner," she called to the closed door.

When no response was forthcoming, she got to her feet and called again, louder this time. "Megan, I'm not going to tell you again."

Silence.

She walked over to Megan's room and knocked on the door. "Megan, are you alright?"

The front door burst open and slammed against the cabin wall. Connie and Isaac stumbled inside. Connie was holding her husband up. Blood gushed from a huge wound in his chest and bubbled between his lips. Isaac's eyes were glazed black orbs and he was barely conscious. Connie glared at Marie. "What are ye standing there for, ye daft cow? Fucking help me!"

The sound of Connie's voice broke Marie's trance. She rushed forward and helped to lay Isaac across the large wooden table in the centre of the room, then closed and bolted the cabin door.

Connie ripped open Isaac's shirt and choked back a sob. While the entry wound was small, the exit wound was the size of her fist. Blood pumped from the gaping hole in her husband's back and his eyes rolled back in their sockets. She turned to Marie. "Get me something to stop the blood. Oh God, Isaac, don't you fucking die on me, you tosser." Marie grabbed a clean white sheet from her bedroom and tore it into makeshift bandages which Connie used to staunch the flow of blood. Then Isaac's entire body shuddered and he lay still.

Connie scrunched her eyes tight closed and turned away from the body of her husband. Marie put a hand on her shoulder, but she shook it away. When she opened her eyes, the grief had been replaced by a cold fury. "We've got to get out of here. He's found us."

The realisation hit Marie like a hammer blow. "Where's James?"

Connie shook her head. "Ah'm sorry. He's gone. Come on, we need to get going. We don't have much time." She looked around the room, then up at Marie. "Where's Megan?"

"In her room. She went in there to play while I made dinner."

Connie strode over to her daughter's bedroom and flung open the door, to find the room empty and the window wide open. She turned back to Marie, her lips curling into a snarl. "Ye were supposed to be watching her, Marie. She's gone, and that fucker is out there, hunting us. If anything's happened to her, Ah'll tear yer fucking heart out."

Marie reeled at her friend's outburst, a wave of guilt and surprise washing over her, and for a moment she didn't know what to say. She shook the feeling off. "Come on, she won't have gone far. I'll check towards the river. You head down to the track. We'll find her, and then get the hell out of here, okay?"

"Alright, but if anything's happened to her..."

"I know, now stop wasting time. You can yell at me when we've found her."

Marie unbolted the cabin door and opened it the smallest crack. The woods were dark and silent. The clearing around the cabin shone in the moonlight, but she could see nothing beyond the first row of trees. She listened for any sound that might help them find Megan or betray the position of their unseen assailant, but all she could hear was the chill autumn wind whistling through the threadbare branches and, in the distance, the lone cry of a solitary owl hunting. There could be no-one there, or the hunter could have the door fixed in his crosshairs. She had no way of knowing.

As she forced the fear down, Connie shoved past her and darted from the doorway, disappearing into the darkness within seconds.

Marie stepped back into the room and undressed as quickly as she could, throwing her clothes into a crumpled pile on the floor. The change swept through her almost immediately. Blinding pain seared through her as her bones splintered and reformed. Fangs burst through her gums as her jaw elongated into a razor-filled muzzle and her ears elongated. After less than thirty seconds, the woman had been replaced by sleek, muscular, brown-furred monster.

She burst from the open doorway and zigzagged her way across the clearing until she reached the relative safety of the treeline. The sounds and smells of the forest assailed her senses, and as she ran, she tried to sort through the myriad sensations.

Connie's scent was distinct, strong and vibrant with a hint of fear. She sensed a family of deer quivering in a thicket to the north, and the musky odour of a female fox slinking back to her den, hoping to avoid the attention of the predators in its midst. Megan's scent was vague, seeming to come from everywhere.

Marie knew instantly what the girl had done. She'd masked her true scent by spraying every bit of undergrowth around the cabin, making her scent harder to find among the others. The girl was playing the werewolf equivalent of hide and seek. She let out a small whine of frustration. She couldn't have picked a worse time to torment her babysitter.

Marie darted through the woods as quickly as she dared, trying to get beyond the range of Megan's scent markers. Once she was outside the circle, she'd be able to loop around its circumference and pick up the girl's scent again, or at least she hoped she could.

A shot rang out to the south west and echoed around the trees before the forest fell silent again. The faintest hint of blood hung in the air. Marie turned towards the gunshot and ran. The trees became a blur and the stench of blood steadily became overpowering, almost sending her wolf into a frenzy before she was able to calm it. She slowed her pace, moving through the forest like a ghost, a soundless mass of hair and muscle. The blood was overloading her sense of smell. Every time she tried to focus on something else, her instincts brought her right back to it.

As she drew close, she crouched in a patch of bracken and strained her senses to no avail. The stench of the fresh blood saturated her mind and her wolf snarled in the back of her psyche, eager to resume the hunt. It was no use. She'd have to get closer and hope the hunter did something to betray his location.

She reached the edge of the bracken and lay flat on her belly. Connie lay behind an ancient oak tree, clutching her left leg in an attempt to stop the bleeding. Part of her thigh muscle had been blown off and fresh blood pumped around her fingers, glistening black in the moonlight.

She looked up and her eyes met Marie's. Connie shook her head almost imperceptibly and nodded in the direction of a thick patch of brambles a few hundred feet away. Megan lay at the edge of the clearing, just before the bramble thicket. A silver bear-trap gripped her rear leg and Marie could see the white gleam of bone through her blood-soaked fur.

Megan sensed Marie and her tail thumped on the ground, despite her agony. Marie let out a low warning growl and tried to locate the hunter. Her senses were still clouded, but a change in the direction of the wind brought another scent to her. Human sweat against metal and wood. Beyond the brambles in a makeshift hide.

She thought of Isaac, lying dead in the cabin, and James, who'd looked out for her when she had first joined The Pack and had become her lover, now a corpse somewhere in the forest. She felt a cold rage build inside her. If Connie and little Megan were to have any chance of survival, she needed to eliminate the threat. She moved away from the clearing, back into the woods. Circling the hidden hunter. Imagining the taste of his blood in her mouth.

The scent became stronger, tinged with fear and anticipation. The bastard knew that there were other werewolves in the area and he was waiting for them to stumble into his trap, oblivious to the fact that the game had changed and he was now the prey.

A thick, sharpened branch slashed out from the darkness and plunged into her side, pinning her against a fallen tree. She yelped in agony and tried to pull herself free as the wound healed around the makeshift trap, but it was no use. She wasn't going anywhere.

The hunter broke cover and moved through the undergrowth, keeping his rifle aimed at her. He moved past Megan, whimpering in the bear trap, towards the tree where Connie lay. He stepped around the tree in a wide arc, with the weapon covering his approach. As he rounded the tree, his shoulders sagged. "Son of a bitch." He scanned the undergrowth for signs of movement, then turned back to Megan and removed an ornate pistol from his jacket.

Megan had reverted to her human form and looked up at the approaching hunter with tear-filled eyes. "Please, Mister. Please don't hurt me. I just want to go home. I just want to..."

The hunter paused and appeared uncertain, then he shook his head, aimed the pistol at the young girl, and shot her between the eyes. Blood and brains sprayed across the mouldering leaves of the forest floor, and Megan slumped to the ground.

Marie screamed and thrashed against the wooden stake embedded in her stomach. The pain was dreadful, but it paled beside her need to tear the hunter into ribbons. The flesh of her abdomen split open and blood poured from the wound, but Marie did not stop. She welcomed the blinding agony and used it to fuel her rage.

The branch tore loose with a wet ripping sound and Marie lurched free of the trap, to stand face-to-face with the hunter. Steven Wilkinson. The man who had stalked and slaughtered dozens of her kind over the last decade. The monster that had just killed Megan in cold blood.

She hurled herself towards him, giving herself to the animal ferocity of her beast. Feeling it rush through her system like a drug. Letting it take control. She covered the distance in less than a second and leaped into the air in a flurry of teeth, claws and muscle.

Marie didn't hear the gunshot. She felt herself propelled backwards in mid-leap, to crash to the forest floor. She struggled to rise, but had no strength in her limbs. Her bones cracked back into place, and her thick brown fur retreated into the pores of her skin. She raised her head and saw the face of the hunter, triumphant, then watched as his face contorted into a mask of terror when distant howling echoed through the forest. He turned and looked at her with disgust in his eyes, then spat on the ground. "Fucking werewolves." Then he shouldered his rifle and walked away into the woods.

Megan lay a few feet away, and Marie dragged herself over to the body of the young girl. She took one of Megan's hands in hers, and gently closed the dead girl's eyes. "I swear to you, Megan. I'll get him. I'll find that fucker and I'll tear his heart out."

Then, with the last of her strength, she laid her head against Megan's chest and let the world go dark.

CHAPTER 1

15th November 2008. Newcastle Airport. 10:30

Gregorz leaned back on the hard wooden chair. He watched in amusement as the red-haired woman wove her way through the milling crowds, three large coffees balanced on a brown plastic tray. A small boy darted between the tables, the woman having to lurch to one side to avoid him. She deposited the tray on the table then sat in the empty seat.

"Ye can get your own bloody coffee next time, Gregorz. If Ah have to dodge out the way of another screaming brat, Ah'm gonna rip the little shit's head off."

The table's other occupant, a tall, grey-haired man in a business suit, picked up his steaming cup and chuckled. "But I think you'd make an exceptional waitress, Connie. Perhaps you've missed your calling in life?"

Connie glowered at him. "Ye can fuck right off, Daniel. Make another comment like that, and ye'll be wearing that damn coffee. It might even improve your cheap suit."

Gregorz leaned forward. "Come now, children, playtime is over. We're here to work. Daniel, have you heard from Oskar's team?"

Daniel nodded. "They landed at around nine this morning, on the Munich flight. Oskar is assessing the situation, but it's not looking good. The moonstruck is in police custody, so it'll be hard for them to get near. *Especially* before the next full moon."

Gregorz scratched his chin. "It's a serious problem, but we have one of our own to deal with. We need to retrieve Marie's body from the hospital, and make sure that no blood samples or DNA tests survive. If things go well, then we'll join up with Oskar's team later on and help them deal with the moonstruck."

Connie blew the foam from her coffee and took a sip. "Ah don't see why we're on corpse clean-up duty. This team's taken down a lot more moonstruck than Oskar's, with fewer casualties. We should be taking care of things while they take what's left of that stupid bitch Marie back to her brother."

"We've been over this, Connie. Oskar has Gabriela and Troy with him. Michael felt that a more subtle approach was called for. It's a delicate situation, and we need to be careful not to make things worse than they already are."

Connie snorted. "Subtle? Is Gabriela going to screw her way to the moonstruck?"

Daniel laughed. "And how would you handle the situation, Connie? With your trademark tact and diplomacy? I suppose you would have us attack the police station head-on and simply kill everyone inside?"

Connie shrugged. "What's wrong with that? Simple, effective, and no witnesses."

Daniel nodded to Gregorz. "See, Connie can be subtle when she feels like it. If you ignore the pile of half-eaten corpses, no one would ever know that we'd been there."

Gregorz shook his head and let out a sigh, very much aware of the nervous glances they were getting from the other people in the coffee shop. He lowered his voice so that it was barely above a whisper. "That's enough. Both of you. We need to focus on the task before us. Marie died over twelve hours ago. While I doubt that an autopsy would have been performed yet, they may have taken blood samples for analysis. Connie and I will retrieve Marie's body from the morgue. Arrangements are in place to ship it back to Russia. Daniel, you will make sure that any evidence is destroyed."

Connie folded her arms. "Does it not make more sense for Daniel to help shift the dead bitch's body? Ah'll take care of the evidence. It's not like Ah haven't done it before."

Gregorz sighed. "Okay, Connie. If you are averse to a little heavy lifting, then Daniel and I will deal with Marie while you take care of the evidence. But please, no killing. We need to be in and out of this hospital without arousing any kind of suspicion. Can you do that for me?"

Connie took a sip from her coffee and gave Gregorz her sweetest smile. "Why of course. Didn't you know? Subtle is ma middle name."

15th November. High Moor Police Station. 13:00.

John wished that he were dead. White hot lances of agony burned into his nerve endings, despite the painkillers. Worse than this, though, was the realisation of what he'd lost, and what was going to happen next.

He closed his eyes and held his head in his hands, seeing the same image play across his mind over and over again. Marie, lying dead on the cold concrete paving slabs, riddled with silver bullets from Steven's Mac-10. A wave of grief surged up from his stomach and he fought to hold back the tears.

Oh God, Marie, you stupid cow. If you'd just told me, then we could have avoided all this. You'd still be alive. Malcolm and the others, too. Deep down, John knew that wasn't true. He realised it as soon as the thought flashed through his mind. Marie might have tried to draw him out, but he was the one that took the bait, infected Malcolm, and killed Billy, Simon and Lawrence. He deserved everything that was coming.

John opened his eyes again, unable to bear the memories, and looked around the room. Its floor, ceiling and walls were solid concrete, walls painted a dull olive green and the floor covered with threadbare green carpet tiles. A table was bolted to the floor, as were the chairs, and the only way in or out of the room was through a heavy steel door. The thick floral stench of cheap disinfectant hung in the air like a cloud.

The door opened, and two people stepped inside, a slightly overweight man in his mid forties, and a younger blonde woman with a severe expression on her face. The man placed an ancient tape recorder on the end of the desk and pressed the record button.

"Interview with John Simpson, tape 1. 15th November 2008.

13.10hrs. DI Fletcher and DC Garner are present in the room, along with the suspect."

They both sat down, and the man leaned back in the chair. "Good afternoon, John. I'm Detective Inspector Phil Fletcher, and this is my colleague, Detective Constable Olivia Garner. Can I get you anything before we start? Tea? Coffee?"

John shook his head.

"No? Alright, then I suppose we should get down to it. My colleague and I were wondering if you'd like to tell us about what happened last night?"

John raised his head and looked into the other man's eyes. "Phil, you wouldn't believe me if I told you. How's Steven? Is he alright?"

DC Garner scribbled something down on a notepad and showed it to her colleague. He nodded and turned back to John.

"Mr Wilkinson is alive, but as I understand it, is critically injured."

John leaned forward in the chair. He had to ask, even though he knew the answer. "And Marie? Is she..."

DI Fletcher shook his head. "If you're referring to the young woman that was found at the scene, then I'm sorry but she was pronounced dead on arrival. You say her name was Marie? Marie what?"

John sucked in a breath. Hearing her name was like sandpaper on his soul. His voice cracked when he spoke. "...Williams. Her name was Marie Williams."

DI Fletcher sat back in his chair and interlocked his fingers behind his head. "I have to say, John, it's not looking too good for you. There were several unregistered firearms found at the scene, including the one that killed Miss Williams, and they have your fingerprints all over them. Not only that, but you were found with half of Mr Harrison's throat in your mouth, lying naked over his corpse.

"Even possession of a weapon like that Ingram will get you five years, and that's before we take the deaths into account. So come on, John, why don't you tell me what happened, so we can sort this mess out?"

John sat back and exhaled a deep breath. "You want to know what happened? Really?"

"No, John. We're just sitting in here because we like the decor. Why don't you start from the beginning?"

John managed a lopsided grin, despite the stitches in his face. "Be careful what you wish for, Phil. You might just get it. You want the truth? OK, I'll give you the truth."

15th November. University Hospital of Durham. 13:00

Doctor Henry Pearce pushed the pieces of grey meat around his plate without any enthusiasm. The food in the hospital cafeteria was barely edible at the best of times, and, judging from the thin gruel on his plate masquerading as Lancashire Hotpot, today was not one of the good days. Of course, given what he'd witnessed during the autopsy of Malcolm Harrison that morning, he doubted that even a meal in a five-star restaurant would have done much for his appetite right now.

The injuries to the corpse had been horrific. In twenty years as a pathologist, he'd never seen anything like it. The police report that accompanied the body stated that the injuries were caused by another man, but everything about the corpse indicated that the terrible wounds were the work of a large animal. Henry honestly could not imagine how another human being would be able to inflict that amount of damage.

The mental image of the eviscerated cadaver caused his stomach to churn, and his mouth filled with the aftertaste of the hotpot. It wasn't any more appetising coming up than it had been going down. He pushed his plate away in disgust, cleared the table, and poured the remains of the meal into the waste bin. From the notes he'd been given that morning, this afternoon was not going to be any better, either. Gunshot wounds never were. He left the cafeteria and moved along the cheerfully painted corridors to the elevator that would take him to the basement pathology lab.

The doors slid open and he stepped out. Here, the bright decoration adorning the public areas was conspicuous by its absence. Instead, cold white ceramic tiles covered the lower part of the walls, while the old beige paintwork above them blistered with age and salt residue from the brickwork. The air smelled thickly of disinfectant and formaldehyde. Harsh fluorescent lighting ran the length of the corridor, buzzing and flickering.

He'd reported the fault to the maintenance department numerous times and so far no one had bothered to come down here to fix it. He'd speak to them again about it, once he'd performed the next autopsy, and his mood was sufficiently foul.

A door swung open, and his assistant, Susan Turnbull, stepped into the corridor. She already wore her hospital scrubs, ready for the afternoon's procedure.

"How was lunch, Henry? Did they manage to come up with something edible today?"

He shook his head. "Not even close. It was the hotpot again, but I have no idea what meat they put in it. *If* it was lamb like they claim, the poor thing must have had something very wrong with it. Are we set for this afternoon?"

Susan nodded. "Jenkins brought the body down from the morgue about ten minutes ago. It's still bagged up, so I've not had a chance to see how bad it is yet," she winked at him, "I thought I'd save the honours for you."

He groaned. "You're too kind. I'll go scrub up, and meet you in the lab. Don't start without me."

Susan smiled sweetly at him. "I wouldn't dream of it, Henry. I don't want to deprive you of all the fun."

Five minutes later, Henry entered the pathology lab. The black body bag rested on the metal table in the centre of the room. He sighed, put on a pair of rubber gloves, and waited while Susan turned on the light above the autopsy slab. Steeling himself, he unzipped the bag.

The corpse was in remarkably good condition. He noted several bites and scratches, but it was nowhere near the horror show that he'd been expecting.

"So, we have a female. Mid-thirties. Hmm, the police report says the cause of death appears to be multiple gunshot wounds, but I can't see any evidence of that, just several contusions that seem to be from an animal attack,"

Susan pursed her lips in annoyance. "It'll be that idiot, Jenkins. He's fucked the paperwork up again. I'm going to put my foot up his arse when we get done here."

"Well, never mind that now. Let's see if we can establish exactly how Miss Williams, if that is her name, really did die. Susan, can you pass me the scalpel?"

Henry took the blade and pressed it against the dead woman's stomach. The scalpel sliced through the flesh easily as he opened her up. Blood welled up from the cut.

"Jesus Christ!"

Susan looked puzzled. "What's the matter?"

"Look, she's bleeding! Dead bodies don't bleed. This is a living person. Get a crash team down here now, and tell intensive care to get ready to receive a patient, while I sew this incision closed. Then tell that cretin Jenkins that I'd like a word with him in my office."

15th November. High Moor Police Station. 16:25.

The door to the interview room swung open, disgorging the two police officers into the corridor.

Olivia turned to her boss. "Well, that was quite a story, wasn't it? Do you believe any of it?"

Phil laughed. "What? That he's a werewolf? Don't be daft. Mr Simpson should really check his facts. Last night wasn't even a full moon. He's taking the piss out of us and angling for an insanity plea, that's all."

"So what do you think really happened?"

Phil shook his head. "Damned if I know. Given that most of the casualties were naked, I'd guess that it was some sort of sick, drug-fuelled sex act gone wrong."

Olivia grinned. "You think they were dogging?"

"That's not funny, Olivia." He smiled in spite of himself. "OK, maybe a little. I don't want a word of what he said repeated. There'd be hell to pay if the press got hold of the werewolf angle. Franks would nail both our arses to the wall."

"Fair enough. So, what do you think we should do next?"

"That's the question, isn't it? I want you to go to the magistrates and get a search warrant authorised for John Simpson's house in High Moor, and, while you're at it, get one for the Wilkinson place as well. I want to have forensics teams in both properties by the end of the day."

"We might struggle for resources. Do you want to pull one of the teams out of the Harrison house?"

Phil considered this for a moment, then nodded. "Yes, but send some uniforms round to Simpson and Wilkinson's first. See if there's anything obvious lying around, but tell them to look and not touch, and not to enter the properties unless there's a clear means of entry. I don't want to risk invalidating evidence because we didn't follow procedure."

"Okay, boss. What are you going to do?"

"Well, I'm going to get a psychiatrist to do an assessment of Mr Simpson, so we can head off the insanity plea that he's working up to. We'll get a blood sample and have them check for drugs. After that, I'll go to the hospital to see if the pathologist can tell me any more about the casualties and, while I'm there, get an update on

Mr Wilkinson's condition. Apart from Simpson, he's the only other witness. Maybe, if he survives, we'll get more sense out of him."

Olivia nodded. "What about Simpson? We've not charged him with anything yet."

"Speak to the CPS before you go to the magistrates, and see if they think we have enough to get him on something. We'll need to get him booked into the court for Monday morning so we can get him remanded into custody. In the meantime, ask a couple of the uniforms to stick him back in his cell. Maybe he'll feel like changing his story after he's had some time to think about it."

Olivia nodded. "Okay, but you'll have to attend the hearing. I've got a scan booked at the hospital."

Phil smiled. "You're still hardly showing. How far along are you now?"

Olivia put her hand against her stomach. "Almost seven months. I'm hoping she doesn't take after her father. Matt's mam says that he was tiny until the eighth month, then piled the weight and size on. Apparently she needed stitches. Not the sort of mental image you want of your mother-in-law. Ever."

Phil winced. "Thanks for sharing. I've met Matt's mother, remember. Come on, let's get on with it. I've got a meeting with the pathologist in an hour, and the old bugger doesn't like to be kept waiting."

15th November. University Hospital of Durham. 17:10

Susan rubbed her eyes and leant back against the cold concrete. The sound of Henry's voice echoed off the unyielding ceramic tiles. The walls muffled the sound so that the details of his conversation with Jenkins were lost, but she could make out enough to tell her she wouldn't have changed places with him for anything. Henry's voice went up another few decibels, meaning she was able to make out some of the words. *Idiot* seemed to be cropping up on a regular basis, as well as *prosecution, criminal negligence* and *fuckwit.*

She massaged her temples. The last few hours had been a blur. No one was certain of the woman's identity, what was wrong with her, or how she'd ended up on the pathologist's table when she was clearly still alive. She'd called an emergency medical team and rushed the woman to intensive care. Henry had ordered a battery of tests to try and determine exactly what was wrong, but they would take time that Susan wasn't sure the woman had. Her vitals were weak, and even in intensive care, they were struggling to keep her stable.

What *she* needed was a coffee. A real one, not the acrid sludge served up by the vending machine. She turned and began walking to the elevator when the doors slid open and three people stepped out, two men and a red-haired woman.

She hurried along the corridor to intercept the strangers. "Excuse me, but you're not supposed to be down here. This area is off-limits to the public."

One of them, a heavy-set man in his forties, smiled and flashed an ID card at her. When he spoke, it was with a thick Eastern European accent. "I'm Detective Sergeant Pawlac, and this is my colleague, DC Braun from Durham Constabulary. We're here with Marie William's cousin, to formally identify the body. Were you not told that we were coming?"

Susan smiled. "Miss Williams, I'm afraid there's been something of a mix-up. I don't want to get your hopes up, but there's a chance that we have some good news for you."

The woman looked at Susan and wiped a tear from her eye. "What do ye mean?"

"The person brought in last night isn't dead. She's in intensive care at the moment, but we aren't completely certain who she is because her injuries don't match the police report. If you'll follow me, I'll take you to her and you can tell us whether she really is your cousin."

The woman looked at Sergeant Pawlac and raised an eyebrow, then turned back to Susan. "That's wonderful news. Please, Ah need to see her. Ah have to be sure that she's alright before Ah call the rest of the family."

Susan frowned. The cousin had almost sounded sarcastic. She shook the doubt away. People dealt with things in their own way and anyway, she was Scottish. They always sounded sarcastic. She smiled her best smile and motioned back along the corridor. "Of course, please follow me."

She walked to the elevator and hit call. The two police officers and the woman followed her into the lift, and she pressed the button for the second floor.

It was large enough to hold a stretcher and a team of medics, and she used it every day, but for some reason a wave of claustrophobia washed over her. Her heart raced and her legs turned to rubber as adrenaline coursed through her system.

Sergeant Pawlac put his hand on her shoulder. "Are you alright?"

Susan flinched at his touch. Waves of gooseflesh surged across her back. "I'm fine, just a little tired." Standing this close, her nostrils twitched at the smell of the man. Not body odour, exactly. An earthy, musk-laden scent that was reminiscent of wet dog. She jumped as her back hit the elevator door. She hadn't realised that she'd been backing away. She opened her mouth, intending to make a joke of it, when the door slid open and she stumbled out into the corridor.

The claustrophobia faded, although her heart still pounded. Cheeks burning with embarrassment, she straightened her smock and attempted a smile. "Please, follow me. She's just down here on the right."

She walked along the corridor as quickly as she could without breaking into a run. *For goodness' sake, Susan, get a bloody hold of yourself.* The urge to walk faster surged up from within on another tidal wave of adrenaline, but she crushed the rising panic and forced herself to take steady, measured steps until they reached Marie Williams' room. She opened the door, letting it swing open. She put out her hand and motioned for the others to go inside. Her heart fluttered again. *For fuck's sake, what the hell is wrong with me?* Susan moved to follow the others, but found herself just standing in the doorway, unwilling to cross the threshold into the dark room.

Marie Williams, or the woman they thought was Marie Williams, lay on the bed with a saline drip attached to her arm. A thick plastic tube ran from the unconscious woman's mouth to a ventilator by her bedside while a monitor above her head displayed her blood pressure and heart rate.

Susan reached out and put her hand on the red-haired woman's arm, then recoiled in shock. Her skin was hot. Not warm, actually hot. "Miss Williams? Is this your cousin?"

The red-haired woman stifled a sob and pushed past Susan, into the corridor. "Ah'm sorry, Ah just...Ah just need a moment. " Then she turned and walked away, back towards the elevator, shuddering with barely suppressed tears.

Detective Constable Braun shrugged his shoulders. "It would have been nice of her to tell us if this woman is her cousin first, but I'm sure she'll let us know when she comes back. So, tell me, what do you think is wrong with her?"

Susan shrugged. "They're running some tests now, but they seem to suspect some kind of heavy metal poisoning. Possibly mercury. Is there anything you might be able to tell us about where she was found?"

Inspector Pawlac shook his head. "I'm afraid that I'm not authorised to comment on an ongoing investigation, beyond what was in the report. There's no need for you to wait. We'll stay here until her cousin comes back, and when we get a formal identification, we'll let you know."

Susan nodded and tried to hide her relief. She really didn't want to wait in that room with these men, even if they were police officers. "I've been meaning to get a coffee. Can I get either of you anything?"

Both men shook their heads, and Susan stepped back from the doorway. She was about to leave when she remembered something. "Oh, should I tell your colleague that you're here when he comes down later? He's with the other one at the minute, but he's got a meeting with Doctor Pearce afterwards."

The two police officers exchanged glances, then Inspector Pawlac turned and shook his head. "Oh, don't worry about that. We'll catch up with him later, and compare notes back at the station."

Susan managed a weak smile and then scurried away towards the hospital cafeteria. She'd never been so relieved to get away from two people before, but she couldn't have said why.

15th November. University Hospital of Durham. 17:30

Colin Jenkins hunched over the microscope and felt the black cloud of anger well up again, burning behind his eyes until all he wanted to do was storm back into Dr Pearce's office and punch him right in his stupid fat nose. *I wouldn't mind, but I didn't do anything wrong.* Out of morbid curiosity, he'd sneaked a look at the corpse when the police brought it in. The woman had been almost cut in half by automatic weapons fire, with exit wounds on her back the size of his fist.

He couldn't tell Pearce that, though. The cranky old bastard was wound up enough. If he found out his lab tech had been checking out the naked dead girl, then he could kiss his job goodbye.

He refocused the microscope and looked at the blood sample taken from the Harrison man that morning. *That can't be right?* The white blood cell count was through the roof, and the red blood cells were stacking in strange groups, in the same way that animal cells sometimes did. The culture was filled with tiny white dots that swarmed through the plasma. He increased the magnification and watched the cells seethe and multiply.

He sat back in the chair. "Shit. The bloody sample must be contaminated." He slammed his fist down on the desk. "Fuck it! Can nothing go right today? Just for once?" He'd have to do it all again before Dr Pearce found out.

He removed the slide from the microscope and picked up another one which held the blood of the mystery woman. He placed the glass under the lens and refocused.

"What the hell?"

He placed the slide from Malcolm Harrison back into the microscope, then put the woman's back in. There was no doubt about it. They both had the same elevated white cell count, and the same cellular infection.

Either both samples were contaminated, or there was something else going on. He reached for the telephone to call Dr Pearce. A hot, slender hand grasped his wrist.

Colin cried out in surprise and almost fell off the chair. He looked at the attractive, red-haired woman holding his arm and managed a weak smile. "I'm sorry, you startled me. I didn't hear you come in. Can I help you with something?"

The woman released his hand and smiled. When she spoke, it was with a soft Scottish accent. "Ah don't know. Perhaps. Did you find anything interesting in the blood samples from last night's victims?"

Colin frowned. "Yes, as a matter of fact, I did. I was just about to call Dr Pearce and get him to take a look. I'm sorry, but, who are you exactly?"

The woman smiled and turned him around to face her. She reached out and stroked her hands across his cheeks, then grasped the side of his head and twisted. The sound of his neck snapping reverberated inside Colin's skull, and a terrible sharp pain flared for a brief moment that seemed like forever. He slumped to the floor, twitching and unable to move or breathe.

As darkness closed in on him, the woman's voice echoed in his ears. "Who am ah? None of yer fucking business, pal. Now, where do you keep the bloody ethanol?"

15th November. University Hospital of Durham. 17:28

Phil arrived just as Doctor Adams was leaving Stephen Wilkinson's room. Phil walked up to him and shook his hand. "Nice to see you again, Bob. How's the patient?"

Doctor Adams closed the door. "He'll live."

"Well, that's the best news I've had all day. Is he in any state to answer questions?"

The doctor shook his head. "Come on, I'll buy you a coffee."

Leaving the room. they headed for the cafeteria. "Well, Mr Wilkinson isn't going to be answering any questions for a while, Phil. He's suffered severe spinal trauma and he's in a coma. There's no way of telling when, or even if, he'll ever come out of it."

Phil exhaled in frustration. "So much for the good news. I was hoping that he'd be able to tell me what happened out there. The suspect we have in custody isn't making any sense and he's the only other person that survived the night."

"That's not the interesting part. I saw Mr Wilkinson three weeks ago. I gave him six months to live, and I was being optimistic. Lung cancer. Inoperable and most assuredly terminal. Yet today, there's no sign of it."

"Really? How is that possible?"

Doctor Adams shrugged his shoulders. "Honestly, I have no idea. I've heard stories about people suffering major trauma and their bodies' healing ability going into overdrive, but never with cancer, and never this quickly. Mr Wilkinson will never walk again, and he may end up spending the rest of his life being fed through a tube, but other than that, he's in perfect health."

They entered the cafeteria and joined the queue for the coffee machine, when Phil felt someone touch his shoulder. He turned and saw the assistant pathologist, Susan Turnbull.

"Oh, sorry to disturb you, Inspector Fletcher. Henry is waiting for you downstairs in the pathology lab, and your colleagues said that they'd catch up with you back at the station."

Phil's brow furrowed in confusion. "I'm sorry, Doctor Turnbull, but which colleagues were those?"

"Inspector Pawlac and Braun, I think their names were. They'd come in with Miss Williams' cousin to identify the body. Of course, I couldn't wait to tell them the good news."

"I'm sorry, Doctor Turnbull, but I'm not following you at all. What good news?"

"Well, the news about Miss Williams being alive after all."

Phil looked at her, open-mouthed. He composed himself, and was about to speak when the fire alarm went off.

Susan huffed. "Another bloody fire drill? We only had one last week."

People detached themselves from the coffee queue, grumbling, and made their way to the fire exit. Phil grabbed Susan's arm as she turned to leave.

"Miss Williams is alive? Where is she now?"

"She's up on the second floor, in the trauma unit. Ward 12, room 2.06. You can't go there now though; we've got to go out to the car park."

Phil wasn't listening. He ran from the cafeteria and threw open the door to the stairs. A tide of people flowed past him, hurrying to get downstairs. Thin wisps of smoke drifted up from the basement, and in the distance he could hear the sound of approaching sirens. He fought his way through the crowds until he reached the second floor. He ran to room 2.06 and threw open the door. The monitor by the bedside screamed an alert and the ventilator was still running; however, there was no sign of Marie Williams.

Phil stepped into the corridor and ran back to the stairs. Thick chemical smoke billowed up from the stairwell beneath him. He put his coat sleeve over his mouth in an attempt to filter out the fumes, and made his way down as quickly as he could. He burst out into the crowded foyer and through the double glass doors into the car park.

The cold clean air burned his chest as he sucked it in. As he looked up at the milling crowd of staff and patients in the car park he caught the eye of a beautiful red-haired woman. She winked at him then moved away through the crowds and out of his line of sight.

CHAPTER 2

15th November. Treworgan Farm, High Moor. 18:16.

Olivia shifted in her seat, attempting to hide her discomfort. Even though she'd been a police officer for more than ten years, there was still something disconcerting about being in the back of a squad car. The iron grill separating any back-seat passengers from the driver made the vehicle feel like a cell. Then there was the bloody baby. The damn thing seemed to delight in lying against her bladder, probably thinking it was a water-bed or something. Of course, she couldn't let the other officers in the car know this. They'd never let her live it down. Instead, she turned to Sergeant Rick Grey, who shared the back seat with her. "How much further is Simpson's house?"

"We should be there in a moment. It's supposed to be up here on the left somewhere. Half a mile down a farm track, back from the main road."

Olivia suppressed a groan. "Maybe we should approach on foot. If there's anyone there, it might not be a good idea to let them know we're coming."

Rick raised an eyebrow. "Good idea. You know you should have gone before we left?"

Olivia's cheeks flushed scarlet. "I did go before we left. It's the baby. You've got no bloody idea what it's like, especially in a car."

"Do we need to stop at the services?"

She shook her head. "No, I'll be fine. Worst case scenario is I squat behind a bush." She tapped on the wire mesh partitioning the vehicle. "And if I catch you with any night-vision gear out, Mark, then you'll get it shoved where the sun doesn't shine. Got it?"

Constable Mark Briggs, the armed response team's operator, laughed. "What? Honestly, Olivia. Do you really think I'd do something like that?"

"Yes. And you'd record it and stick it on YouTube or something for a laugh. I know you too bloody well, mate." She looked at Paul Patterson, the unit's driver, who was trying to hide a smirk. "That goes double for you, Paul. Remember, I know your wife."

Paul raised his eyebrows in an attempt to look innocent. "Nothing to do with me, Olivia. I'm staying well out of it. Never mess with a pregnant woman. Especially if she's a copper and has access to firearms. Oh, hang on, I think this is it."

The police car slowed down then turned onto a gravel drive. The car bounced as a wheel went through a pot hole.

Paul's smirk became a grin. "Sorry about that, Olivia." Then he veered to the right and hit another.

"Paul, if you make me piss myself in the back of a squad car, I'll make what remains of your life a living hell. Jesus, what the fuck is that?"

The police car ground to a halt in a crunch of gravel and dust that swirled in the twin beams of the headlights. They could just see a large dark stain covering the centre of the track right in front of them.

Rick leaned forward in his seat. "What the hell! I hope that's not what it looks like. Paul, put a call in. Mark, get the gear out of the back. Olivia, you stay here."

Olivia bristled. "Bollocks will I. This is my case, and in case you've forgotten, I did two years on armed response. I'm going up there with you. Now stop wasting time and get me a vest and a Glock."

Rick shook his head. He'd seen Olivia like this on plenty of occasions and knew there was no point in arguing. "OK, but you know the score. Stay behind me and Mark, and try not to shoot us up the arse."

They walked to the back of their vehicle where Mark was passing out the weapons and protective gear in silence. After donning vests and helmets, the team checked and loaded their weapons. Only then did they move to investigate the dark patch in the road.

Olivia crouched down and examined the mark. She'd been praying that it was just an oil patch, but once she got close there was no mistaking it - dried blood, dotted with small chunks of meat, and smeared where something had been dragged through it.

A small glimmer of white caught her eye, reflecting the beam from the headlights amid the dried gore. She looked closer and, for a moment, couldn't work out what it was, then she made the connection, a wave of nausea washing over her. It was a severed human thumb.

Rick put his arm on her shoulder, but she brushed him away. "I'm fine, Rick. Really."

He nodded and withdrew his hand, then turned to Mark. "Talk to Paul. We're going to need a forensics team here, and we're going to need some backup. Get the area sealed off, and tell Franks that we're going to need that warrant yesterday. Then, we're going to take a little walk and see what's been going on at that house."

15th November. Seven Bells Hotel, Durham. 19:04.

Marie floated in warmth and darkness. Images played across the theatre of her mind: a jumbled subconscious narrative that followed no real logic, but nevertheless made perfect sense somehow. She could hear voices, muted, as if a radio was on in the next room. The voices became louder, clearer. Awareness began to leak into her protective cocoon, but instead of opening her eyes she remained still, regulating her breathing to feign sleep until she could work out where she was and who the voices belonged to.

"What part of 'no killing' was I not clear on?" said a man's voice, deep with a thick Eastern European accent and clearly angry.

"What the hell did ye expect me to do? They had her blood under a microscope. Ah only just got there before the lab tech called his sodding boss." A woman this time, with a Scottish accent and an indignant tone.

"So your solution was to break the lab tech's neck and then burn the fucking hospital down?"

"Ah, the hospital's fine. Only the basement labs and the morgue were damaged. By the time they figure out that it was started deliberately we'll be far away from this shit hole."

Both speakers sounded familiar, but Marie struggled to place who they were. Realisation dawned slowly, eliciting a groan: Gregorz and Connie. Michael must have sent a team to retrieve her. Marie opened her eyes and attempted to sit up. "Do you two mind keeping it down? How the fuck is anyone supposed to sleep with that almighty racket."

Connie, to her credit, managed to keep her snarl in check. "Ah see Sleeping Beauty's finally woken up."

Gregorz got up from the chair and walked to the bedside, then took her hand. "How are you feeling?"

"Like shit. My head feels like it's wrapped in cotton wool, while the rest of me appears to have been run over by a truck. Other than that and a dry mouth, I'm fine."

Gregorz picked up a glass of water from the bedside cabinet and passed it to her. "Can you remember what happened? What did the moonstruck do to you?"

She shook her head. "There wasn't any moonstruck. I got silver-shot."

Connie walked across the room and stood at the end of the bed. ""What in Christ's name happened here, Marie? This was supposed to be a simple recruitment. How could ye fuck things up so badly?"

Marie felt a familiar anger bubble up, but forced it back down. "There were other factors. Steven fucking Wilkinson for one. He's the bastard that shot me."

Connie's face turned purple. "Wilkinson? Here? Where is he now?"

Marie propped herself up on her elbow and fought through the wave of nausea that hit her. "How the fuck should I know? He almost cut me in half with a Mac-10. If it makes you feel any better, by the time I got there, Malcolm had made a nasty mess of the bastard. I'd be amazed if he was still alive."

"Ye should have torn the fucker's throat out the second you saw him. After what he did to my Megan, how could you not?"

"It was on my list. I had other things to worry about, and to be honest, I thought he was already dead until he started shooting."

Connie opened her mouth to reply, but was silenced by a look from Gregorz. He turned to Marie and frowned. "Perhaps you'd better start at the beginning. What happened?"

"Before I could make contact with John, he got into a fight with a local dickhead called Malcolm Harrison. He punched John in the mouth, and John's teeth broke his skin. Next full moon, he turned."

"I thought you said there was no moonstruck?"

Marie shook her head. "No. Worse. He turned wild. Slaughtered his family and a few locals, then ambushed me when John and I went looking for him. What happened to John? Is he alright?"

Gregorz sighed. "Simpson survived, but is in police custody. This is a critical situation for us, Marie. Moonstruck or not, if he doesn't change before the next full moon, his beast will do it for him. I don't have to tell you what that means."

Marie sat up. "We have to get him out of there. Out of the country and back to The Pack."

"Oskar is handling that particular problem."

"Then I need to be with Oskar's team. Where are they now?"

"You're in no fit state to go anywhere, Marie. You can hardly stand, and in case you hadn't noticed, your wounds have stopped healing. The police will also be looking for you by now. You are to stay hidden until we can arrange passage back to Russia."

"So when's the rescue going to happen?" She looked at Gregorz, then to Connie. Neither of them would meet her gaze. "You've got to be kidding me. They're not going to attempt a rescue. They're going to fucking assassinate him, aren't they?"

"The order's been given. You know how it works."

Marie pushed herself up into a sitting position. "That's a load of shite, Gregorz, and you know it. I want to talk to my brother, and I want to talk to him now."

15th November. Treworgan Farm, High Moor. 19:16.

Silently, Rick and Mark moved along opposite sides of the track, weapons raised. The outline of the house up ahead was just visible through the skeletal tree branches: the track, which wound its way through a small wood leading to the courtyard, was blocked by a white Transit van. Rick motioned to the other man, dropped to one knee and took up a covering position. He then moved to the side of the vehicle and made his way to the driver's door. Cautiously, Rick pulled it open.

The vehicle turned out to be empty, apart from discarded coffee cups and crisp packets in the foot-wells and an empty packet of cigarettes on the dashboard. Pervading the vehicle's interior was a foul smell. Rick signalled Mark, who nodded and moved closer to the vehicle, weapon trained on the van's back doors. Rick followed him, making sure to keep out of his partner's line of fire. He nodded, counted to three, and opened the doors.

The stench of spoiled meat billowed out like a miasma, its source a heavy-duty black plastic sack nestled in the van's interior. Dark liquid pooled beneath it, filling the grooves in the corrugated floor. Rick took out his pocket knife and slit the sack open: he instantly regretted his decision as a mass of blood, bone and tissue spilled across the van and onto the road. He took an involuntary step backwards, simultaneously trying not to vomit. The body was human, but almost unrecognisably so. Rick couldn't fathom how someone could inflict that kind of damage on another person. The man's head had been torn in half, for Christ's sake, cracked open like a walnut.

He took a second to compose himself then activated his radio. "Control, we have a body in a white ford Transit van, approximately one hundred yards from the house. It looks to be the remains of a white Caucasian male, but it's hard to be certain. No sign of movement from the property. Moving to check the barn next."

The cold hard knot of fear tightened in his stomach, filling his veins with ice. The tips of his fingers felt numb, and his heart pounded in his ears. He felt glad that DI Fletcher had arrived with the backup and that he'd made Olivia stay at the track's entrance. He hadn't caught the details, but he got the impression that something had occurred at the hospital where last night's bodies had been taken.

Rick teetered on the edge of a precipice, the ground falling away beneath his feet. This kind of thing didn't happen around here. Sure, there were the usual: fights that got out of hand, petty theft, robbery and smack-heads with re-commissioned pop guns which were more likely to blow up in their owner's hand than fire. But all this shit they'd had to deal with was unbelievable, and the fact that they had a suspect in custody hadn't done much to calm Rick's nerves. He took a deep breath, pushed down the fear, and focused on the job at hand.

He signalled to Mark, and the two officers moved into the woods. The barn loomed up before them: a large, wooden-framed building, with rotted walls and a heavily rusted corrugated iron roof. Its door stood open, creaking on ancient hinges as it shifted in the breeze. Rick's every instinct told him to avoid the open doorway, so he crept around the other side of the building while Mark took up a covering position behind him.

He saw it as soon as he'd rounded the corner - a gaping hole in the barn's side. The rotten walls had splintered into long, viciously jagged shards, as if something (or someone) had burst through it with tremendous force - or had been dragged through.

He moved closer, aiming his tactical light into the hole. The wood was bloodstained, and one of the lower boards had something snagged on it: it looked like a party streamer, pointing back into the tree-line and out of sight. He shone the narrow beam onto the object, realising as he did so that he was looking at someone's intestines. It was all he could do to stop himself from falling on his knees and emptying his stomach all over the crime scene.

He heard Mark coming closer but waved him away. He walked unsteadily up to the hole, shining the light through. The lower half of a man's body lay just inside. Rick knew that if he followed the unravelled guts, he'd find the rest.

"We've got another one. There's...there's half a body in the barns, with a trail of intestines heading back into the woods. It looks like this one was dragged through the wall, I..."

An electronic beep pierced the silence. Rick looked through the hole once more, trying to locate its source. The beep rang out again, and he saw the trouser pocket of the half-corpse glow in the darkness.

"Control, it looks like one of them had a phone on them. Mark and I will check the main house, but it's quiet as a grave up here. It looks like no-one's home. No-one alive, anyway. Get forensics ready to move when we give the all-clear."

15th November. The Angel, Durham. 21:32.

Gregorz strode through the busy city centre streets, heading for a meeting with Oskar. If circumstances had been different, he would have liked to spend more time in Durham, if only to appreciate some of the architecture. The cathedral and castle dominated the city, especially at night when floodlights illuminated it. The magnificent buildings stood proud on the skyline for miles around, although at ground level the ancient streets had been 'developed', with orange and brown brick shopping centres clinging to the old stone like an obscene fungal growth. Gregorz considered it nothing less than vandalism.

Streams of young men and women in various states of inebriation and undress staggered past him. One girl, dressed in a PVC nurse's uniform, stumbled into his path and threw up over his shoes. He considered hurling her from the stone bridge into the fast-flowing river below, but quickly reminded himself of his purpose and the need for restraint. He'd have to have another talk with Connie about that later.

He walked away from the bustling centre, turning off into a side-street. It was mostly residential, with a couple of shops here and there. A gaggle of young people, all sporting long hair and motorcycle jackets, were standing outside a bar, smoking cigarettes. Heavy metal music reverberated incongruously along the old narrow street. Gregorz sighed. Of course this is where Oskar would want to meet. He could sniff bars like this out in a five-mile radius, knowing that Gregorz hated them.

He eased his way past the crowd at the door and pushed it open. The noise hit him like a solid wall. Dozens of conversations, screamed over music so loud it made his ears ache. People were squashed together as they jostled to get back to their seats, laden with drinks, or pushed their way through to the bar. One teenager, a dark-haired youth with half of his face concealed by his fringe, sat underneath the pool table while one of his friends, a tall, blonde boy in a denim jacket, passed drinks down to him. The air stank of sweat and leather, with a faint hint of marijuana beneath.

He considered leaving and texting Oskar to rearrange the meeting, but then he caught sight of Troy. He could hardly miss the big American. He was six-and-a-half feet tall, with a close-cropped blonde buzz-cut. In a place like this, he stood out more than Gregorz was comfortable with. The problem was, Troy stood out everywhere. Gregorz pushed his way through the crowds until he arrived at the table where he found Troy sitting with Oskar and Gabriela.

Oskar raised a bottle of dark brown liquid. "Ah, Gregorz, I'm glad you could make it. Would you like a drink? This local beer is quite good. Gabriela, would you mind getting a bottle of...what did they call it again? Oh yes. Dog. Would you get Gregorz a bottle of Dog?"Gabriela got to her feet, and eased her way into the crowd, which shifted and parted to allow her to get to the bar. She returned minutes later with a cold beer, which she put in front of Gregorz and returned to her seat without so much as a word.

He picked up the bottle and took a mouthful. "Have you seen the news, Oskar?"

The Norwegian nodded. "It's unfortunate that those bodies were discovered. The moonstruck is well guarded, meaning it will be even more difficult to get to him. This situation is getting too much attention and I'm sure I don't have to tell you how dangerous a position we are in. This could get worse than 1996 if it escalates any further. Did you get anything from Marie?"

Gregorz took another swig. "She's adamant that Simpson isn't moonstruck, but based on the news reports, that's looking less likely."

Troy raised an eyebrow. "You think she's protecting him?"

Gregorz shrugged. "I don't know, and to be honest, I don't care. Her face is all over the news at the moment, so I'm going to keep her out of sight for a few weeks and then get her back to Russia. She can explain herself to her brother."

Gabriela snorted. "Even if she is harbouring the moonstruck, do you think her brother will abide by the law? He's soft when it comes to her. Weak."

Oskar raised his hand. "That's enough. Michael is our pack leader, and he will deal with matters according to the law, or face the consequences. Until he goes against that law, he is our alpha and you will treat him with respect. We have more pressing matters to attend to. Did you get anything else from her, Gregorz?"

He took another mouthful of the ale, enjoying the flavour. "Yes — she said that Stephen Wilkinson is involved and he silver-shot her. I don't know what he did, but she's not healing like she should. She also said that he was a casualty, having been badly mauled. However, there's been no mention of him in news reports. I'll get Daniel to look into it in the morning."

Troy let out a whistle. "Jesus. Wilkinson? How the hell have you kept a leash on Connie?"

"It's not been easy. Daniel is currently babysitting them both -

I'll try to keep them from killing each other or doing something equally stupid tomorrow, while Daniel checks into Wilkinson's involvement. I'm sending Connie back to Moscow. She's got too much personal involvement in this, and she wasn't behaving rationally before she heard about Wilkinson. I dread to think how she'd behave in the field now."

Troy grinned. "We heard about the hospital. You can't deny the girl's got a refreshing directness. Plus, if she hadn't torched the evidence you might not have made it out with Marie."

Oskar laughed. "Dear Connie is a blunt instrument, one you aim and then get out of the way. I'm not sure why you brought her, if I'm honest."

Gregorz nodded. "We thought we were coming over to retrieve a corpse. As you say, the job changed and she's no longer the right tool. Do you know how you're going to solve the Simpson problem?"

Oskar raised his bottle to Gregorz and took a long swig. "Yes. When you speak to Michael, you can tell him that John Simpson will be dead within the next thirty-six hours."

CHAPTER 3

15th November. Seven Bells Hotel, Durham. 22:35.

Marie paced the floor of the tiny hotel room. Daniel sat in the corner reading a book while Connie lay on the bed, watching *The X-Factor* on a small flat-screen TV. As the programme went into an advert break, she craned her head to look at Marie, a snarl on her lips.

"Can you pack that shite in? Ye're driving me mental. Sit yer arse down before ye wear a hole in the fucking carpet."

Marie stuffed her hands in her pockets and flopped down in the other chair. "When's Gregorz coming back? He's been gone for hours and I need to talk to Michael."

Connie rolled her eyes. "He'll be back when he's good and ready, and not a second before. Now settle down and shut the fuck up. Ah'm trying to watch telly."

The door handle twitched. Daniel dropped his book, motioning for Marie to get into the bathroom. Connie sprang from the bed and positioned herself to one side of the door. The lock clicked and it swung open. Gregorz stepped inside, with a mobile telephone held to his ear. He nodded to Daniel and held the phone out. "You can come out now, Marie. Your brother wants to talk to you."

The bathroom door burst open and Marie grabbed the phone from him, quickly putting her hand over the mouthpiece. She looked at the others and waited for a moment. "Any chance you lot could piss off and let me talk to my brother in private?"

Connie looked at the TV. The adverts had ended, and the show's theme music was playing. "Oh, ye've gotta be fucking kidding. Ah'm gonna miss the sing-off. Can't ye just stand outside?"

Gregorz picked up the remote control and turned the TV off. "Connie, Daniel, let's give Marie some time to talk things over with her brother."

Daniel shrugged, picked up his coat and stepped out into the corridor. Connie gave Gregorz a pleading look, then huffed, grabbed her jacket, and stomped after Daniel. Gregorz turned to Marie. "We'll be downstairs in the bar. I discovered a wonderful local beer that I think Daniel would appreciate. Take your time. I'm sure you both have a lot to talk about." Then, without another word, he followed the other two, closing the door behind him. Marie sat down on the bed and put the phone to her ear.

"Michael?"

"Fucking hell, Marie. You don't know how good it is to hear your voice. When I heard you were dead..."

Marie cut him off mid-sentence. "Cut the crap, Michael. Why did you order a hit on John, instead of an extraction?"

"You have to be kidding me? Have you seen the news? John's a fucking celebrity. The UK's latest serial killer. His face is all over every TV station, newspaper and website in the civilised world. There's no way we could get him out of the country, and even if we did, he'd still be recognised wherever we took him."

Marie's knuckles tightened around the phone. "So that's it? You're just giving up on him?"

The line was silent for a moment. "Do you have any idea how serious this is? One of the papers has already started calling him "The Wolf Man". If he changes in police custody, then it's over for all of us. It'll make what happened in Czechoslovakia seem like child's play. You told Gregorz that he's not moonstruck earlier. Is that true? Because the news reports from John's farm sound a lot like the work of a moonstruck to me."

"They had him tied up in a fucking chair and were beating the shit out of him with a hammer. I'd have done the same thing. So would you."

"So it's just a coincidence that this happened on a full moon? Don't lie to me, Marie. You know what the penalty is for harbouring a moonstruck. I won't be able to help you if this comes out later."

"He's something else, Michael. He told me that he brought the change on himself, before the moon was up, because Billy was going to take his eye out. And when he came after me the following night, he changed and killed Malcolm without a full moon. I think he's learning to live with his beast."

"But is he moonstruck?"

Marie clenched the phone and took a breath. "He was. He isn't anymore."

Michael's voice turned hard. "It makes no difference. Given the circumstances, I'd have to order the hit irrespective of who it was, even if it was you. You know what'll happen if they find out what he is. You've seen it. We'd be hunted down. Those of us who've survived would spend our lives hiding in the shadows or fleeing to the forests like frightened beasts. I won't allow it. Not again."

Marie held the phone at arm's length, with her hand over the receiver as she tried to stifle her sob. She wiped her eyes and brought the phone back to her ear.

"Marie? Are you there?"

"Yes, I'm here."

"Good. I'm only going to tell you this once. Don't fuck me about on this. It's too important. There's too much at stake. You keep your arse out of sight until we can get you out of the country and don't get in Gregorz or Oskar's way. If you do, then I won't be able to help you. Do you understand?"

Marie stared at the faded floral wallpaper and gritted her teeth. The plastic casing of the phone creaked as she tightened her grip. The urge to throw the device at the wall swelled almost irresistibly. Everything that Michael had said was right. She'd hunted down and killed people for acting on the same urges she was having now. There was nothing she could do to save John. Killing him was the right move. In that instant, her rage evaporated into a thick, cloying fog of resignation and despair. Tears moistened the corners of her eyes. "Yes, Michael. I understand. I'll do as you say."

17th November. High Moor Police Station. 07:30.

John lay on the cell's hard bed, watching the world come back to life. The sky turned from a muddy orange to a dismal flat grey that leeched the colour and energy from everything beneath it. Even the birds were unimpressed, their songs muted as if they lacked the enthusiasm to greet the cold, wet morning. He could sympathize.

The sound of jangling keys caught his attention, but he remained still until the steel cell door creaked open. Four police officers entered the room, armed with pepper spray and batons, keeping as much distance from John as the confined space would allow.

One of them moved forwards and held out a set of handcuffs. "Face the wall and put your hands behind your back. Don't try anything funny or we might be forced to break a couple of ribs while restraining you. Got it?"

John swung his legs off the bed, taking amusement in the fact that all four officers took an involuntary step backwards. He stood, faced the wall, and moved his arms behind him. Rough hands grasped his shoulders and wrists, pushing him against the cold concrete wall as the handcuffs locked into place.

He tried to turn his head and found his face forced against the wall. Deep within him, the wolf growled. He forced the beast down with difficulty. "Do I not get a shower before I'm dragged into court? I've not washed or shaved for three bloody days and in case you hadn't noticed, I fucking stink."

One of the police officers, a squat, foul-tempered thug called Carter, grabbed John's shoulder and snarled in his ear. "Does this look like a hotel to you? Get a fucking move on. DI Fletcher wants you at the court nice and early."

Carter and another officer frog-marched John from his cell and down a short corridor to another secure holding room. Two private security guards stood chatting with the duty officer, and an armoured prisoner transport van sat in the garage area. Reinforced shutters giving access to the rear of the police station was the only other way out. When John and his escorts entered, the two security guards and the duty officer stopped their conversation and stared at him.

Carter nodded to one of the guards. "Alright, Frank? Got a celebrity for you this morning. You take good care of him, now. From what I'm reading in the papers, this bastard bites."

Frank nodded. "Don't you worry, mate. If the prick tries anything like that, then I'll pull his teeth out, one by one. Paperwork's all sorted, so we're good to go." He nodded to John. "Your carriage awaits, your majesty."

The two police officers bundled John into the rear of the van and secured his handcuffs to a chain in the floor. The van's only other occupant was a young man: pale with dirty jeans, and missing one of his front teeth. He looked up from the floor at John, then back at his feet.

Frank and the other guard climbed into the rear of the van, closing the doors behind them. John heard the click as the lock engaged. After Frank had banged twice on the van's side panel, the vehicle's engine started and pulled out of the police station.

The pale man glanced up at John. "Drugs?"

"Excuse me, what?"

"Did the fuckers get you for drugs? You look a bit strung out."

Frank laughed. "Whitey, you are in the presence of a celebrity. Mr Simpson here allegedly killed five people. Tore most of them apart with his bare hands and his teeth."

Whitey sat back in his seat, his mouth hanging open. "Fuck me, is that true?"

John arched his eyebrow. "Allegedly."

Whitey shuffled further away from John. "Shit, I didn't mean any offence, mate. We're cool? Yeah?"

John nodded. "Don't worry. We're cool."

The journey to the magistrate's court took a little over twenty minutes, but to John it felt like hours. Whitey had lapsed into a worried silence, while Frank whistled the theme tune to *Mission Impossible* over and over again. The other guard turned his baton over in his hands and kept a cautious eye on John. When the van arrived, John and Whitey were shoved through a set of metal doors and into another holding area. Once the paperwork was processed, they were taken to adjoining cells in the basement.

As soon as the guards left the room, Whitey got up from the bench and walked over to John. "Is this your first time, mate?"

John nodded. "Yeah. I take it that you've been here once or twice before?"

"Yeah, once or twice. Your brief should have told you what was happening. Unless you took the duty solicitor?"

"Some bloke called Jarvis, I think. He sat down once with me, but to be honest, I wasn't paying much attention."

"Jarvis? You need to get shot of that useless wanker, and quick. He's a waste of fucking space. It won't matter much this time around, though."

"Why not?"

"This is just the magistrates, mate. They aren't even proper legal professionals. Just power-crazy twats that like to lord it over the peasants. They'll take one look at you, shit their pants, and pass the whole thing up to Crown Court. All they'll want from you today is a guilty or not guilty, then they'll take you back to your nice, cosy cell."

John exhaled and lay back on the bench. "Any idea how long we'll be sitting here?"

Whitey smiled a lopsided grin. "You might as well get comfy, mate. These daft tossers like to take their time."

17th November. High Moor Magistrates Court. 11:13.

Phil sat at the front of the courtroom, arched his back, taking pleasure in the loud pop as his spine realigned itself. He'd lost count of the number of hours he'd spent on hard wooden benches in dingy little courtrooms like this, waiting for the magistrates to pull their bloody fingers out. He'd specifically requested Simpson's case to be pushed to the front of the queue, to try and avoid the swarms of reporters. The magistrate had ignored him, and the first case, some junkie up for aggravated burglary, had dragged on for the best part of two hours. Then the magistrates had buggered off for tea and biscuits.

The situation made Phil uneasy. Simpson should be secure enough in the holding cells, but something was gnawing on his nerves. They'd found more bodies at Simpson's house over the last twenty-four hours, and some of them looked like they'd been in the ground for a very long time. Forensics couldn't give him an exact date yet, but they'd guessed they'd been there for at least twenty years, maybe more. If that was the case, then Simpson would have been nothing more than a child when they died. That implicated his parents, but they'd been dead since the mid-nineties.

Then there was Steven Wilkinson's involvement. For the life of him, he couldn't work out where he fitted into the puzzle, or how his lawyers had managed to get his name withheld from the press. They didn't even have a search warrant for the bastard's house yet. He massaged his temple and sighed. The more information that came to light about this case, the less sense it made.

The door to the chambers opened and the magistrates shuffled out to take their seats. A few moments later, two police officers escorted Simpson to the dock and secured his handcuffs. The room had been silent, but now was buzzing with an uneasy murmur as people in the public gallery held fast, hushed conversations, and pointed at the man who'd brought so much death to their town. Predictably, the room was packed. Phil recognized some of the faces, but not all: the usual mixture of local journalists and old dears with too much time on their hands. He caught a glimpse of a red-haired woman sitting at the rear of the room. He couldn't make out her face from here, but before he could adjust his position for a better look, the magistrate called order and proceeded with the case.

Simpson's court appearance was a routine matter. The magistrates just had to remand him in custody after the duty solicitor gave the "not guilty" plea, and refer the case to the Crown Court in Durham, although one of the magistrates, a retired dentist called Ferguson, had looked ill as he read the case notes. Simpson kept his eyes pointed at the floor and only spoke to confirm his name. The whole thing was over and done with in twenty minutes, when Simpson was taken back to the holding area.

As soon as the magistrates left, Phil got to his feet and rushed to the rear of the courtroom, looking for the red-haired woman who, naturally, was nowhere to be found.

Phil had a sick feeling in his stomach - his every instinct screamed that something was wrong, but the pieces wouldn't fit together. He stood frozen for a moment, finally leaving the courtroom and making his way to the building's holding facility.

17th November. Weardale Café, High Moor. 14:02.

Oskar sipped his latte and observed the world through the café's rain-streaked window. People hurried along the street, dragging small children and shopping carts behind them, while others huddled in shop doorways to avoid the worst of the downpour.

The only sounds were the low murmur of conversation from other occupants of the café, and the hiss of car tyres on the wet tarmac outside. He checked his watch. It wouldn't be long now.

He took another sip of his coffee and smiled. There it was - the prisoner transport vehicle detailed to ferry John Simpson to Durham Prison. He reached into his pocket and removed his phone. He sent the message he'd prepared earlier to Troy and Gabriela, after which he left the café, got into the hire car parked outside, and started following the armoured van.

They drove through the town, past abandoned shops and rows of small terraced houses, out to the dual carriageway leading to Durham city. Oskar felt his pulse quicken, his beast rousing itself from slumber - he could almost imagine it wagging its tail in anticipation.

Soon. Be patient.

The armoured van was five cars ahead, so he slowed down to allow two more vehicles to pass before joining the flow of main road traffic. Gabriela would be around the same distance ahead of the van by now. The noose was tightening around Simpson, and he had no idea. This would all be over in moments. Oskar smiled and waited for Gabriela's signal.

The line of traffic ahead came to an abrupt standstill; the rows of brake lights stretching out through the grey drizzle like a neon snake. The prison van had stopped directly opposite a junction, Gabriela timing her breakdown to perfection, but then Oskar had expected no less from her. It was time to close the jaws of the trap. Picking up his phone, he texted a single word to Troy.

'Now.'

A blare of horns came from the adjoining road as the twin headlights of a petrol tanker blazed through the rain and burst through the traffic, accelerating towards the junction on the wrong side of the road. Oskar unbuckled his seatbelt and removed the vehicle's ignition keys, then bringing his wolf fully awake and holding it just below the transformation threshold. Time slowed, the world taking on a monochrome cast. He heard cries of alarm from the occupants of the other vehicles as the tanker hurtled toward the junction, the click of door-locks as people scrambled to get clear. Children screamed, their mothers frantically trying to free them from car seats. Oskar looked up at the tanker and saw Troy, grinning like an idiot, sitting atop the corpse of the tanker's driver.

The petrol tanker slammed into the side of the prison van.

The impact hurled Troy through its windshield, sending him sailing over the crash barrier and down a slight slope leading to the fields beyond. The momentum of the massive tanker had pushed the prison van against the steel barrier, crumpling the side of the van. The tanker, with a dead man's foot still planted on the accelerator, hadn't slowed down, instead mounting the side of the armoured vehicle as if it were a ramp. The tanker's storage vessel ruptured, spilling fifty thousand litres of petrol onto both the road and the prison van. Oskar smiled, taking a phone from his pocket and dialling a prepaid cell phone they'd picked up the previous day. Expectantly, he braced himself.

The bomb that Troy had planted on the tanker was crude and small, little more than a firework with a detonator connected to a phone. It was more than enough. The device ignited the fuel from the stricken tanker, exploding in a searing fireball that appeared to expand in slow motion, consuming the vehicles closest to it. The roar of the flames mingled with the screams of the trapped, while the people who'd managed to escape their vehicles staggered ablaze along the roadside until they collapsed to the ground and burned. One child, wrapped in fire from head to foot, still carried a burning teddy bear for a few agonising steps before the flames consumed her.

Oskar opened his car door, removing a silver stiletto from his jacket, and stepped out into the inferno.

The heat was intense, but now that the initial fireball had passed, had become manageable, at least in the short term. Oskar raced through the flames, ignoring his blistering skin and stinging eyes. The heat, smoke and noise confused his senses, his wolf whining at the back of his mind, but he pressed on until he reached the wrecked van.

The back doors had buckled with the impact of the crash and now lay open. Three corpses, little more than blazing skeletons, lay strewn across the inside. Oskar swore under his breath, then leapt over the ruined crash barrier. He rolled down the embankment to extinguish his blazing jacket, picking himself up and running alongside the road until he reached the spot where Gabriela's car had 'broken down'. He opened the rear door and got into the back seat.

Troy sat in the front passenger seat, picking shards of glass from his forehead. He turned to Oskar. "All done?"

Oskar shook his head. "No, Simpson wasn't in the van. Even a fire as intense as that would not have killed him so quickly and there was no wolf scent. Was Connie certain that Simpson left the court?"

"She couldn't be sure. He was in court with the others, but she thought the cop in charge of the investigation might have recognised her, so she scrammed."

Oskar sighed. The plan had been perfectly designed and executed, yet Connie had still found a way to ruin things. Gregorz should have sent Daniel, a fact that he'd make very clear when he spoke to him later on.

Gabriela started the car and drove away from the inferno behind them. "So what the hell do we do now? That was our only shot at Simpson before the next full moon. How are we going to get to him and destroy his body when he's locked up tight in a high security prison?"

Oskar removed his ruined jacket and smiled at her. "Don't worry, my Italian beauty. I have a plan. Tell me, how do you feel about doctors?"

CHAPTER 4

5th December. Aykley Heads Police HQ. 11:25.

Olivia balanced the stack of folders on her left arm, holding them in place with her chin while she struggled to open the office door. She'd only given the documents a cursory glance after retrieving them from the archive, nevertheless, she hoped that they might provide the breakthrough they'd been looking for. Phil was not going to believe some of the things she'd managed to dig up.

The door swung open, two uniformed officers stepping through it. Olivia nodded a greeting and stuck her foot into the open doorway before it swung closed. Sighing, she pushed the door all the way open with her backside while struggling to control the paperwork.

The office was open plan, with only the short partitions on each desk offering any sort of privacy. The levels of background noise made her ears hurt. Constant telephone ringing mingled with the low thrum of the heating system and dozens of different conversations until it all blended into a dull roar.

She had no idea how anyone managed to concentrate in here. Putting her headphones on was the only way to block it out, drowning out the noise with music, otherwise she'd never have been able to keep her train of thought long enough to accomplish anything.

Phil's desk was at the end of a row, by a window overlooking the car park. He sat hunched over his PC, a cold cup of coffee on the desk next to him. Olivia made her way along the row, grabbed an empty chair, and slapped her folders down on his desk.

Phil looked up from his screen. "Jesus, Olivia! You scared the life out of me!"

She grinned. "Yeah, sorry about that, boss. You were off in your own little world, but I thought you'd like to see this."

He picked up the first folder, opened it, and skimmed through its contents, finally turning to her with a confused look. "What am I supposed to be looking at?"

Olivia's grin turned into a smug smile. "These are the case files from the High Moor beast attacks in 1986. Take a look at the name on the report."

Phil flicked through the folder again. "Steven Wilkinson? Our comatose friend in the hospital?"

"It gets better. Carry on reading."

He scanned the papers and flicked past a couple of faded photographs, then stopped. "Is this real?"

"It most certainly is. Sergeant Steven Wilkinson was the officer who saved the life of those boys at the scout camp, including one John Simpson. We've been looking for something to tie the two men and I think this qualifies. Not only that, but the boy who later died in hospital was called Michael Williams, brother to David Williams, who was the first victim and..."

Phil exhaled tiredly and sat back in his chair. "Marie Williams. Our mysterious vanishing witness. Olivia, I could kiss you."

She screwed up her face. "I'd rather you didn't. You haven't shaved and you have coffee breath. What do you think Wilkinson's solicitor will make of this?"

"I'd say the little weasel is going to shit his pants. We've got solid evidence linking the suspects and he can't block the search warrant of Wilkinson's place anymore, no matter how many friends he has in high places. I'll give you the pleasure of delivering the message, if you like?"

"Oh yes. Can I get the little scrotum down here so I can tell him to his face?"

"I think that under the circumstances, that would be quite appropriate." He picked up his coffee mug and took a sip, making a face and putting it back on the desk. "I think I'm getting somewhere with our other mystery woman. I've been going over the CCTV tapes from the hospital and the court."

"Are you still on about this? Phil, there is no shortage of red-haired women in High Moor, and even if the same woman was at the hospital and court, it doesn't necessarily mean anything."

"All I know is that I saw that woman when Marie Williams disappeared, and the next time I saw her was at John Simpson's court hearing. If I hadn't sent him back to the nick in a squad car, then he'd have died in that wreck with the others."

"We've been over this. The autopsy on the driver said it looked like he'd had a heart attack. You're chasing ghosts, when you should be concentrating on this new evidence."

"I appreciate your concern, but you're wrong. Here, take a look at this from the hospital. She's being very careful to avoid the cameras, but she gets caught for just a second, right here."

He paused the video and expanded the screen until a pixelated image of a woman's face filled the screen. He dragged the window across onto his second monitor and called up another video file.

"Again, you can see her entering the building. She's being careful to avoid the cameras, but she couldn't get past the one near the metal detector without looking suspicious." He hit pause and expanded the image. This one was clearer and showed a woman in her mid-thirties or early forties with shoulder length red hair.

"That's the same woman I saw at the hospital. No other cameras get a clear shot of her the entire time she's in that building, and she leaves just before the end of Simpson's hearing. She's got something to do with this, Olivia. I'm sure of it."

Olivia sighed. "OK, print that out for me and I'll make some quiet enquiries at the local hotels and B&Bs. Maybe something will turn up. By the way, did you get anywhere with those bogus police officers?"

Phil was about to reply when his telephone rang, a look of irritation on his face. "DI Fletcher. This had better be important." Moments passed, and while she couldn't hear what was being said on the other end, she could tell by the reddening of Phil's neck that he didn't like the message. He slammed the phone down without another word and turned to Olivia.

"Simpson's shrink has been to the courts and requested he be transferred to a secure unit pending assessment. It seems that, in his infinite wisdom, the judge agreed and signed the papers."

Olivia's mouth fell open. "What the fuck? Why are we hearing about this now? We should have been told about this as soon as the hearing was scheduled."

Phil's face twitched. "Yes, we should have, but it seems that we didn't get the memo."

"For fuck's sake. Those tossers never bother to tell us anything. Can we do anything about it?"

Phil shook his head. "No. It's a done deal. They're moving him next week, on the twelfth, once all the paperwork is sorted out."

"At least those secure units are safe. Simpson won't be going anywhere. The security in those places puts Durham nick to shame."

"Yeah, as long as there aren't any more accidents *en route*."

Olivia took out her phone to update her calendar and frowned.

"What?"

She shook her head. "Oh, nothing, just a funny coincidence, really. The twelfth is the night of the next full moon."

5th December. Dr. Miller's Office, Newcastle. 16:43.

Phil pushed the door open with enough force it slammed against the wall. The receptionist raised an eyebrow at his show of aggression, and then turned back to her computer. Phil strode across the room and stood in front of her desk. "I need to see Doctor Miller. It's urgent."

If the woman heard him, she made no sign. Instead, she continued tapping away at the keyboard.

"Excuse me, my name is Detective Inspector Fletcher, and it's vital that I speak to Doctor Miller right away." When the woman still refused to acknowledge his presence, he leaned over the desk and turned off the power to her monitor, noticing that the vital work she'd been doing involved a soon-to-end auction on eBay. For a hat.

A look of supreme irritation etched itself onto the woman's face and she glared at Phil. "Do you have an appointment?"

"No, I don't. It's a police matter and it's urgent. Is he in his office?"

"He's with a patient, and when he finishes up here, the office will be closing. If you would like me to make an appointment, then I believe he has a free slot at the back end of next week. "A look of pure evil flashed across the woman's face. "Or maybe it was the week after."

Phil felt an overwhelming urge to reach across the table and slap the old woman. With what felt like a feat of superhuman willpower, he forced himself back under control. He placed both hands on the desk and leaned forward. "Look, I could make life very difficult for you and we could spend the next half hour arguing about it, at which point I'm pretty sure that your auction will have ended and you'll need to go and find another disgusting hat instead of working. Or, you could call Doctor Miller, tell him that I'm waiting outside, and then get back to whatever it was you were doing. Your choice."

The receptionist's face twisted and after a moment, she picked up the telephone and rang through to the doctor's office. Phil heard it ring several times before it was answered. "Yes, Doctor Miller. There's a police officer in reception to see you. He says it's urgent. Yes, of course. I'll send him right in."

Phil smiled at the sour-faced woman and strode past her. He knocked twice on the door, and when the doctor answered, he strode into the office.

The doctor's office was just as Phil had imagined it would be. A large, expensive desk made of dark, polished wood, dominated the room, and rows of bookcases filled with heavy medical volumes lined two of the room's walls. To the right was another door, marked as the treatment room, while medical certificates adorned the wall behind the desk, along with a framed print of a kitten gripping a branch for dear life, with the caption "Hang in there, Baby!" written across the bottom. Doctor Miller himself was a thin, pale, and unassuming man. His hair was untidy and his shirt creased, with the top button undone. He got up from his chair and offered Phil a limp, sweaty handshake.

He sat back down and regarded Phil. "Please, take a seat. So, DI Fletcher, what brings you all the way out here?"

Phil sat down in a leather chair, noticing that it was quite a bit shorter than the one Doctor Miller sat in. He'd seen this tactic before. Chief Inspector Franks used it when he wanted to make people feel uneasy and inferior. Not the sort of behaviour he would have expected from a psychiatrist. "Well, to be honest, Doctor, I wanted to know why the hell you went behind my back and made arrangements to have John Simpson transferred to a mental institute?"

Doctor Miller gave Phil a weak, knowing smile. "If I remember correctly, Detective Inspector, you contacted me and requested that I perform a psychiatric evaluation on Mr Simpson prior to his trial. Unfortunately Durham Prison is not the most conducive environment for me to make any kind of assessment. True lycanthropy, where the patient believes they actually transform into a wolf, is rare, and we need to know whether he truly believes what he is saying, or whether he's making it up to try to plead insanity. I decided, as his doctor, that he needed to be taken out of the prison environment to a secure unit where I could assess his condition properly. That is what you asked me to do, is it not?"

Phil leaned forward in his chair. "I asked you to assess Simpson. I didn't ask you to cut me out of the fucking loop, go straight to the judge, and push through a court order to have him moved."

"I assure you, everything is completely above board. You can check the paperwork if you like. I did notify your station of my intent last week. I can hardly be held responsible if your colleagues didn't pass the message on. Now, if there's nothing else, I still have a patient and you are eating into her valuable time. If you need to speak to me again, please call Martha on reception and have her make an appointment for you."

Phil got to his feet. "Look, Doctor. I think you're making a mistake. I have reason to believe that the incident with the petrol tanker outside of High Moor last month may have been an attempt on Simpson's life. Not only that, but for someone who claims to turn into a monster every full moon, don't you think that transferring him on that very day could be potentially damaging to your patient?"

Doctor Miller shook his head. "If I could have got the paperwork through sooner, then I would have had him under observation in the secure unit well before then. It's vital that he's in the proper environment on that night, so that he can be restrained or medicated if necessary. It should also give us valuable insights into the nature of his condition. Now, I really must get back to my patient. Thank you, Detective Inspector. I'll be sure to keep you informed from now on."

Phil got to his feet and made to leave. "Please make sure you do, Doctor. I don't need to remind you that this is a high-profile case, and I need to know exactly what's happening with my suspect at all times. I'm glad I can count on your co-operation."

Doctor Miller was already moving towards his treatment room, so Phil let himself out. Martha the receptionist didn't even look up from her computer as he left and made his way back to the car park. Something was bothering him, but for the life of him he couldn't work out what it was. He'd been feeling that a lot lately.

He reached into his pocket for cigarettes that he'd not carried in ten years, shaking his head in disgust when he realised what he'd been doing. He got into his car and drove away.

***

Doctor Miller closed the door of the treatment room and walked to the window, where he stood until the police officer had driven away. Turning to the dark-haired woman sitting on the couch, he said, "He knows. I could see it in his face. He suspects."

In a single sinuous movement, the woman rose from the sofa and put her hand on the doctor's shoulder. He flinched at her touch. "The policeman knows nothing, and it had better stay that way. If he comes around asking questions again, then deal with him, just like you did this time. Do you understand?"

Doctor Miller nodded. "Yes, I understand." He looked up into her eyes. "Please, I've done what you asked. Can I see my family now?"

The woman smiled and pushed him down onto the sofa. "Don't worry about your family, Wesley. You just be a good boy and sit quietly over there. Once your receptionist leaves, I'll take you home to your wife and children. I'm sure my friends have been taking very good care of them."

12th December. Durham Prison. 07:30.

The reveille bell echoed around the cell block. John's eyes snapped open and he sat upright in bed. His brow was sticky with sweat and his heart raced. He'd been dreaming, reliving the fight with Malcolm over and over, feeling the hot gush of blood on his tongue and the sweet taste of his enemy's flesh. He forced himself back to the present and shook off the memory, aware of the dissatisfaction lurking in the back of his mind.

John's cellmate, a man called Jonesy, peered down from the top bunk. "Fuck me, you don't half make a racket when you're asleep. You must have had a nightmare-and-a-half last night. I tried to wake you a couple of times, and you just opened your eyes and stared at me like I was meat. Scared the shit out of me."

John's fear of the coming night coiled and writhed in his stomach. He managed a sheepish grin. "Oh, shit, sorry, mate. Last night's dinner can't have agreed with me."

Jonesy clambered off the bed, stark naked, and stumbled across to the toilet, then sat down. "Yeah, tell me about it. I swear it's given me the shits 'n' all. I can feel my guts sloshing around. Oh, here we go."

John buried his face in his pillow and tried to ignore the noises coming from the other side of the cell. It was going to be a long half-hour before the doors were unlocked to let them out for breakfast. Thirty minutes in which to agonise over the details of his plan and to let doubt gnaw the edges of his already tattered nerves.

There was no way he could get out of this prison before moonrise that night. It was early tonight —17:38 on the dot, just after the cell doors were unlocked and the prisoners let out for their evening's free association. The entire block would be out in the communal areas, playing cards and gambling their daily allowances away. Almost a hundred men would be torn to bloody ribbons and no-one would be able to do a thing about it.

They'd know the truth then. The world would know. There was nothing that he could do to change that. There might just be a chance to save the lives of the other inmates. That's *if* the plan worked, *if* he didn't go on to make things even worse.

Jonesey let out a satisfied grunt, accompanied shortly afterwards by a liquid splattering. "Ah, better out than in, that's what my Dad used to tell me."

John buried his face deeper in the pillow. This close to the change, his senses had heightened, and right at this moment an enhanced sense of smell was the last thing he needed.

The automatic door lock clicked open and John dived through the cell door, out onto the steel walkway beyond, almost colliding with one of the prison officers.

Officer Phelps glared at him. "Watch where you're going, Simpson." He stuck his head into the open cell and withdrew it at speed. "For Christ's sake, Jones. Wipe your arse and get dressed. Breakfast's in five minutes."

"I can't, guv, got the shits, guv. Must have been that manky tuna casserole we 'ad last night."

"I don't give a fuck. Stick a bloody cork up it if you have to. I want you out of that cell and downstairs in two minutes or you're on report. Again."

The sounds of grumbling came from the cell. The toilet flushed, then after a few seconds, flushed again. The handle was pushed two or three times in quick succession, making Jonesey swear under his breath. Ten seconds later he stumbled out with one shoe still in his hand and his shirt on inside out. He sniffed his hand, shrugged, and turned to the officer with a wide grin plastered across his face. "There we go, guv. All ready. Are they doing the marinated quails' eggs this morning? Or is it the deep-fried slop for a change?"

The officer shook his head. "Well, why don't you get your arse down there and find out? And for fuck's sake, Jones, wash your hands before you set foot in that dining area."

As the officer walked away, Jonesey winked at John. "Mr Phelps will make someone a lovely mother one day."

They made their way down to the morning roll-call, then filed into the dining area. The blocks were brought in, one at a time, with A -Block usually the first through the doors. A few officers stood around the periphery of the room, keeping a close eye as the inmates queued for food.

John picked up his breakfast: fatty bacon with a couple of forlorn sausages drowned in baked beans. He grabbed a mug of coffee and followed Jonesey to a table in the centre of the room.

The adrenaline coursed through his body, making his stomach do somersaults and his heart hammer. *Fuck it. Now or never.*

He turned to Jonesey and smiled. "I'm really sorry about this, mate..." Then he slammed his hot cup of coffee into the other man's face.

Jonesey screamed and fell to the floor, holding his hands to his scalded face. John leapt to his feet and began kicking the prone man in the ribs, feeling the bones crunch under his feet.

Within seconds, the guards had swarmed over John and pounded at him with their batons, forcing him to the floor. John's beast snarled and tried pushing its way to the surface.

His body had become slick with sweat and he could feel the first itching of the transformation begin at the tips of his fingers and back of the jaw. Still the blows rained down, breaking his concentration, giving the beast more of a hold. "No more," he panted. "Please, no more."

The beating stopped and his hands were forced behind his back. Cold metal restraints gripped his wrist. He was dragged to his feet. John shoved the snarling wolf back into the deepest recesses of his mind, feeling relief flood through him as the itching subsided and his temperature returned to normal.

Mr Phelps lifted John's head and looked into his bloodshot eyes. "Now, Simpson, I know Jones is an arsehole, but that's no excuse to beat the shit out of him and spoil everyone's breakfast." He turned to one of the officers holding John's arms. "Get him cleaned up, get the doc to check him over, and stick the bastard in isolation. He can bloody well rot there until his remand hearing as far as I'm concerned. And someone get Jones down to the infirmary before he bleeds all over the floor."

The other inmates glared at John with murder in their eyes. Jonesey was popular here, having a knack for getting hold of certain luxury items. John's attack hadn't gone down well, but he didn't care. As he was dragged away, he grinned at them through bloodied teeth. It didn't matter what happened next. His plan had worked like a charm.

CHAPTER 5

12th December. Market Tavern, Durham. 11:35.

Gregorz pushed open the door, smiling at the rush of warmth from the bar. He stepped inside, closely followed by Daniel. The interior was dimly lit, with old stained-wood floors and an oak counter that was probably close to a hundred years old. The pub smelled of old wood infused with decades of spilled alcohol and cigarette smoke. Rickety wooden tables stood on the dance floor, with small laminated menus laid on their surfaces.

The lunchtime crowd had not yet arrived, so the place was almost empty, except for a couple of under-age boys in the corner nursing pints of watered-down lager, who cast suspicious, furtive glances at the newcomers. Gregorz made his way to the bar, ordered two glasses of cola, then moved away from the main area with Daniel, to an alcove where Oskar, Troy and Gabriela waited. Without a word of acknowledgement, Gregorz and Daniel took their places at the table.

Oskar sipped from a glass of iced water, then smiled at Gregorz. "Is everything in place? Have the arrangements been made?"

He nodded. "They have, but there's been a complication. Daniel found Wilkinson alive. At the hospital and under police guard."

Oskar arched his eyebrow. "That does complicate matters. How do you propose to deal with it?"

"We'll have to infiltrate the hospital again and take care of him before he turns. It sounds like he's in a coma, so it shouldn't be too much of a problem. The guard will be difficult, but not impossible."

Oskar nodded. "Please tell me that you are leaving Connie at home for this job."

Gregorz laughed. "Yes, she knows nothing about this. Connie will be escorting Marie into some nearby woodlands so she can change. As far as she's aware, Steven Wilkinson died from his wounds, and Daniel and I are providing your team with logistical support."

"Good. This situation has got out of hand and needs to be brought back under control."

Troy drained his drink, wiping his mouth with the back of his hand. "The weapons shipment arrived this morning. Your team's allocation will be in the trunk of your car by the time you get back to it." He winked at Daniel. "There should be enough there for even the two of you to put an old cripple down."

Daniel ignored the American and spoke to Oskar. "Do you know how you're going to get to Simpson? The police will be cautious after the last time."

Oskar smiled. "Don't worry, my friend. You take care of your little problem. The Simpson situation is well in hand."

Gregorz stood up. "I'm glad to hear it. Come on, Daniel. We have things to do. Good luck, Oskar."

Oskar smiled. "Luck? Luck won't even come into it."

12th December. Aykley Heads Police HQ. 16:18.

"What do you mean, he's gone on holiday? Do you know where? Well, did he leave a contact number? A mobile? A fucking email address? Anything? Well, thanks for nothing." Phil slammed the phone down and glared at it, imagining what it would be like to wrap his hands around Dr Miller's receptionist's turkey-neck and squeeze until her face turned blue and her eyes bulged out of her smug self-satisfied face.

Olivia entered through the double doors at the end of the office, took one look at her boss's face, and then beat a hasty retreat towards the coffee machine. He was about to join her when the phone rang again. He grabbed it from the desk and hit himself on the side of the head with the receiver. "What?"

"Erm, DI Fletcher? This is Dave down in forensic IT. You said you wanted to know when we pulled anything off that phone?"

Phil massaged the growing lump on his head with his free hand. "Phone? What phone?"

"The one they found at the Simpson house. On the body of...hang on...I've got his name here somewhere."

"You mean Simon Dobbs? What did you find? Anything useful?"

"I think you're going to want to see this for yourself, sir."

"Can it wait? I'm trying to get hold of Simpson's doctor."

"No, sir. I think you're going to want to see this right away."

Phil let out an exasperated sigh. "Okay, I'll be right down."

He locked his computer and headed towards the exit. Olivia was trying to sneak back to her desk without attracting Phil's attention. "Olivia, come on. They've got something for us downstairs."

Olivia rolled her eyes, took a sip from her drink, and followed Phil into the corridor. "What's up?"

He shook his head. "No idea. Forensics say they've gotten something from Simon Dobbs' telephone. They say we need to see it for ourselves."

Olivia tutted. "This better not be another one of those bloody YouTube videos. The last one Dave showed me put me off my dinner. Did he show you the one with the giant spot? Never seen anything so gross in my entire life."

"I was spared that one. If this is more of the same, then Dave will get a size ten planted right up his arse. I've been trying to get hold of Doctor Miller all day, and that bitch of a receptionist says that he's taken his fucking family on holiday and can't be contacted. Can you believe it?"

"Nothing that weasel does surprises me anymore. I've been chasing up some hotels and B&Bs in High Moor, but no luck tracking your mystery woman, by the way. Maybe she's just a local. I'm waiting to hear back from a couple in Durham, but I'm not holding out much hope. Did you see the inventory from Wilkinson's place yet?"

"Yeah. The evidence lads are having a fit, trying to find somewhere secure to store all those weapons. His solicitor's being unusually quiet about the whole thing, but it looks like there are enough unregistered firearms in that house to lock our comatose cripple up for a few decades. It looks like the Mac-10 was his, and Simpson's prints are all over the place."

Olivia raised one eyebrow and grinned sardonically. "Woo-hoo. Another win for the good guys. Let's see if Dave has any more good news for us."

The IT Forensics lab was situated in the basement level at police headquarters. Phil rang the buzzer and waited to be let in. It didn't take long. Dave virtually flung open the reinforced door and ushered them both inside to where an LCD monitor sat on a desk, surrounded by cables and pieces of circuit board.

The monitor was plugged into a desktop PC with its case open, and Simon Dobbs' telephone was connected to a USB port. Dave grabbed two red plastic chairs and placed them next to the table so that Phil and Olivia could sit down. The man was a bundle of nervous energy.

"OK, so we went through the contents of the phone. Most of it was pretty standard stuff. A few home-made porn pics. You know the sort of thing? Anyway, what was really interesting was a video file created on the night of Mr Dobbs' untimely death."

Olivia frowned. "Cut the shit, Dave. Just get on with it. Some of us have more important things to do than watching home-made porn on a dead bloke's phone."

"Oh, right. Of course. Now, the camera on this phone is pretty low spec, but you need to bear in mind that what you are seeing is raw, unedited footage. I checked the digital signatures on the files and they have not been messed with. In this instance..."

"Dave!"

"Oh, sorry." He reached over to a mouse and clicked play, then stepped back to allow Phil and Olivia an unobstructed view of the screen.

It showed an image of Simon Dobbs, dressed in a badly-fitting balaclava. He swore to himself, then turned the phone around so that the camera was pointing the other way.

John Simpson was tied to a chair in the centre of a room. Fresh blood covered his battered face and stained his clothing. White fragments of bone jutted out through the fabric of his T-shirt and from his ruptured knees. Another masked man removed a knife from his pocket and brought it up to John's face. "I'm going to take one of your eyes now, John. Just the one. I want you to be able to see what we've done to the rest of you." The tip of the knife pushed into John's cheek and sliced through the flesh in a slow, deliberate line towards his left eye.

John thrashed against his bonds, his body going into violent spasms. The chair toppled over and crashed to the floor.

The image on the phone shook and Simon Dobbs' voice wavered as he spoke. "Billy? What's happening to him? Is he having a fit or something?"

"I don't know. I've hardly touched him yet. Get the tape off his mouth. He might be having trouble breathing."

The image moved around John as Simon crept closer. His hand reached out and removed the strip of tape from John's mouth. "There you go, mate. No harm done, eh?" The image focused on John's face. The cut on his cheek had vanished and his eyes were a bright feral yellow. "Oh Jesus...he's...it's..."

Simon backed away, the camera still aimed at John's thrashing body. John's jaw dislocated with a loud snap and the front of his skull seemed to warp and shift. Then the video file ended and the screen went black.

Olivia put her hand to her mouth. "Jesus, what the hell was going on there?"

Dave grinned, barely able to contain his excitement. "I told you that you had to see it for yourselves... "He turned to Phil. "So, DI Fletcher, what do you think?"

Phil exhaled, not realising that he'd been holding his breath. "I really don't know... Has anyone else seen this video file?"

"No, not yet anyway. I thought you'd want to be the first."

"Dave, let me be clear about this. Nobody else is to watch that file without my express permission. I don't know what we just saw happen, but the press would have a field day with that footage, and Franks would have our heads on a pike. You say that the file hasn't been altered in any way?"

Dave looked crestfallen. "No, it's the raw footage. If the files had been altered then the digital signature would have changed. There's no way that it's been tampered with."

"Thank you, Dave. We'll be in touch, but in the meantime, remember. No one sees that file without my say-so. I don't want anyone even knowing about it. Okay?"

Dave's head dropped and his bottom lip puffed out slightly. "Alright. I got it."

Satisfied, Phil turned to Olivia. "Come on, we need to go and have a talk."

Phil and Olivia got to their feet. Leaving the IT lab, they walked the length of the corridor, going into a small meeting room at its end. Phil shut the door behind them.

"Was that for real, boss?"

Phil leaned against a table and ran his hand across his thinning scalp. "I don't know. The eyes could have been contact lenses. We didn't get a good look at his face until that close-up, so he could have already been wearing them. The thing with his face could have been crap on the camera or any number of other things. If nothing else, we've got a motive for what Simpson did to them."

Olivia shook her head. "Got to be honest, I can't really say I blame him, after watching that. He'd have a pretty good case for self-defence."

"Self-defence would be beating them up and driving them off.

Simpson chased each one of them down and tore them to pieces. It's understandable to an extent, but it's still murder."

"So, you don't think that we just watched a video of our suspect starting to turn into a werewolf, then?"

Phil exhaled. "I honestly don't know what to think. I'm not at the point of believing in werewolves, but there was something going on with Simpson."

"What are we going to do?"

"Well, the first thing I'm doing is getting on the phone to Durham nick. If Doctor Miller isn't around to take charge of his prisoner, then we need to keep him where he is, preferably in isolation. At least for tonight."

"You mean, until after the full moon."

Phil nodded. "Yes. Until after the full moon."

12th December. Durham Prison. 15:05.

John lay on the hard metal cot and waited. His new cell was small, barely eight feet by five, with only a metal bunk and small table (both of which were fixed to the floor), a steel toilet, and a chair made from reinforced cardboard for furniture.

The walls were made of old salt-encrusted brick, curving above his head to form a dome, and painted a flat white that reflected the glare from the fluorescent tube on the ceiling.

The only natural light came from what could euphemistically be called a window: a steel grille with small cubes of reinforced glass fitted in it. It seemed to be more metal than glass, and the weak grey light from outside was overpowered by the flickering phosphorescent glare of the overhead tube. The only way in or out of the cell was through a sturdy steel door on the wall opposite the window. In many ways, it reminded John of the secure basement in his secluded Welsh home. He wondered if the police had been there, and what sort of state it had been left in. He sighed. It was all irrelevant. He knew he would never see the place again.

The full moon was less than two hours away. This close to the change, his senses were aflame with sensation, and he found that he could map the entire wing out in his mind using only sound and smell. The low muttering from the convicted child murderer at the end of the hall. The laboured breathing of the drug dealer two cells along, asleep in his cell and unaware of the cancerous rot taking hold in his lungs. John smelled the sickly odour with every exhalation the sleeping man made. The sound of a door opening and several pairs of sturdy shoes ringing against the vinyl floor. Getting closer. The key jangled in the lock of John's cell.

No!

John sat bolt upright as the door swung open and Mr Phelps, flanked by two other prison officers, stood in the open doorway. Mr Phelps had a pair of handcuffs in his hands. The other two guards carried batons and pepper spray.

"Rise and shine, Simpson. Turn around, face the wall, and extend your hands behind your back."

John got to his feet and backed away from the prison officers. "What's going on?"

Mr Phelps took a cautious step into the cell. "What's going on is that you are going to turn around and extend your arms or these gentlemen behind me will assist you in doing so."

"You can't take me out of here. Not until tomorrow. Just lock the door and walk away. Please."

The three men took another step into the confined cell, and John found his back pressed against the wall. Mr Phelps smiled. "Last chance to do this the easy way, Simpson."

John's shoulders sagged and he turned around to face the wall. He couldn't risk another confrontation. Not this close to the full moon. Rough hands grasped his shoulders and the cold, unyielding metal of Mr Phelps' handcuffs clamped around his wrists. The officer backed out of the cell while the other two guards grabbed

John's arms and dragged him into the corridor.

"Please, put me back in the cell. Just for a couple more hours. Then you'll see."

Mr Phelps stepped in front of John, a sneer playing across his face. "In a couple of hours, you'll be tucked up, safe and sound in the nut-house where you belong." He nodded to the guards. "Get this piece of garbage out of my sight. We don't want to keep the van waiting."

12th December. University Hospital of Durham. 16:18.

Daniel drummed his fingers against the steering wheel of the rented car and waited. Part of the hospital car park had been cordoned off to accommodate the builders working on restoring the pathology lab, and it had taken him over twenty minutes of driving in circles before he'd found a place to park. Even then, he'd had to cut off another vehicle that had been making for the same space. The driver of the other car had gotten out of the vehicle and stormed over to him in a rage. Rather than risk confrontation, Daniel had simply apologized and handed the irate man a twenty pound note, which seemed to satisfy him.

He was not comfortable with returning to the hospital. Too many people had seen them last time. He was certain that the police officer guarding Wilkinson would have been briefed on the two men and the red-haired woman who visited Marie before her disappearance.

It would have made more sense for someone from Oskar's team to take care of Wilkinson, while he and Gregorz joined the assault mission against Simpson. Oskar could show flashes of pure inspiration when planning attacks, but all too often his arrogance meant that he sometimes made bad decisions. As far as Daniel was concerned, this was one such instance.

He checked his watch. Gregorz had been inside the building for over an hour, posing as a hospital porter, and the lack of subsequent communication was making him nervous. The moon would rise soon and he could already feel its effects. He could smell the traces of cigarette smoke in the upholstery of the vehicle and make out fragments of conversations from the people standing in the hospital foyer. His limbs buzzed with power, while at the back of his mind, he could feel his beast's desire to run, hunt and kill.

It was a mistake to leave the assault so late. Wilkinson was comatose and crippled. Helpless. When the moon came up and he transformed for the first time, all of that would change. His wounds would be healed, and they would have to deal with a newborn, moonstruck werewolf in a crowded hospital full of CCTV cameras.

Again, it had been at Oskar's insistence that they delay the assault until the last possible moment. He feared that Wilkinson's death, if discovered too soon, might jeopardize their attack on Simpson. Gregorz had argued with Oskar for over an hour but had eventually relented when Oskar had called Michael and asked for him to make a ruling.

His phone vibrated on the dashboard and he snatched it up to check the message. One word. Restaurant.

A grim smile played across his lips. "Finally." He reached across and picked up the black canvas bag from the passenger seat, then stepped out of the car and made his way towards the main entrance of the hospital.

The foyer bustled with activity and people queued three-deep at the receptionist's desk. Daniel made his way through the crowds and veered off to the left, taking the staircase to the second floor where the restaurant was located. Gregorz sat in the far corner of the room, with his back to the rest of the patrons. Daniel bought a coffee from the vending machine and threaded his way through the room, sitting on a table adjacent to his team leader.

He took a sip from his cup and grimaced, then put it down on the table and leaned back on the plastic chair. "I was beginning to worry about you, Gregorz. How are things looking?"

"It's as we suspected. Wilkinson is in a private room, with a single police officer stationed outside. None of the cameras have a direct line of sight to the doorway, but there is one at each end of the hallway, and there is a nurse’s station almost directly opposite the room."

"I take it you have a plan to distract the nurses and policeman?"

Gregorz took a drink from his cup and nodded. "I think a more constrained version of Connie's plan will be the most effective."

"So you are not intending to burn the hospital down? She will be disappointed."

"I think a small, easily-contained fire may serve our purposes better. We should be able to get to Wilkinson and deal with him in the initial confusion." He nodded to the bag at Daniel's feet. "You have everything?"

"Yes. We have some silenced nine millimetres and I made up the solution before I left the hotel. I have to say, though, just handling it makes me nervous. I almost wish that we could deal with Wilkinson in a cleaner way than injecting him with that foul substance."

"Just remember who you are dealing with. Wilkinson has slaughtered our kind for decades, without any mercy. Connie's daughter was only eight years old, and it didn't stop the bastard from shooting her in the face. Silver particles suspended in acid is almost too good for him. If it were up to me, I'd simply lock him in a room with Connie for a few days and leave the manner of his demise up to her. Unfortunately, that is not my decision to make."

Daniel checked his watch and reluctantly took another drink from the plastic cup. "We have less than an hour before moonrise. When do we make our move?"

"We wait for Oskar's signal. Once he's sure that they have Simpson where they want him, we can take care of our mission."

"Well, then let's hope that Oskar doesn't take too long."

12th December. Seven Bells Hotel, Durham. 16:25.

Connie paced back and forth, then stopped by the door to the room and put her hands on her hips. "Can ye not get a bloody move on? The moon will be up in an hour, and Ah don't want ye changing in the fucking car."

Marie picked up a towel from beside the sink and dried her wet hair, leaving dark streaks of dye across the white fabric. She was as keen to get out of the hotel room as Connie was. After spending almost a month inside it, with only Connie's sparkling company and daytime TV to distract her, she felt more than a little claustrophobic in the cramped surroundings. "I'll just be a second. Just need to get this eyeliner on and I'm good to go."

A sneer played across Connie's face. "Do ye not think yer a bit old to pull off the goth girlie look? Ye'd have been better off going for 'middle-aged mum'. Ye've already got the arse for it."

Marie gave Connie the finger and applied thick strokes of eye make-up to her face, giving her eyes a sunken appearance. Satisfied, she put down the eyeliner and picked up her jacket from the hanger. "OK, all done. Let's get this over with."

"About fucking time. The car's parked across the street, and before you ask, Ah'm driving."

"Whatever. Let's just go."

The two women stepped out of the room into the hotel's dingy corridor and walked to the staircase, descending to the ground level. Marie was about to open the door into the foyer when Connie put her hand on her arm and shook her head. When Marie looked confused, Connie whispered, "Coppers. Outside. Ah can smell the bastards. Ye wait here and Ah'll see what's going on."

Connie stepped through the fire door into the reception area, while Marie stood against the wall and peered through the glass. As Connie had said, there were three uniformed police officers standing at the reception desk, along with a blonde woman in a business suit. They turned to Connie as she walked through the door, and the woman stepped forward to offer her hand.

"Miss Hamilton? Or is it Mrs? I'm afraid that it doesn't say which on your registration form."

Connie spoke with a calm tone, all traces of her accent gone."Yes? Can I help you? Is something the matter?"

The blonde woman smiled and shook her head. "No, nothing to worry about. I was just wondering if you would mind if I asked you a few questions?"

"Of course. I don't mind, but right now isn't very convenient. I'm supposed to be meeting someone and I don't want to be late. Could we arrange something for Monday, perhaps? I'd be happy to come down to your station and have a chat at, say, 2pm?"

The blonde woman nodded and smiled again. "It really wouldn't take very long. I just need to establish your whereabouts on the fifteenth of November, at around five-thirty in the evening."

Connie shook her head. "I'm sorry, but without checking my schedule I'm afraid I really couldn't say. Things have been so busy that the days just seem to run together. Look, I really hate to rush, but can we do this later? I have a rather pressing appointment, and I don't want to keep my client waiting. Can we do this on Monday?"

"Of course, I'm sorry to have kept you. I'll be at High Moor station on Monday afternoon. Just come to reception and ask for DC Garner. Olivia Garner."

Connie nodded and shook her hand. "Thank you for being so understanding. I'll check my diary and let you know what I was up to when I see you."

Marie stepped away from the door and made her way to the end of the corridor, then slipped out of the emergency exit into the dark alley beside the hotel. She stood in the shadows, watching as Connie left the hotel and walked along the road towards the city centre. The police officers stood by the doorway for a moment, speaking in low voices as they watched Connie glide through the crowded streets. The uniformed officers got into a police car and drove away, while the woman pulled up the collar of her coat and hurried after Connie.

A few minutes later, Connie clambered over a stone wall at the rear of the car park. "Bastards have made us. Oskar and his crew better finish the job tonight, because it's time for us to get the hell out of this shit-hole." She started to walk across the road to where her rented car was parked, then turned back to Marie. "Well, are ye coming, or do ye just fancy changing in the middle of the fucking town centre?"

CHAPTER 6

12th December. University Hospital of Durham. 17:35.

The first thing that Steven noticed was the noise. Far away and indistinct, but insistent. It tugged on the threads of his awareness and punctured the peace of the darkness in which he floated. The next thing he noticed was the pain. A hot glow that started from the smallest coal in the centre of his back, growing in size and intensity until his body burned. It filled him, lighting up every nerve ending in a white blaze of agony. Fire crackled along his spine, fusing ruined bone and reconnecting the shredded nerves. He screamed, but the sound never left his lips. Instead, it reverberated inside his mind, combining with the pain into waves of absolute torment. Consuming him. Burning away everything that he had ever been. Turning him into something else.

His eyes snapped open, and he gagged at the hard plastic pipe in his throat. His body was slick with sweat, soaking through the polyester pyjamas so the material stuck to his skin. An alarm rang outside: the air stank of death, even beneath the overpowering stench of disinfectant. He tore the ventilator tube from his swollen throat and, still disoriented, swung his legs off the bed and pulled the IV drips from his arm.

He was obviously in a hospital, but the reason eluded him. He tried to think through the drug-induced cloud in his mind, but all he saw were fragments. He remembered the school. He'd been doing something in a school with...

The memories surged back, memories of he and John Simpson sneaking into the school to confront the monster that had once been Malcolm Harrison. The short-lived battle, the terrible pain as the werewolf crushed his spine with its jaws. He looked down at his legs and wiggled his toes.

"Oh fucking hell. How long have I been here?" He stumbled to the window and pulled back the blinds. It was dark outside. The neon pinpricks of the city's streetlights shining against a velvet background, while to the east, the first sliver of the full moon rose above the cathedral.

"Oh no."

His body began to spasm and he fell to the floor, dragging the ventilator with him. He tried to stand, to hold back the raging, alien presence in his mind. "God, no. Please. Not here."

Bone daggers burst through his gums, filling his mouth with a bloody froth, while his jaw dislocated and the ends of his fingers split open in a spray of gore, to allow dark black talons to emerge. His skin itched and burned as hair burst from his pores and flowed across his body.

He was vaguely aware of the door to his room bursting open and two dark silhouettes standing in the doorway. Then the world turned red.

12th December. Waldridge Fell Country Park. 17:35.

Marie removed her clothes and put them in the boot of the hire car. Connie's were already in a crumpled heap next to the steel strongbox that held the team's tactical kit. She stepped away from the vehicle and closed the boot, rubbing her arms to ward off the biting cold. Connie stood stark naked in the bushes that separated the car park from the open fell beyond. Clouds of condensation billowed from her body. She smirked at Marie's discomfort.

"Are ye feeling the cold, petal? Ah thought your lot didn't mind a wee chill. Get a bloody move on before some poor bastard catches a look at your bare arse waddling across the car park."

Marie jogged across the open tarmac to where the other woman stood. "Connie, I'm sure I've told you before, but please do me the favour of fucking off. I'm not in the mood for your shit."

Connie puffed out her bottom lip. "Aw, pet. Are ye upset because Oskar and the others are putting yer little moonstruck boyfriend down? Ah bet he's on his knees, begging for his life right this second."

Marie shoved the other woman with both hands, sending her back a few steps. "I told you. Pack it the fuck in."

Connie grinned and her eyes became two flat, green phosphorescent disks. "Ah, get over yourself. Ah'm just playing around. Come on, the moon will be up any second. Let's get away from the road so we can change."

Marie exhaled and nodded her acceptance. The two women made their way through the hedgerow into a small willow coppice bordering the moors. The ground was cold and wet under Marie's bare feet. Twigs caught between her toes, and a patch of brambles left bright red scratches across her legs. Frost had begun to form on the open expanses of grassland. Each blade glimmered in the starlight and crunched under Marie's feet. The lights of the city illuminated the sky to the south-east, while the first white glow of the new moon shone from the horizon.

Connie's change had already begun. Marie turned her head so that she wouldn't have to witness it. Connie could transform from human to beast faster than anyone she'd ever met, but it didn't make the sight any less disturbing. In some ways, the ease with which Connie turned made it worse. As if she were closer to the bestial side of her nature. Within moments, the transformation had completed and a huge russet monster stood in the clearing beside her. Marie suppressed a shudder as Connie sniffed the air and then slipped through the trees, into the darkness.

The moon came into view, bathing Marie in a cool white light. She closed her eyes and waited for her beast to break through.

Nothing happened.

Marie's heart fluttered, the first instinctive realization that something was wrong. She searched her feelings for that other presence, her constant companion since she was eight years old, but found no trace. She closed her eyes and steadied her breathing, then willed the change to happen, but it had no effect. Her wolf was gone. For the first time since she was a little girl, she was alone. She choked back a sob and tried to contain the grief that welled within her.

Then, a few hundred yards to the north, she heard Connie howl and her blood ran cold. Somehow, she was human. And The Pack had very specific rules about how to deal with humans who knew of their existence. Connie's senses, now that she'd turned, would register this in a matter of seconds, if they hadn't already. Marie's heart lurched as adrenaline surged through her system, then she turned and sprinted back towards the parked hire car.

12th December. University Hospital of Durham. 17:30.

Gregorz sipped his coffee and suppressed a grimace. Vending machine coffee was vile at the best of times, but with the full moon approaching, his enhanced senses were able to pick out the individual flavours and chemical tangs from the foul black liquid. He picked up his phone and checked it for a message from Oskar, even though he'd done so only seconds before.

Daniel shifted on the hard plastic chair. "Gregorz, we need to move. Now."

He nodded. That they were leaving things so late was absurd, but the orders had been explicit. The consequences of ignoring them, especially if it put Oskar's mission at risk, would be severe. "We'll give Oskar another minute."

"You said that five minutes ago. The moon will be up in another five, and we'll have a much more serious problem to deal with. There are cameras here, Gregorz. Lots of cameras. If a moonstruck tears through a hospital and they film it, then it will be over for all of us. Forget Simpson. He's contained. Even if Oskar fails to complete his mission, the casualties will be limited and there is still a chance to fix it. This is where the most damage could be done, and we have to deal with it. Right now."

Gregorz picked up the phone again and exhaled. If this went wrong, then he would have to live with the consequences, but if they sat here and did nothing, then disaster was assured. "You're right. We've already waited too long. Make your way to Wilkinson's room and I'll arrange the distraction."

They both got up from their seats. Daniel hefted the canvas holdall, nodded to him, and made his way out of the restaurant while Gregorz headed for the staircase to the floor below. The urge to race down the stairs rose within him, but he forced himself to stay calm. He walked quickly through the outpatients area to the toilets, then opened the door and stepped inside.

The toilets were empty apart from a man urinating in the far cubicle. He was whistling to himself, and did not seem to be finishing any time soon. Gregorz checked his watch and sighed. He had only minutes before moonrise. Not nearly enough time. He walked over to the cubicle, grabbed the back of the man's head, and smashed it into the porcelain tiles. The tile cracked under the impact, and the man slid to the floor, unconscious. Gregorz grabbed a toilet roll and several handfuls of paper towels, stuffed them into a waste bin, then, with the aid of some lighter fluid, set the bin alight. Smoke and flames billowed from the waste receptacle. Moments later the smoke detectors triggered the fire alarm. Gregorz slipped from the toilets and made his way up the central staircase to rendezvous with Daniel.

The hospital was in pandemonium. So soon after the last fatal fire, everyone was taking the alarm very seriously indeed. Nurses directed patients and visitors to the nearest fire exit and began the arduous process of moving those who were unable to move themselves. He pushed his way through the tide of people to reach Daniel. The German's eyes said it all, and Gregorz knew it too. He'd felt it the same moment as Daniel. The moon had risen. Instead of a quiet assassination of a comatose man, they had to cope with a newborn moonstruck werewolf in a crowded hospital. Daniel handed him a pistol, then they opened the door to the darkened room and stepped inside.

Wilkinson's transformation had just completed. The creature crouched on the tiled floor, snarling at the intruders. Saliva dripped from razor-sharp fangs, and its muscles tensed. As Gregorz and Daniel raised their pistols, the creature lashed out with a huge, taloned claw and hurled the ventilator at them. It smashed into Daniel, knocking him back into Gregorz. His pistol discharged as the ventilator hit, and the window behind the bed shattered, spilling shards of glass onto the pavement below. The beast regarded them for a moment, as if it understood what it faced. Just as Gregorz brought his weapon to bear, it snarled once more, then leaped through the broken window. For a fraction of a second it was silhouetted against the rising moon. Gregorz took his shot, then the beast disappeared from sight.

Daniel picked himself up. "Did you get it?"

"I don't know. It was fast. Faster than a newborn should have been, and it knew. Somehow the damn thing understood what those guns meant. Have you ever seen a moonstruck run before?"

Daniel shook his head and walked to the window, looking out onto the gravel path surrounding the hospital, and the trees beyond. "There's no sign of it. Come on, we should get out of here. I'll try and pick up its scent once we are outside."

"Just like the good old days, eh, Daniel?"

Daniel tried to smile, then shook his head. "If you ask me, my friend, the good old days were vastly overrated."

12th December. Finchale Road, Brasside. 17:35.

John squeezed his eyes closed and tried to control his breathing. He'd been bundled into the prisoner transport van, and two guards had shackled his ankles and wrists with handcuffs. A chain had been passed through both sets of cuffs and fastened to a steel ring on the floor of the van. The two guards had climbed in beside him, and the vehicle had left the prison on the five-mile journey to the secure unit.

That had been an hour ago. The Friday evening traffic around Durham City had been even slower than usual, with the freezing conditions causing a number of accidents, clogging the roads of the city with frustrated commuters. It had only been when it turned off the main road on the way to Frankland Prison and its psychiatric assessment unit that the van managed to pick up any speed at all. Of course, it was all too late now. The moon would be up in a matter of seconds, and despite the restraints, the interior of the van was too small for the two men locked in with him to escape the ferocity of his wolf.

He felt it trying to push through, and he erected well-practiced, familiar walls in his mind to try and slow the beast's progress. Not that they had ever made any difference. He'd not even been able to hold the transformation back for long enough to save his parents. The beast was not happy about John's attempts to restrain it. He felt some of its emotions leaking through into his own consciousness. Surprise, confusion, and grief, like a mistreated dog that had been lavished with love for once in its life, before being discarded and abused once more. The hurt the beast felt quickly changed into anger at the betrayal, and it hurled itself against John's feeble barriers with renewed strength, fuelled by the rising moon. John's teeth itched and sweat poured from his body, soaking through the prison clothing.

One of the guards reached across and put his hand on John's shoulder. "Here, mate, are you alright?"

***

Oskar crouched in the bushes and smiled as the headlights of the prison van approached. He let out a low whistle to signal Troy and Gabriela. They would place the traffic lights on the road to prevent any other vehicles from interrupting them, and then take up their positions. Troy would make his way down the road to help him take care of the Moonstruck, while Gabriela would transform and chase the creature down if it got past them.

It was time for him to complete his part of the plan. He crept from the undergrowth and deployed a strip of spikes across the road, just as it passed under a stone railway bridge, after which he retreated to cover once more and drew his weapon.

It was at times like these when he felt the most alive. He could visualize the disparate parts of his plan coming together before him, like the components of a complex machine. He'd left nothing to chance. Not this time. While Frankland Prison was only a mile away, the radio jammer that he'd activated in the rear of their rented van would ensure that no call for help would reach the authorities. The red traffic lights were positioned a quarter of a mile away on either side of the bridge, and there were no pedestrians. Not any more, at least. An old man had been walking a decrepit Labrador along the roadside a little while ago, but Gabriela had taken care of them, dragging the corpses into the woods, out of sight.

The headlights of the approaching van flared as it crested a slight rise in the road, then started down towards the tunnel. Oskar tightened his grip on his weapon in anticipation, running his tongue across his dry lips. The van would hit the spikes in three seconds. Two. One.

***

All four tyres on the vehicle exploded simultaneously, and John's world turned upside down. He hardly felt his arm break, nor the shattered bone slice through his flesh and clothing. His head struck the floor and then he flew forwards, to crash against the rear wall. He opened his eyes, but could not focus on the face of the security guard standing over him, or make out the words coming from his mouth. The world was distorted, as if he were seeing and hearing it from underwater. He concentrated, trying to bring it all back into focus. The sound came back gradually, as if someone was turning up the volume on a muted television set.

"It's alright, mate. We've crashed, and it looks like your arm's broken. I'm going to undo your restraints and try and get you more comfortable until the ambulance arrives." The guard banged on the rear wall adjoining the driver's compartment. "Mike. We need an ambulance in here. The prisoner's got a broken arm and god knows what else."

The driver's muffled voice replied after a moment. "The radio's out. Crash must have knackered it. I can't get a mobile signal either, so I'm going to go and get some help. OK?"

John fought to clear his head and remember where he was. As the guard unlocked the ankle and wrist restraints, his memory returned and he looked up at the man with horror in his eyes. "Oh

God. What have you done?"

Then the full moon crested the treetops outside, and John's transformation began.

The broken bone in John's arm slid back into place and the flesh around the wound closed up. The guard took a step backwards to join his companion, who was trying to open the buckled door. Blind terror was etched across the man's face, and the stale air inside the vehicle stank of fear.

John's bones began to snap and reform, while the colour drained from his vision, leaving the van's interior cast in a stark monochrome. The beast was like a tsunami of blood and rage, roaring up from the deepest parts of his subconscious.

He tried to remember what Marie had told him. To work alongside the monster. Accept it, and so retain a measure of control. He opened himself to the wolf, realising too late that the beast was not interested. This was its time, not his, and it was in no mood to compromise.

John attempted to fill his mind with mental images of them working together, two parts of a single entity. For the smallest fraction of a second, John sensed a change in it. Some of the fury abated, and he sensed that he'd caught the monster's interest.

Then one of the guards squirted pepper spray into the werewolf's eyes.

***

The tyres of the van exploded as they crossed the spikes. The vehicle swerved to the left, the driver over-compensating for his loss of control. The metal wheel-rims screamed against the road, spraying the air with a shower of sparks, before the vehicle flipped onto its side and slammed into the solid stone walls of the tunnel.

Oskar opened his mind and brought his beast to the surface just as the moon crested the horizon, barely holding his transformation in check. He heard Troy running along the side of the road towards his position. The large American's scent was distinct, a heavy animal musk combined with sweat and gun oil. Gabriela's scent was, in part, masked by the stink of leaking motor oil and blood that emanated from the prison van. She was circling around from the east, through a small patch of woodlands.

The driver clambered out from the wreckage and limped along the road towards the prison, presumably to bring help. He wouldn't get far. His route took him straight past where Gabriela lurked. She'd be glad of a brief distraction before the main event.

Muffled screams came from within the prison van, along with a furious, bestial roar. The screams soon stopped, to be replaced by a wet, tearing noise. The stench of blood threatened to overpower Oskar's senses and drove his own beast into a frenzy. It was so distracting that he didn't notice that Troy had arrived until the big American put his hand on his shoulder.

"Looks like the sheep took too damn long to wander into the trap. Why are these things never easy? I'd rather have just put a bullet through Simpson's head and be done with it."

Oskar smiled. "It's unfortunate that he turned before we could get to him, but it doesn't change the plan. Besides, it's better this way. Purer."

Troy sighed. "Harder and more dangerous, you mean." The American turned away from his alpha and moved towards the overturned van, his pistol trained on the buckled rear door. Oskar moved alongside him, aiming his own weapon at the now silent van. Rivulets of dark blood ran from the wrecked door frame, running down the white paintwork to drip onto the road, mingling with the growing pool of black oil on the tarmac.

He transferred his pistol to his left hand, and with his right, grabbed hold of the door handle, ready to pull it open.

The door flew off its hinges, smashing into Oskar's face and throwing him to the ground. Something flashed past him. Something big and incredibly fast. The sense of raw power that he got from the moonstruck terrified him. He'd been hunting the beasts for two decades, but he'd never seen one so fast, or so powerful, in all that time.

Troy managed to squeeze off two shots before the beast was on him. The monster leaped into the air, reaching out for him, but Troy was close to the change himself, and he rolled beneath the slashing claws with ease, bringing his pistol to bear as he did so.

The werewolf didn't stop. Instead of turning to attack Troy, it leaped over a low wooden fence and disappeared into the trees. Troy fired his weapon at the fleeing monster, then engaged the safety catch and put the pistol into the pocket of his hooded top. He ran to the ruined van and helped Oskar to his feet. "Did you see that? It should have torn me apart."

Oskar dusted himself down. "Are you complaining? You'll need to get after it. I've never seen a moonstruck that big before. Gabriela might struggle to contain it alone."

Troy began to remove his clothes, passing them to Oskar as he did. "It took off to the northwest. Any idea what's up there?"

"Open fields, hemmed in by the river. There's a ruined abbey on the river bank, and a caravan park, along with a footbridge, over the river. Try and contain it before it gets to the caravans. If you can't, then drive it over the bridge. I'll clean up here, then take the van and block its escape route."

Troy nodded his understanding as he passed the last of his clothes to Oskar, then began to change. His spine elongated in three distinct snaps, and he fell forward to all fours as his leg bones twisted into their new shape. His ears stretched out into ragged triangles, while fangs forced their way out of the werewolf's muzzle. Troy had not so much as broken stride during the transformation, and by the time he'd gone ten paces, the change had completed. The huge, blond werewolf sniffed the air and let out a howl of triumph as it caught the scent of its prey, then it leapt over the fence and vanished into the woods in pursuit.

Oskar watched Troy leave, then hurried to retrieve the spiked strip and brass casings from Troy's pistol. He made his way through the tunnel to where their hired van was parked, disengaged the radio jammer, and set off to retrieve the fake traffic lights. He realised, as he put the keys in the ignition, that his hands were shaking and his heart still pounded.

He pushed the fear down, but it remained a nagging presence, turning his stomach and flooding his system with adrenaline. He'd never seen anything like the creature that John Simpson had become. He prayed that Troy and Gabriela could finish the job alone, because he found that he did not relish the thought of encountering that monster again. Not one little bit.

CHAPTER 7

12th December. Waldridge Fell Country Park. 17:42.

Marie's lungs burned as she sucked in gasps of the frigid night air. The moonlight filtered down through the trees, providing just enough illumination for her to make her way through the small woods on the edge of the fell, for which she was grateful. The smallest trip or stumble could mean her death.

Gregorz or Daniel would have at least talked to her and consulted with Michael before making any decisions. Connie was another story. She'd never forgiven Marie for what had happened to her daughter. If she was honest, she'd not forgiven herself, either. Where the others would have been reasonable, to a point, Connie would delight in the chance to interpret pack law as she saw fit.

Brambles slashed at her skin while branches and stones stuck into her feet as they impacted on the cold ground. She ignored the pain and tried to control her breathing in an attempt to calm the rising wave of panic in her gut. She made out the first orange twinkle of the streetlights through the trees and almost cried out in relief. Then Connie howled. Somewhere close, off to her right.

There was no way that she could beat Connie to the car park. She'd be cut to ribbons before she got another ten feet. She stopped running and looked around for anything that could be used as a weapon, knowing that it would be all but useless against the werewolf stalking her.

The undergrowth rustled to her left, and her straining ears picked up the faint hint of a snarl barely held in check. Her eyes fixed on a broken tree branch - eight feet long and almost nine inches across, ending in a jagged point where the branch had split from the tree. Marie dropped to her knees, grabbing for the branch, just as the bracken parted and Connie pounced.

Marie's instincts took over. She grasped her makeshift spear and rolled forward in a single, sinuous movement, bringing the branch up into Connie's stomach. The werewolf's momentum carried it over Marie, slamming it into the old elm tree behind her. The impact as the monster hit the floor forced the jagged piece of wood straight through the werewolf's back, trailing a glistening black loop of intestine behind it. The beast howled in agony, snapping at the wooden stake that impaled it.

Marie wasted no time. She scrambled to her feet and sprinted through the last of the trees, onto the hard gravel of the car park. Luck was on her side for once. She grasped the cold metal handle of the car door, yanking it open, and threw herself inside.

With trembling hands, she retrieved the keys from the glove compartment, feeling a wave of relief when the engine started first time. She put the car in reverse and slammed her foot down on the accelerator, whipping the car round to face the exit in a cloud of dust. Then Connie burst from the undergrowth.

The werewolf's fur was stained black with blood, but there was no sign of any injury. The wound would have healed as soon as the branch was removed, although Marie could not help but hope that some sharp fragment was still lodged inside, slicing through organs with every move it made. The creature stalked towards the car, fangs bared, with hatred glistening in its glowing green eyes. Marie shifted into first gear, planted her foot on the accelerator, and aimed the vehicle directly at the enraged monster.

For a terrible moment, as the car hit the werewolf, Marie thought that she was going to lose control. The impact jarred her, and the steering wheel lurched in her hands, while the beast's blood splattered across the windscreen. She grasped the wheel in a death grip, holding on for her life as the werewolf disappeared under the vehicle with a satisfying crunch of breaking bones. Marie twisted the wheel, sliding sideways onto the main road, before she straightened the vehicle and accelerated away from the car park with a tortured squeal of rubber.

She checked the rear view mirror, but the road behind her was empty. She breathed a sigh of relief. By the time Connie healed enough to give chase, she'd be a mile or more down the road. Not that she could be complacent. Connie could be particularly single-minded when her blood was up. Marie had no doubt that she'd be giving chase, tracking the scent of the car for as long as was practical. She'd have to put a few miles between them before she could risk stopping to retrieve her clothes from the car boot. Then all she would have to do is figure out what the hell she was going to do next.

12th December. Aykley Heads Sports Ground. 18:00.

The red tide in Steven's mind began to recede and, for the first time since the change had begun, he was aware of himself. Trees flashed past in a blur, and his—*its*— shoulder burned in a white hot blaze of agony. The beast's thoughts filled his mind in a tumble of emotions and images..

Run. Hide. Kill. Eat.

The werewolf was weakening from blood loss, and its mind swam with confusion at its conflicting urges. Steven could visualize its memories. The werewolves bursting in on him mid-transformation, for the newborn beast had instantly recognized the intruders for what they were, and had known fear.

The crack of a pistol being fired. The pain as the silver bullet struck home. The building terror at the knowledge that it was being hunted. The creature scent-marked the trees around the hospital, then darted over a busy road to the surprise of the passing motorists, into another small, wooded area.

OK, you fucker, let's have a little talk.

Steven forced himself up through the layers of the creature's consciousness like a drowning man clawing his way to the surface, then folded his will around the raging, but weakened, alien presence. The werewolf struggled to free itself from his grip. It snarled and snapped at him, but Steven just tightened his grasp and forced the beast down. The transformation began almost immediately.

If anything, the experience was worse going from wolf to human than it had been from man to beast. The savage fangs pushed their way back through his gums, feeling as if a dentist was drilling all of his teeth at once, without the benefit of anaesthetic. Black talons forced their way under his already forming fingernails, while every bone in his body splintered and reformed, flowing like liquid into their original shape.

The worst thing, however, was the itching burn across every inch of his skin, as thousands of coarse black hairs pushed their way into his flesh. He cried out in agony, but his vocal chords were halfway between human and werewolf, so all that escaped his lips was a strange combination of howl and scream.

Then, after what felt like hours but was in fact just a few seconds, the transformation finished. He lay in the cold, wet dirt and brought his trembling hands up to his face to reassure himself that he didn't still have a muzzle and fangs. The wound in his shoulder screamed in outrage. He pulled the last, tattered remains of the hospital smock over his head with his uninjured arm, and craned his neck to assess the damage. The bullet appeared to have passed straight through without hitting bones or vital blood vessels, and although the exit wound was ugly, it was nowhere near as bad as it could have been. If his would-be assassins had been using hollow points, or something like his mercury rounds, then things would have been a hell of a lot worse.

He folded what was left of the smock and tried to wrap it around the exit wound, where the blood flow was heaviest, grasping one sleeve with his teeth while he knotted the other around it with his free hand. It wasn't much use as a bandage, but it was better than nothing, and would hopefully keep him from bleeding to death. Assuming he didn't die of exposure first, of course. The temperature had to be below freezing. Frost was forming on the mouldering blanket of leaves beneath his bare feet, and an icy wind whipped through the trees. If he didn't find some shelter and some clothes pretty sharpish, then he'd be in trouble. Assuming that he could get away from the pack of assassins stalking him, that is.

He tried to put together the pieces in his mind. He'd obviously been brought to the hospital after the incident at the school, and the nearest major hospital to High Moor was in Durham. If his fragmented memories were to be trusted, he'd headed east, towards the rising moon, after the escape from the hospital. He grinned. He knew exactly where he was. He'd worked here for almost fifteen years.

The Durham Constabulary Headquarters at Aykley Heads lay less than half a mile east of the hospital. And just to the south of the main building was the Aykley Heads Recreation Ground, the private sports club that served the people working at the police HQ.

The place would be quiet at this time on a Friday night, with most of the officers either getting ready to deal with the inevitable drunken riots in the city centre or heading home after a long shift. If he was lucky, there would only be one or two people using the facilities. Wincing at the pain, he got to his feet and pushed his way through the undergrowth towards the distant glimmer of the sport centre's lights.

Steven emerged from the trees after five anxious minutes of making his way through the woods, listening out for any sign of pursuit.

The sports centre lay across a playing field with the skeletal outlines of goalposts visible against the light spilling from the building. The centre itself was a squat, ugly building, made from pebble-dashed concrete panels and steel.

There were two cars parked outside, a silver Mercedes and a bright yellow Smart Car. His hearing, still enhanced from the transformation, picked out the sounds of a squash ball being slammed against a wall. Perfect.

He ran across the field as quickly as his injury allowed, keeping himself low and ensuring that he kept the main bulk of the building between himself and the front door. Being discovered now would be awkward.

Steven made it across the field without incident, and flattened himself against the cold concrete wall. The squash game continued, but now that he was close, he realised that something was wrong. The grunts of exertion from within were not made by men. Two female police officers were working the stress of the week off, complaining to each other about their colleagues and taking out their pent-up aggression on the squash ball.

Which meant that the only clothes inside belonged to women. And it meant that discovery would be so much worse. He shook his head. "For fuck's sake, that's just bloody typical." Then he made his way around to the front of the building and slipped inside.

The sounds of the squash game echoed around the cold concrete floors of the building, reflecting from the walls until it sounded like dozens of balls were suffering in place of these women's workmates.

"Do you know what the twat said then?" WHACK!

"No, what did the wanker do this time?" SMACK!

"He said I should wear tighter trousers because my arse looks fat in baggy ones."WHACK!

"The fucking tosser!" SMACK!

Steven kept low and hurried to the women's changing rooms. He breathed a sigh of relief. Neither of the women had bothered to use the lockers. The chances of a casual thief deciding to rob the police gymnasium were fairly remote. The women's clothes lay across the slatted wooden benches, with thick winter coats hanging on the pegs above.

Steven grabbed the biggest coat, and the bag beneath it, then ran from the changing rooms toward the car park, pulling on the coat as he did. He flung open the doors, when his nostrils picked up a heavy, animal musk from the west. They'd found him.

Steven fought the panic bubbling up from his stomach, and shoved his hands into the bag, discarding handfuls of loose tampons and pieces of makeup until he found a set of keys. He fished them out from the bag and pressed the unlock button on the key fob.

A surge of pure relief washed over him when one of the cars lights flashed, swiftly replaced by dismay when he realised that he'd unlocked the Smart Car instead of the Mercedes. Still, in his position, he really couldn't afford to be picky. He sprinted barefoot to the parked car and forced his frame inside, then started the engine and accelerated away.

He looked over his shoulder, fearful of pursuit. From the darkness of the playing field, his gaze was met by two sets of glowing green eyes.

12th December. Finchale Priory. 18:05.

Gabriela burst through a hedge and darted across a field. The crops had long been harvested, and the loose soil shifted beneath her paws as she ran, throwing up a lingering stink of the manure the fields had been sprayed with in late September. She suppressed a shudder at the thought of scrubbing it out from under her fingernails later. The moonstruck was heading straight for the ruined Priory to the northeast. She picked up Troy's unmistakable scent to the southwest as he pursued the other werewolf. He was gaining on the bipedal creature, but would not get to it before it reached the caravan park and more witnesses. She'd have to head it off before it got that far. With her ears flattened to her head, she accelerated her pace, hoping that she'd make it in time.

The ease with which the moonstruck had escaped Oskar and Troy bothered her. By rights, John Simpson should have been chained up in the back of the prison transport, and it should have been a simple matter of putting a bullet through his brain. Instead, another of Oskar's brilliant plans was unravelling before her eyes.

She respected her team alpha, but was not without her own ambitions. When this was over, she'd have to think about how she could use his repeated failure to her own advantage. Before that, though, there was the small matter of John Simpson. How hard could it be? He was just another rabid moonstruck, waiting to be put out of his misery. It was nothing they had not dealt with a hundred times before, even if this bastard was making things difficult. At least he was out of police custody. The hard part was over. Now all they had to do was kill him.

She reached the corner of the field, making a decision. In front of her was another ploughed field. It would be the most direct route, but the soft ground would slow her progress, reducing the likelihood that she would intercept the moonstruck in time. To her right, through another hawthorn hedge, was the small road that serviced the caravan park and the Priory's visitor centre. It was less direct, and there was always a chance that she'd run into someone, but she should be able to get ahead of Simpson. She hurled herself at the hedge, bursting through without losing a step, then tore along the dark lane as fast as she could manage.

The ruins came into view at the end of the road. She made out the darker silhouettes of crumbled walls and towers, outlined by moonlight reflecting from the ancient stones.

To her right, the warm glow of the lights in the caravan park spilled out through the darkness, encroaching on the cool silver moonlight until it was overwhelmed. She heard the sounds of a dozen television sets, playing through the flimsy walls. Smelled a dozen different meals being cooked. A dozen families with no idea of what lay just beyond the relative safety of their caravans.

She leapt a fence and angled herself back to the north. The moonstruck was close now, its raw animal reek assailing her nostrils. The creature stank of blood and death, and she was eager to feel its throat in her teeth.

Then she saw it. It was bipedal, like all moonstruck were, caught halfway between man and wolf. An abomination. The monster was covered in thick brown fur and used its arms in tandem with its legs to hurl itself forward, almost falling onto all fours in an effort to gain more speed. It was working, too. Troy burst from the tree line, struggling to keep up with the creature, let alone catch it. She needed to slow it down.

Instinct took over, and Gabriela veered off to the right to intercept the beast. It seemed to register her presence for the first time, and changed direction to increase the distance between them. Heading for the ruins, it leapt over a low stone wall then vanished from her sight.

A long, savage howl tore through the silence of the night. She heard the televisions in the caravans turn off, almost in unison. The exterior lights on the caravans flicked on. Faces pressed up against the glass with hands cupped around their eyes, trying to locate the source of that awful sound. Electronic beeping from dozens of telephones, all dialling the same number. She suppressed a snarl and vaulted the wall into the ruins, not expecting the heavily muscled, clawed arm to slash out from the darkness as she jumped.

Claws tore through her chest, but thankfully they glanced off her ribcage and did no real damage. She was hurled against a stone wall and fell to the floor, momentarily dazed.

That was all the time Troy needed. He leaped over the wall with a roar of rage and crashed into the hulking moonstruck werewolf. The pair of them thrashed on the floor, gouging and biting at one another.

Gabriela got to her feet and paused to assess the battle. There was no clear shot at the moonstruck. The combatants were moving too quickly. Whenever she thought she saw an opening and prepared to pounce, the moonstruck would shift position, and Troy would end up between them. She whined in frustration. When this was over, she'd make Troy pay for this. After she'd finished fucking him, anyway.

The battle moved into what would have once been the centre of the Priory. Now only jagged parallel walls stood, with neatly-tended grass filling the area where wooden pews once would have been. Teeth tore at flesh, and talons raked jagged wounds through hair, skin and muscle. Blood splashed across the grass, staining it black.

Simpson hurled Troy against one of the stone walls, but Troy angled his body, and instead of crashing into the stone, he used the wall as a springboard to hurl himself back at the monster, jaws agape. The moonstruck's arm slashed out, passing through Troy's open mouth, tearing through the inside of his throat with vicious claws. Its other hand grabbed the underside of Troy's muzzle to prevent him from biting down, before ripping his entire lower jaw away.

Troy went limp, impaled on the moonstruck's arm like some obscene, twitching glove. The werewolf howled in fury, and ripped its arm free from its fleshy prison, bringing a trail of internal organs with it. Hair retreated back into pores. Bones snapped, reforming the ruined corpse from wolf to man. What remained of Troy slumped to the floor. Then the moonstruck turned to Gabriela and snarled.

Gabriela weighed her options. The urge to throw herself at this monster that had killed her pack mate and lover was almost overwhelming, but the simple fact was that Troy had been among the strongest of them, and the creature before her had torn him apart as if he'd been nothing. She was faster than Troy, but the moonstruck was no slouch either. If it managed to grab her, then she'd be finished. She needed help. She needed Oskar.

She curled back her lips and snarled a challenge to the blood-soaked moonstruck, then feigned an attack at its flanks. The creature responded as she'd predicted, changing its stance and lunging forward. Instead of returning the attack, however, Gabriela darted away from the beast and dashed through a hole in the wall.

She landed in a vaulted undercroft, beneath the main section of the Priory. Stone pillars supported the ornate arched roof, and the remains of inscriptions, long since faded through exposure to the elements, decorated the thick sandstone roof arches. Moonlight shone through a doorway at the far end of the room, and she started running toward it, just as the moonstruck crashed through the opening, dislodging several stone blocks in the process.

Gabriela ducked her head down and ran as fast as her four legs were capable. The heavy musk of the moonstruck filled the enclosed space like a cloud, and the smell of Troy's blood in its fur inflamed her senses. She heard the monster's breath and the clack of its claws against the flagstone floor. The creature was pursuing her and, impossibly, was gaining. An icy finger of fear ran down her spine as she realised that the moonstruck was not only stronger than her, but was faster, too.

She leaped through the doorway onto a hard gravel path, then bounded over a metal handrail onto the top of one of the Priory's exterior walls. The bridge lay to her north, just beyond the ruins. In the distance, she heard the first sirens and knew that the authorities would arrive soon.

Even if she and Oskar were able to destroy the moonstruck, there would be no time to retrieve Troy's body before they arrived. She shook off the thought, knowing that she had more immediate problems to deal with. She leaped from the wall, just as the moonstruck swiped at her. She landed on the neatly-manicured grass, and bolted for the footbridge, praying that Oskar was in position.

The moonstruck was right behind her. She zigzagged her way across the lawn, doing her best to anticipate and avoid the creature's attacks. The beast snarled in fury as its talons met empty air. Gabriela had felt the air shift behind her that time. It was getting closer, and she knew there was no way she could avoid it for much longer.

She changed direction again, ducking under the moonstruck's outstretched arm and leaving a deep slash across its thigh, hoping that would be enough to slow it down. Then she ran flat out for the bridge with the enraged monster on her heels.

The bridge was narrow and much longer than she would have liked. Wooden boards set on long iron girders, held above the river by five stone columns. She extended her senses, trying to find any sign of her alpha on the opposite shore, but the roar of the river beneath her drowned out any noise, and her nostrils were filled with the stink of the blood-soaked monster pursuing her.

She'd made it halfway across when she saw Oskar step from the trees with his weapon raised. Her heart fluttered at the sight. She'd never been so glad to see anyone in her entire life. Oskar would blow the cursed thing's brains out, and then they could work out what to do next.

She tried to urge one last burst of speed from her tired body when she felt hot breath on the back of her neck and a flash of searing pain across her back. Her legs gave out beneath her and she crashed onto the bridge. She struggled to regain her footing, but her back legs wouldn't work. The pain in her back flared into a sunburst of agony, and she realised that the moonstruck had severed her spine.

The creature plunged its claws through her back and lifted her from the blood-drenched wooden boards. She felt its fetid breath on the back of her neck, and she knew that it was over.

As long as Oskar takes the fucker out, then I'll die happy.

Her vision began to fade, and she looked up to the far side of the bridge, expecting to see her alpha preparing to blow the beast's head off, but Oskar had gone. She had just enough time to feel a wave of despair at her abandonment before the moonstruck tore her in half.

CHAPTER 8

12th December. Finchale Road, Brasside. 19:00.

Olivia started to realise how bad things were when she turned off the main road towards the prison and saw the traffic. The line of stationary cars stretched for over a quarter of a mile, while dozens of irate commuters argued with the uniformed officers as to why they were not allowed to go home. There was only one access road to the Brasside estate, and from what she'd heard over the radio, it seemed unlikely that the forensics teams would be finishing up any time soon.

She flashed her ID at a uniformed officer, and he waved her through on the opposite side of the road, much to the irritation of the stranded motorists. One of them pulled out of line and tried to follow her, but the police officer moved into the centre of the road and blocked him. Olivia sympathized with the man to some extent, and didn't think that the harsh rebuke from the uniform would do much to improve his mood.

She passed a row of houses, curtains open and faces seeming to peer from every window, before heading back into the open countryside. It was then that she saw the crime scene for the first time. The front of the tunnel beneath the train tracks was covered in a heavy white sheet.

Halogen lamps blazed from inside the tunnel, and she saw the outlines of the forensics officers, in their white suits, working within. Dozens of police officers stood around at the periphery of the crime scene, while a helicopter roared past them, flying to the north to search for Simpson in the fields and nearby woods.

She parked her car behind an ambulance and got out. The two paramedics stood by the rear of their ambulance, smoking cigarettes in trembling hands. That wasn't a good sign. She made her way towards the largest group of officers, when Rick noticed her and stepped forward to meet her.

"How bad is it, Rick? I heard some things over the radio and it sounded like a fucking disaster."

Rick shook his head. "It's beyond a disaster. So far we've got six confirmed dead and there's no sign of Simpson."

Olivia's mouth fell open. "Six? Jesus Christ."

"Yeah. The two guards in the prison transport were torn apart in the back of the van. And I really do mean torn apart. The forensics guys are struggling to work out which part goes with which body. The driver was found with his throat torn out in the woods past the tunnel, along with some poor old bastard who'd been out walking his dog."

She frowned. "That's only four. What about the other two?"

"They are about a mile up the road, in the ruins of Finchale Priory. One of them...one of them had his lower jaw torn off and part of his digestive tract pulled out through his neck. The other one was on the bridge. Well, half of her was. We think the lower half must have fallen in the river and been washed away, towards the city. Oh yeah, and both of the bodies at the Priory were found stark bollock-naked."

"Fuck."

"Yeah, my thoughts exactly. Best we can tell, Simpson took off over the footbridge into the woods. The chopper crews are searching for him with the IR gear, but they've not found anything bigger than a badger yet."

"Is Phil here?"

Rick motioned towards a riot van with his head. "He's in there. Using it as a temporary control room. He's not in a very good mood."

Olivia let out a long sigh. "He's not the only one." She reached over and put her hand on Rick's arm. "Why don't you go and get a cup of tea or something? You look like shit. I take it your team was on point again?"

Rick's face contorted into a grim smile. "What do you think?

Apparently, because we were lucky enough to bring Simpson in the first time, that automatically means that we're the most experienced. I've got to tell you, Liv, I wish I'd just put a bullet in that cunt's face when I had the chance. I can't believe that one bloke could do those things to another human being."

Olivia hugged him. "I know that you've been through it the last few weeks. If you need anyone to talk to, you know where I am."

Rick gently pushed her away. "Won't Matt mind?"

"Matt will be fine. He knows that we are ancient history, and he knows that sometimes coppers need to talk about stuff to other coppers. I mean it, Rick. Give me a call if you want to talk."

Rick gave a small, sad smile. "Thanks, Liv. I appreciate it. Now, you'd better not keep the boss waiting."

She smiled at him, then turned and walked towards the riot van. As she approached, Phil got out from the rear doors, took out a cigarette, lit it, and inhaled about a quarter of it in a single drag. That wasn't good either.

"I thought you quit those years ago."

Phil looked up and, for a moment, looked like a schoolboy caught smoking by his parents, before his face darkened once more. "I did. As of today, I'm taking them up again, and if you breathe a word of this to Sharon, then I'll make sure you never hear the end of it."

She shrugged. "Fair enough. They're your lungs, just don't do it anywhere near me. I don't want the baby getting poisoned by your bad habits."

Phil looked at the lit cigarette, took another long drag from it, then dropped it into the earth and ground it under his shoes. "Did anyone tell you what we've got here?"

She nodded. "Yeah, Rick filled me in on the gory details. I'm sorry, Phil, but something's not right with this situation."

Phil's right eyebrow arched at the comment. "Well, of course there's something not bloody well right about it. There's no way that van crashed without some outside assistance, which either means that Simpson has someone working with him, or that someone wanted him dead so badly that they didn't care about how many people they killed to get to him."

"And judging from the trademark naked corpses, I'd say the latter is more probable. Oh hell, I forgot to tell you..."

Phil's phone rang and he raised his hand to silence her. "What? Say that again? You have got to be fucking kidding me. Well, check your bloody security tapes. It's not like he just got up and walked out of there on his own. Yes, call me when you find something."

He hung up the call and clenched the phone so hard that Olivia thought he might shatter it. "Do I dare ask?"

"It seems that Steven Wilkinson has gone missing from the hospital, and his whereabouts are currently unknown. According to the officer that was supposed to be guarding him, there's some evidence of a struggle in his room, and the window's broken. There were also two brass nine-millimetre casings on the floor. We now have officially no suspects in custody, no witnesses, and no fucking leads. Oh yes, and apparently Franks is on his way over here, just to put the icing on the fucking turd."

Olivia stood silent for a moment, to absorb the new information, then looked up at Phil and in spite of the circumstances, managed a sly smile. "Well, I wouldn't say that we don't have any leads. You know your mysterious, red-haired woman? I think I might have found her."

12th December. Handy Storage Ltd. Newcastle. 19:00.

Marie glanced over her shoulder, half-expecting to see Connie's eyes shining out from the shadows. She typed a six-digit number into the keypad beside the heavy shuttered door. The keypad chirped as she entered the final digit, while the red light above the keys turned green. She reached down and pulled the shutters up to her waist, then ducked inside.

She struggled to find the light switch in the darkness, feeling a momentary sense of panic as her hand groped the cinderblock wall. She was still not used to the loss of her night vision. Before, it would have been a simple matter to bring her wolf up to the surface of her mind so that her senses were enhanced. Now, she felt as if she'd gone blind and deaf. Steven Wilkinson hadn't just come close to killing her. He'd maimed her. Taken away a part of her. A part that she'd come to depend on more than she'd realised.

Her hand found a cold metal tube on the wall, and she traced it down until she found the light switch at its end. Two banks of fluorescent tubes flickered into life, flashing a cold, lifeless light across the storage unit. Feeling much happier now that she could see, Marie pulled the shutters closed behind her.

The storage unit was piled high with heavy duty cardboard boxes, the detritus of her mother's life. When she'd gone into the home, Marie had stored her things here, hoping that one day she would recover and be able to live on her own again. That hadn't happened.

Joan Williams had wasted away in the care home, not responding to anyone, or anything. The few times Marie had managed to visit, her mother had not even registered her presence. The old woman, with the stench of death about her, had stared out of the window, where the care assistants had left her that morning. She'd been like that since her father had died. Well, since Marie had killed him, anyway.

The doctors said it was a heart attack, but Marie had been the cause of her father's fatal cardiac arrest, and to this day she felt no guilt about it, save for what it had done to her mother. The bastard had it coming.

This would be the last time that Marie came here. She supposed that the police would find out about it, sooner or later. Even if they didn't, Michael knew that the storage unit existed, if not the exact location. It would be too dangerous to ever return. In many respects, she was taking a hell of a risk by being here now, but it was not like she had a choice.

She tore open one of the boxes and retrieved a large leather satchel from within. Her escape kit - a completely new identity: passport, driver's license and credit cards, all in the name of Suzy Neale, along with around twenty thousand in cash, split evenly between US dollars, pounds, and euros. While she used fake identities as a matter of course when on missions for The Pack, this one was something that she'd set up herself, just in case she ever had to disappear.

She'd never intended to leave The Pack or do anything to betray their trust. They'd taken her in when she was a lost soul in her teens, wandering around Europe in search of other werewolves. The Pack had saved her from the moonstruck that she'd blundered upon. They'd given her a home, reunited her with her brother, and had become the family she'd always yearned for.

The Pack was home, and that was another thing that Steven Wilkinson had taken from her. She could never go back. Not now that she was human. Michael would argue with the others, demanding that her life be spared, perhaps even jeopardizing his own in the process. There was no hope for John, either. Oskar's team were as efficient a group of killers as she'd ever met, and that meant he would already be dead. Cut down in a hail of silver bullets while chained up in a prison van. She had no-one else to turn to. She was alone again, and the surge of emotions almost brought her to her knees.

She slapped herself across the face. "Sort it out, you silly bitch. This is no time to be feeling sorry for yourself. You've got what you came for, now let's get the fuck out of here."

She held her breath for a moment, then, as she turned to leave, something caught her eye in the open box. She reached in and took out a faded Polaroid photograph. Five children, jostling each other, with innocent, happy smiles spread across their faces. David stood in the middle of the picture, his arms folded and a serious look on his face that never reached his bright eyes. Michael was pulling a face, while John had his arm up behind her brother's head, making a pair of antennae with his fingers. She was squeezed in between John and Michael with a huge grin on her face, and a gap where one of her teeth was missing.

They'd taken this picture with David's camera, on the afternoon she'd officially become part of the gang. The day she'd kicked Malcolm Harrison in the balls. The day that David was torn apart by a moonstruck werewolf in the woods near their home.

Shaking away the flood of memories, she dropped the photograph into her bag, opened the shutters, and turned out the light. When she brought the steel shutters down again, there was a sense of finality to the loud clang of metal against metal. Slinging the strap of the bag over her shoulder, she hurried back to the car. Newcastle airport was a little over five miles away. With any luck, in a few hours she'd be airborne and far away from the police and The Pack.

She put the bag onto the passenger seat, fastened her seatbelt, and started the engine. The radio came to life as the engine caught.

"The police are still refusing to comment, but unofficial sources have said there are at least three people confirmed dead, and that John Simpson appears to have escaped from police custody. Police advise the public not to approach Simpson, and to call the police immediately if he is sighted. He is to be considered armed and extremely dangerous."

Marie turned the radio off. Could John have gotten away from Oskar? Might he still be alive? She opened the glove compartment and took out an Ordnance Survey map of the area.

If John had escaped, then the chances were that he'd be wounded. The police would expect him to behave like a man, and would end up looking for him in the wrong places. She might not have her wolf anymore, but she'd had years of training. Years of experience hunting moonstruck werewolves. She traced her finger along the lines of the map and made some rough calculations. The moonstruck would try to get back to its territory so that it could lay low and allow its injuries to heal. It would avoid any built-up areas, so would most likely follow the patches of woodland around to the north-west before cutting back south, towards High Moor. It wouldn't get there before dawn, but it would not be far away when the sun came up, and she had a pretty good idea which route it would take.

She sighed. It was stupid for her to even consider going after John. Even if he'd gotten away from Oskar's team, they would not be far behind. It was an unnecessary risk. She should stick to her plan, drive to the airport, and not look back.

Marie's shoulders slumped. She couldn't leave. If there was a chance that she could save John, then she had to take it. She'd been alone before, and the thought of it brought a damp sparkle to the corner of her eyes. Tomorrow morning, when the sun rose, she'd intercept John and get them both to safety. Before she did that, though, there were other arrangements that she'd need to put in place. It was going to be a busy night.

12th December. Durham Train Station. 20:00.

Gregorz and Daniel were the first to arrive at the rendezvous point in the far corner of the car park, away from the glare of security lights. The station was on the top of a hill, overlooking Durham city centre, and was relatively quiet at this time of night, with only a couple of taxis parked in the bays. Most of the commuters were safely home, and only occasional groups of young men and women arrived at the station, for a night out in the glittering city below. Sirens still rang out in the night, and the roads beneath seemed to be filled with flashing dots of blue and red light. The moon loomed large overhead, and Gregorz could feel its influence, tugging at a deep, primordial part of him. He held the beast in check. From what he'd heard on the news report, Oskar's mission had been even less successful than his own. They would have to work out their next moves, and, unfortunately, they would have to report the situation to Michael. That was not a conversation he was looking forward to.

A pair of knuckles rapped against the passenger window. Daniel raised his eyebrows and lowered the window.

"My, Connie, I do like your new look."

Connie did have a new look. She wore an ill-fitting leather jacket over a dark green top and a short leather miniskirt. The jacket only just hid the blood that stained the green fabric black around the shoulder and neckline. Her hair was dishevelled and she kept scratching at her stomach. "Ye can go suck a leper's cock in hell, Daniel."

Gregorz leaned across. "I take it that you've not had a good night. Where's Marie?"

Connie's eyes blazed, and as she ranted, flecks of saliva sprayed from her lips. "Ah wish Ah fuckin' knew, because then Ah'd be eating the bitch's heart."

Daniel could barely contain his smirk. "I take it that the girls night out did not go well?"

"Not if ye call the cunt spearing me through the stomach with half a tree, then running me over in the car and pissing off with ma clothes a good night. Ah had to kill some little slag in Chester-le-Street for her clothes, or Ah'd have been coming here in the nude."

Daniel's attempt at suppressing his amusement failed and he started to chuckle, despite the situation. Gregorz frowned at him, then turned back to Connie. "And why would Marie resort to such drastic measures, Connie? Perhaps something you did? Something you said?"

"She didn't change. The moon was up, shining right on her pretty little face, an' fuck all happened, even though she's been locked in a hotel room for the last month. Ah couldn't smell any trace of a wolf on her. She smelt human. Like food. And the law's pretty specific about dealing with humans who know about us."

Gregorz snarled. "There could be any number of reasons why Marie didn't change, Connie. That does not give you the right to attack another member of this pack without provocation, and I'm not sure how Michael is going to take the news that you tried to hunt his little sister. Now get in the car and keep your mouth shut. I don't want to hear another word out of you unless I ask you to speak."

Connie opened the rear passenger side door and flopped into the back seat. She opened to mouth to say something, but then thought better of it and instead lapsed into a sullen silence. Satisfied that he'd made his point, Gregorz turned back to face Daniel. "Have we heard anything from Oskar or the others yet?"

The German shook his head. "No, but then it is still early. How many bodies did the news say there were?"

"At least three on the last report, but with the numbers expected to rise."

Gregorz considered this for a moment. "The casualties are most likely the guards and driver of the prisoner transport. Those were expected. It may be that the moonstruck is giving them a little more trouble than anticipated, and they're having to chase it down."

Daniel exhaled. "Well, it won't be like they were the only ones to let a moonstruck get away from them tonight."

Connie's brow wrinkled. "What other moonstruck? Ah thought that... Oh, ye bastards. Ye absolute pair of motherfuckers. Ye went after Wilkinson, didn't ye? Ye went after the bastard that killed my daughter and ye left me out of it. Worse, ye let the fucker escape."

Daniel turned around to face her. "Connie, we..."

Her lips curled up into a snarl. "Shut it, Daniel. Ah want to hear it from Gregorz. Is that what you did?"

Gregorz nodded. "We discussed it with Michael and Oskar. If it had been up to me, I would have let you have him. The timing of the hit was sensitive, though, and we weren't sure you would have been able to restrain yourself. In the end, the decision was taken out of my hands."

Connie's face turned purple, and she was about to tell her team alpha exactly what she thought, when a set of headlights flashed on the approach road and a white transit van pulled up alongside. Oskar got out of the van and climbed into the car, beside Connie.

Gregorz looked from Oskar, to the van, then back to the Norwegian. "Troy? Gabriela?"

Oskar shook his head. "Both dead. The moonstruck was like nothing that I've ever seen. Huge, strong and fast. Worse than the creature in Prague. At first, the thing just ran. I've never seen a moonstruck run from a fight before, and it took us by surprise. It was past us before we could react. Troy and Gabriela pursued it while I cleared up the scene and headed around to intercept. By the time I got there, it was already too late. The moonstruck had killed them both and the police were already arriving."

Gregorz massaged his temples. "So the police have both Troy and Gabriela's bodies. I'm not sure that this day could get any worse."

Connie gave a slight cough. "There was something else, Gregorz. The police showed up at the hotel before we left. They didn't see Marie, but they got a good fucking look at me. I'm supposed to go into the station on Monday to answer a few questions."

The vein in Gregorz' temple began to twitch, and the team alpha's jaw clenched. For a moment he said nothing, then he turned around to face Oskar and Connie. "Things have gone too far. In two decades hunting moonstruck, I've never known an operation to go this badly wrong." He reached into the alcove beneath the car radio and retrieved his telephone. "We need to talk to Michael. We need to let him know what's happened."

CHAPTER 9

12th December. Nauchnnyy proyezd, Moscow. 22:03.

Michael sat alone in the dilapidated office, drumming his fingers on the desk while glaring at the telephone. He barely looked up when Steffan entered the room and took a seat opposite him.

Steffan pushed a bottle of vodka across the table. "Here, while we wait, we may as well have something to take the edge off things."

Michael shook his head and pushed the bottle back to his friend. "I need the edge right now. I have to stay sharp. I'll relax when we hear back from the teams in England. Then we can take care of that bottle of Zyr."

Steffan gave a slight shrug of his shoulders and poured two shots anyway. He raised a glass to his alpha before swallowing the clear liquid. "You worry too much, Mikhail. Two of our best teams are working on the situation. They have done these things many times before. They will take care of the moonstruck and return home with little Marie, yes?"

In spite of things, Michael could not help but grin. "You know she hates it when you call her that?"

"Ha, secretly she loves it. There is a little smile in her eyes when I say it, it's just not easy to notice with all of the anger and indignation that she hides behind."

"I'll take your word for that, but I wish I shared your confidence about the problem in England. I don't like the reports I'm hearing from over there. This is too public. It should have been a quiet clean-up mission, not a fucking media frenzy. We've not been at risk like this since 1966."

"Mikhail, you are my alpha, and you are also my friend. I tell you, Gregorz will call you as soon as he has any news." At that moment, the telephone chose to ring, and Steffan smiled. "You see?"

Michael looked at the telephone with a mixture of relief and apprehension. He reached across and pressed the loudspeaker button. "Gregorz, I'm here with Steffan. What's the situation over there?"

The telephone crackled and there was a pause before Gregorz spoke. "Not good. Troy and Gabriela are dead and Simpson escaped. The police have their bodies, Wilkinson managed to evade us, and your sister has run off. Oh yes, and apparently the police have tracked us to the hotel we were using as a base of operations."

A wave of nausea bubbled up from Michael's stomach. "So you're telling me that you managed to fuck up every single aspect of your respective missions? What the hell happened?"

Oskar spoke next. His voice seemed different, without his usual arrogant tone. The Norwegian sounded shaken, which was something that Michael wouldn't have believed possible. "Simpson was too powerful. I've never seen a moonstruck like that before. He tore through Troy and Gabriela like they were nothing. By the time I arrived to back them up it was all over."

"And the Wilkinson hit? How did you manage to screw up killing a crippled, comatose old man?"

This time, it was Daniel who spoke. "We waited as long as we could for Oskar's message, but it didn't arrive. By the time we got there, he'd already changed. He escaped through a window and fled. We gave chase, but by the time we caught up Wilkinson had transformed back to his human form, stole a car and got away."

"He turned himself back? So he's not moonstruck, then?"

"Gregorz managed to get a shot off before it escaped. The silver may have weakened it enough for Wilkinson to take control. At least, that's what we think happened."

"And what about the police? How in God's name did they manage to track you down?"

Connie's voice crackled through the speaker. "They spotted me at the hospital an' the courthouse. It must have been enough for them to get a description, so that Garner bitch could go round the hotels in the area."

"Is there anything back in that hotel that could make things worse?"

Gregorz sighed. "No, we cleared the room out before we left. If things had gone to plan, then we all would have been on the first flight out of the country."

Michael wiped his hand across his face, shaking his head while he tried to work out how best to proceed. Steffan pushed the shot glass of vodka across the table, and this time, Michael took it, downing the liquid in a single mouthful.

"OK, this is what you're going to do. Gregorz will take Daniel and track Simpson. Don't engage until the sun comes up and he transforms back. Then, once he's human, move in and finish the job. Oskar will have to infiltrate the hospital and get rid of Troy and Gabriela's bodies.

"Connie, I want you to take care of the police problem. Anyone who's seen your face and knows your name needs to be taken out, quickly and quietly. This is as big a fuck-up as I've ever seen. The only positives are that Simpson is no longer in police custody, and Wilkinson didn't tear through the hospital on camera. Believe me when I say that none of you have heard the last of this. I'll be having a very long talk with each of you when you get back here."

Connie's voice crackled through the speaker. "What about Wilkinson and yer sister? She didn't change when the moon came up, an' she stuck half a fucking tree through ma stomach."

"Marie will go to ground somewhere. She's not a priority. The same goes for Wilkinson. If he's not moonstruck, then he's not an immediate problem. When this is over, you are more than welcome to track the fucker down and rip his head off, but I expect you to carry out the mission first. Am I making myself clear?"

Each of the voices at the other end of the line murmured their assent and Michael disconnected the call. "Fucking hell, Steffan, what's going on over there?"

The older man poured them both another drink. "The situation is not ideal, but as you said, it could be worse. There is still time for them to clear up this mess before it attracts any more attention. What I am most interested in is what are you going to do now? Will you speak to the others?"

Michael picked up the glass and drained it. "No, not yet. I'll see what the situation is in the morning. I'd rather have something positive to say before I go and speak to the Council."

"And if things are no better in the morning?"

"Then God help us all."

12th December. Steven's House, High Moor. 21:08.

Steven turned off the main road onto the maze of narrow lanes leading to his home. He'd driven from Durham via a circuitous route, determined to avoid CCTV cameras or police patrol cars. Durham Constabulary didn't take it kindly when criminal acts were committed against one of their own, especially when that act had taken place inside the grounds of their headquarters.

Coppers tended to get riled up over things like that, and Steven didn't fancy trying to explain what he was doing in a stolen car, naked apart from a woman's heavy winter coat, to some overzealous traffic constable.

He'd driven in silence the whole way, turning the situation over and over in his mind. He was a werewolf. One of the monsters that he'd spent the last two or more decades hunting. When it happened to Carl, the American hadn't been able to cope with it. He'd locked himself away in a hotel room for almost a month, drinking scotch and writing down everything that he thought Steven would need to know about hunting werewolves. Then the old bastard had blown himself to pieces.

Steven couldn't help but wonder whether he was destined for a similar fate, once the reality of the situation had sunk in. He couldn't afford to dwell on those thoughts now, though. Not with at least two pack assassins on his tail.

If the large, two-legged variety of werewolf was bad, then The Pack's murder squads were so much worse. As smart as a man, and damn near immune to silver. Normal silver bullets were not going to do the trick. If he had two of them to worry about, then he'd need his special ammunition. The ones with the silver particles suspended in mercury. Pack killers.

First things first, though. Before he did anything, he needed a hot shower to remove the last lingering musk of the werewolf. Then he could take care of his wound properly, have something to eat, and find out what the hell had been going on in the month he'd been unconscious.

He pulled up to an imposing set of metal gates, flanked by ten-foot-high granite pillars and high stone walls. The gates were wrapped with yellow crime scene tape and were firmly locked with a heavy steel chain. Steven swore under his breath and drove past the entrance to his home. He'd been stupid to come here. There was no way he could get through the gates without a bolt cutter to remove the chain, and there was no other way for him to get in.

He'd fortified his home to make it as difficult and dangerous as possible for a werewolf to even get onto the grounds. The walls were sheer-sided and topped with vicious silver spikes, each one coated with a mixture of grease and wolfsbane.

Even if he made it over the wall, the house security systems would register his naturally higher body temperature as soon as he got within fifty feet of the property. Then it would arm the property's defences. He'd be lucky to get past the ultrasonic sirens, remembering the effect they'd had on John.

There probably wasn't another place on the planet that would be more difficult for him to get into. His home was lost to him, and judging from the crime scene tape, he'd have been under arrest from the moment the police searched the property. There were far too many illegal weapons inside for it to be any other way.

He slammed his fist down onto the steering wheel. "Fuck!"

This was useless. He needed time to think, to understand what was going on. He kept an isolated cottage out in the hills of Weardale. There were clothes, food, and some weapons there, and the police would probably not know about it. It was registered under the name of Carl Schneider, and there was no documentation linking him to the property. He should be safe there, at least for now. Give him a bit of space to work out what his next move was going to be.

He turned the car around and drove back the way he'd come. It would take him less than an hour to reach the cottage and, despite the latest setback, Steven felt a little better knowing that his hot shower was still on the cards. He reached down and turned on the radio. It was tuned to a local station, playing seventies and eighties hits. With the heater cranked all the way up, he started to relax a little.

He'd driven for around twenty minutes when the music was interrupted by the station's evening news bulletin. The first headline snapped him straight back into reality.

"Six people confirmed dead after John Simpson escapes from police custody."

He turned the radio off, unable to listen to the full report. He'd have to deal with the information, but not now. He couldn't. Six people, probably all with families, were dead, and it was his fault. Everything that had happened in the last month was down to him. All because he'd been a sentimental fool and had let nostalgia get the better of him. All because he'd not put a bullet between John Simpson's eyes the moment he'd shown his face in High Moor. He had to put it right, or at least try and stop things from getting any worse, and the way to do that suddenly seemed so simple. He had to kill John Simpson.

13th December. Mill Woods, High Moor. 08:04.

John's eyes snapped open as the first weak rays of the sun filtered through the wood's bare canopy. The cold of the December morning penetrated his entire body, a heavy numbness that seeped into his bones, robbing him of his strength. He pushed himself into a sitting position, wincing at the bomb-bursts of pain that flashed across his wounds. His body was covered in dozens of deep scratches and bites. Four parallel tears crossed his chest, and a piece of flesh was missing from his thigh.

Fortunately, while the injuries were deep, none of them were bleeding anymore. At least, not yet. John tried to stand and his battered body roared in outrage. He ignored the pain. As bad as it was, it was nothing compared to the agony of transformation, so, werewolf or not, he needed to warm himself up, and quickly.

The only problem was, he had absolutely no idea where he was. The dark skeletons of the deciduous woodland stretched out before him in all directions, with no sign of a footpath. The brown, frost-covered fronds of dead bracken rose almost up to his knees and filled the gaps between the trees for as far as he could see. The only thing approximating a path was the trail his wolf had torn through the undergrowth, but instinct told him that the last place he wanted to go was where his monster had been the previous night. Instead, he pushed through the bracken, heading in the direction that his monstrous other self had been going.

What the hell happened last night?

The last thing he remembered was being in the back of the prisoner transport. There had been a crash, after which he'd changed. Then, there was the usual hole in his memories. One thing was certain, though. The police would be searching for him, and if he didn't get the hell out of the area, then it would only be a matter of time before they found him. And that didn't bear thinking about.

Then there were the wounds. They weren't healing, which meant...

"Oh shit."

The realisation hit him like a hammer blow. He should have known that The Pack would have come after him, but he'd not even considered it until now. From what he knew of them, there was no way they would allow a werewolf to remain in police custody. It would only take until the next full moon before the world had proof that werewolves were real. They'd do whatever it took to stop it. And that meant that unless he'd killed them last night, then they were most likely on his trail. He really had to get out of here.

He tried to pick up the pace, pushing his way through the undergrowth, ignoring the slashing of hidden brambles against his bare legs. John tripped and stumbled through the foliage, a wave of fear beginning to envelop him.

He continuously cast nervous glances over his shoulder, expecting to see a pack of werewolves hot on his tail, but the woods were empty, and the only sounds were morning calls of birds and the whistle of icy wind through naked trees.

After what seemed like forever, he escaped from the bracken's clutches onto an area which, while not exactly a footpath, was fairly clear of obstacles. The floor was covered with a carpet of slimy brown leaves that squelched under his bare feet, and the ground started to fall away on a slight gradient. John stopped and strained his hearing. He wasn't sure, but he thought he could hear running water, somewhere off in the distance.

Then he heard the howl. Long, mournful, and somewhere very close. He thought it might have been to his left, but he couldn't be sure. Frantic eyes scanned the trees for any sign of movement, and he searched around for anything he could use as a weapon.

A second howl answered the first. This time, from his right. The sound of this one was different: deeper, as if made by a larger beast. He spun around and thought he caught a flash of movement between the trees, but by the time he focused on the area, the woods were silent and still once more.

Then, from directly behind him, he heard a savage, guttural growl.

13th December. Olivia's House, Bear Park. 09:17.

Matt Garner wiped the sleep from his eyes and shambled down the stairs in search of coffee. With Olivia pulling an all-nighter, he'd stayed up until the early hours of the morning, watching Asian horror films and eating the burnt remains of the dinner he'd prepared earlier that night. He risked a glance into the living room and groaned at the empty bottles of beer and the half-drained bottle of scotch. He'd need to get that cleared up before Olivia got home, or she'd make his hung-over existence even more miserable than it already was. It was bad enough that he'd promised to paint the nursery today. The thought of the paint fumes made his head swim and his stomach churn.

He stepped around the piles of empties and opened the living room blinds, squinting at the weak grey light filtering through the slats. The street was quiet for a Saturday morning; just a few people wandered past on their way to the shops. Spider webs of frost spread across car windscreens parked outside. He was glad he didn't need to go out - it looked bloody freezing.

Matt walked away from the window, turning the heating up as he stumbled towards the kitchen. There were only two things that could make him feel better at this point - black coffee and a large bacon sandwich, dripping in tomato sauce. His stomach growled at the thought, and before long, bacon sizzled in the frying pan and a large cafetière of coffee brewed on the worktop. He poured himself a large mug of the black beverage and immediately felt better as the hot, rich liquid flowed down his throat. What he really wanted was a cigarette, but Olivia would string him up by his balls if she caught so much as a whiff of one on him.

He flipped the bacon over again, waiting until all the fat had crisped up, then slid it between two thick slices of bread. He regarded his culinary triumph with something approaching reverence, then, satisfied, took a large bite, washing it down with another mouthful of coffee.

Heaven.

At that point, the doorbell rang and spoiled his perfect moment. Matt looked at the sandwich and thought about leaving it on the work surface until he dealt with the unwanted caller. Then he noticed Mr Whiskers, their large ginger tomcat, slinking between the stools, and knew that if he took his eye off the sandwich for a second, then the bastard cat would make off with it. He took another bite as the doorbell rang again, and trudged to the front door, his culinary triumph still in hand.

A beautiful red-haired woman stood on the doorstep. A thick woollen coat covered her almost down to her knees, and her eye makeup was streaked with the tracks of recent tears. Matt's irritation at the unwanted visitor evaporated. "Can I help you?"

The woman sniffled. "Is Olivia home yet? She said Ah should meet her here when she got back from work."

Matt was suddenly very conscious of his attire. T-shirt and boxer shorts was not the sort of first impression that Olivia would want him to make with her friends. He opened the door. "Please, come in. She probably won't be too long. There's some fresh coffee in the kitchen. Help yourself, and I'll run upstairs and sort myself out." He opened the door and the woman stepped past him, into the hallway.

"Can I take your coat, Miss...?"

"No, Ah'll keep hold of it for the moment if that's okay. And it’s Connie. Ma name’s Connie."

Matt waited until Connie had gone past him into the kitchen before he raced upstairs. There was a pair of tracksuit bottoms in the laundry that weren't too dirty. He reckoned he could get away with those, along with a clean T-shirt and a few swigs of mouthwash. He hurried into the bedroom and began dragging clothes from the washing basket when he became aware of a presence behind him. He turned to see the woman standing in the doorway to the bedroom. "Erm, the bathroom’s just down there on the left if you want to freshen up."

Connie's face contorted into a predatory smile. "Ah think I'm ready for ye to take ma coat now," she said, as the heavy garment fell to the floor, exposing her naked body.

Matt staggered backwards, aghast. "Is this a fucking wind-up? Olivia will be back any second."

Connie took a step forward. "Oh, dinnae ye worry. We've got plenty of time for what Ah've got in mind."

CHAPTER 10

13th December. Mill Woods, High Moor. 08:25.

John froze in place, only slowly turning around to face his death. A huge, black werewolf emerged from the bracken, its teeth bared. A moment later, it was joined by another creature, this one even bigger, covered in thick grey fur and a look of feral hatred in its eyes. He backed away from the creatures, knowing that it was a futile gesture. They could be on him in seconds if they wanted to, but they seemed to be toying with their prey, savouring every last second of his terror. He looked around frantically, searching for some means of escape or a weapon, but even the lowest branches of the nearby trees were out of his reach and there was nothing that he could use to defend himself. All of the fallen wood around him was well on the way to being rotted. He was out of options.

In desperation, John called out to his wolf. He threw open his mind and tried to induce the transformation through sheer force of will. Nothing happened. The presence in his mind was silent, no doubt satiated from the long night of carnage. He was on his own.

The werewolves were closer now, approaching cautiously. The grey creature moved away to his left, trying to flank him, while the black monster stalked forward, its muscles tensed, ready to pounce. John closed his eyes and waited to die.

The explosion almost knocked John off his feet. A loud crack rang out and for a fraction of a second he could see the veins of his eyelids as his world turned red. He felt a warm, wet trickle of blood run from each ear, and the air was heavy with a sulphurous stench. John opened his eyes, just in time to see the two werewolves cut down by automatic weapons fire. Bullets slammed into their bodies and the creatures flew backwards as miniature explosions of blood and fur erupted across their flanks. John looked up to the source of the gunfire, expecting to see armed police officers bearing down on him.

Instead, what he saw was Marie. Somehow still alive, and firing an assault rifle into the twitching bodies of the two werewolves. The magazine on the weapon emptied, and she replaced it in a single, fluid move before resuming fire. When that mag emptied, she rushed over to John's side, her eyes filled with concern. She said something. Her mouth moved, but all John could hear was the ringing in his ears. Marie shook her head in frustration, grabbed his arm, and hauled him after her, down the slope.

She set a fast pace, almost going at a sprint through the trees. John felt something tear on his side, and warm blood oozed from the reopened wound. Even on his best day, he would have struggled to keep up with Marie, but with his injuries, he was already falling behind. Marie glanced back over her shoulder, and seeing the difficulty he was in, waited for him to catch up, weapon trained on the woods behind them.

When he reached her, she put her hand on his arm, and spoke in a muffled voice. "Come on, we need to keep going. That won't stop them for long and we've still got a long way to go before we get to the car."

"Marie, I can't believe you're okay. The last time I saw you..."

"Save your breath for running. We can talk later. Now move your fucking arse."

They sprinted down the hill, leaping over fallen trees without breaking stride. John's lungs burned with the exertion, but he knew that if he fell behind then he was as good as dead.

As his hearing returned, the sound of running water became clearer, and the overpowering stink of the stream, polluted with the waste from hundreds of houses, filled his nostrils. They were running straight toward it. Then John heard something else. A howl echoed through the trees, followed by another moments later.

Marie's voice was strained, almost on the edge of panic. "Come on. There's not far to go. Run faster."

John did his best to obey and pushed his aching body harder. More of his wounds tore open, releasing new waves of agony. His entire torso felt slick with blood. The stink of it threatened to overpower the stench of the polluted stream, and somewhere deep in the lowest reaches of his mind, something shifted and stirred.

They broke clear of the trees. The gradient of the slope steepened as it made its way down to the stream. A small metal bridge spanned the water, and beyond that, John could see the outlines of houses through the trees. He recognised this place. The housing estate beyond the tree line was where he'd parked his car, when he and Marie had gone to rescue Steven from Malcolm Harrison. He was back in High Moor.

Marie reached the bottom of the slope and sprinted across the bridge, with John right behind her. When she reached the other side, she stopped and risked a glance backwards.

Two pairs of green eyes shone from the undergrowth at the top of the embankment. One of the pairs winked out, and a couple of seconds later, Gregorz stepped forward.

His body was covered in fresh blood, and there were still some bullet holes that hadn’t yet healed properly. From the expression on his face, he was obviously in a considerable amount of pain, yet when he spoke, his voice was steady.

"Marie, don't be a fool. No one has to know about this. Give up the moonstruck and come back with us, and I promise you, it will all be okay."

Marie positioned herself in front of John and raised her assault rifle. "I can't fucking go back, Gregorz. Did Connie tell you what happened to me?" Her lips curled into a sneer. "Yeah, of course she did. I'd be put to death, no matter what you or Michael say, and you know it."

The old man shook his head. "You don't know that. Your condition could be temporary. If it is, then you are throwing away your life and your family for no reason."

Marie's shoulders tightened and she pulled the AK-47 into her shoulder. "It doesn't matter, Gregorz. I'm not letting you take me back there, and I'm not letting you take John."

"For the love of God, think about what you're doing. Simpson is the most wanted man in the country. His face is all over the news, and the police will be setting up checkpoints by now. You won't get five miles before they catch you, and then we'll be back where we started. Think about that. Think about the deaths you will cause by doing this."

"You know me, Gregorz. You helped train me, and you know what I'm capable of. They won't find us, and you know there's no way you can reach us before we're out of the trees. I love you like a father, so please, don't make me shoot you again."

"Please, I'm begging you. If you do this, then you know what it will mean. You know what Michael will be forced to do. Daniel and I won't mention what just happened. You have my word on that. Come home with us, Marie, before you make things worse than they already are."

A tear rolled down Marie's cheek and, for a second, the barrel of the assault rifle dropped toward the floor. Then she clenched her jaw and her eyes turned cold. "No, it's already too late. Let us go, Gregorz. We'll disappear and no-one will ever hear from us again."

The old man dipped his head, unable to look her in the eyes. "I'm sorry, Marie, but you know that I can't do that."

"I know. Goodbye, Gregorz. Tell Michael I'm sorry."

Marie and John walked backwards to the edge of the woods, never taking their eyes from Gregorz. As they reached the periphery of the trees, where the woods gave way to the neatly mowed lawns of the housing estate, Gregorz stepped back into the woods and out of sight.

Marie took off her jacket and draped it over John's shoulders, then hurried him to a gold Ford Focus. She cast a nervous glance around to make sure that they hadn't been seen, then opened the boot. "Get in and don't fucking argue."

John opened his mouth to say something, but, suddenly very aware of his naked, bloodstained body, climbed into the boot without any objection. Marie closed the rear hatch behind him, and a few moments later, started the engine and drove away.

John lay in the cramped compartment, wriggling around a heavy steel box in an attempt to get comfortable. It was pitch dark inside, but after searching around, he discovered a mobile phone that had fallen down behind the wheel arch, that provided at least a little light.

Marie's voice called out. "You alright in there, John?"

"Yeah, I'm just great. Is it really you? I saw you dead. The fucking police said you were dead."

"I know. I was, or at least, pretty damn close to it."

Well, what the hell happened?"

"Isn't it obvious? I got better. I'm a pretty difficult lass to kill, in case you hadn't noticed. Now, we've got a long drive ahead of us. I'll stop in about twenty minutes so that we can sort your wounds out and get some clothes on you. Until then, I'm going to need you to stay quiet, especially if we get stopped. OK?"

"Okay. Thank you, Marie. I can't believe you came back for me."

"Yeah, well, don't worry about it. Just get as comfortable as you can and keep quiet until we get where we're going."

"Marie?"

"Yes, John."

"Did that Russian say something about Michael?"

Marie let out a long, exasperated sigh. "Yes, John, he did. I can see that we are going to have to have a very long talk. I'll tell you everything, but for now, please keep your bloody mouth shut and try not to bleed all over the boot."

13th December. Olivia's House, Bear Park. 10:02.

Olivia wiped her eyes and tried to concentrate on the road. Phil had spent most of the evening trying to simultaneously organise the search for John Simpson and avoid Chief Inspector Franks, with varying degrees of success. She'd been glad for an excuse to get away from the tense atmosphere, so took Rick and his team with her to the hotel where she'd spoken to Connie Hamilton earlier that day. The manager was more than happy to oblige and opened the room for them, but the place was empty.

The beds were made; only a wet towel, streaked with black hair dye, gave any indication that the room had been occupied. Deflated, she'd called in a forensics team to do a thorough sweep, and then began the laborious task of interviewing the staff. It was there that she got lucky. Despite the twin room being registered under a single name, one of the maids said that there were actually four people living in the room.

The mysterious Connie Hamilton, along with another woman and two men. The men matched the descriptions of the bogus officers last seen with Marie Williams, and apart from the hair colour, the age, and appearance, the female occupant was a fair match for Marie herself. She also had a name. Gregorz Pawlac, whose credit card had been used to pay for the room. All of which was great, except for the fact that no one knew where any of them were.

She'd returned to the office and typed up her report, leaving it on Phil's desk before heading home. She needed a shower, then about twelve hours of uninterrupted sleep. She couldn't help but smile to herself as she left the countryside behind and entered the outskirts of the small town where she and Matt lived.

Rows of identical, red-brick terraced houses lined the main road through Bear Park. Old colliery workers' cottages with two bedrooms, one reception room and, in some instances, an outside toilet. Her home was a little further up, on the left-hand side. The first house on the end of the terrace, opposite a used car showroom.

She loved the little house. They'd bought it a year ago, straight after they were married. At the end of a small block of four, and backing onto open fields, it was her sanctuary where she could hide away from the stresses of her job, watch crappy movies with Matt, and lock the world outside. Plus it was only fifteen minutes from the police headquarters, which made her morning commute a doddle.

She parked her car on the pavement and grabbed her bag from the back seat, frowning as she realised that the blinds in the living room were still closed. That meant that Matt was either still in bed, or was playing on his Xbox, probably in nothing but his pants and T-shirt. She didn't have the energy for an argument. If he wanted to do that all day, then he was welcome to, as long as he didn't wake her up. She retrieved her keys from her handbag and let herself into the house.

"Matt, are you up?"

The house was silent. She listened out for any sign of life - Matt's distinctive snores, or the sound of the shower being used, but the only noises she heard were the cars passing on the road outside. Maybe he'd just gone to the shops or something. She took off her coat, kicked her shoes into the corner behind the front door, and hung her bag from the back of one of the kitchen stools.

A cafetière, half-full of coffee, stood on the work surface. She put her hand against the side of the glass container and discovered that it was lukewarm. It was not like Matt to leave his coffee. It was usually the first thing he did when he got up, even before feeding the cat.

She glanced down at the cat bowl, and discovered that it was full. Again, probably nothing, but certainly unusual. Most mornings it was an effort to make it down the stairs without the large animal tripping you up as it wove between your legs. You couldn't move for him until he'd been fed. Olivia felt the first real stab of concern. Maybe something had happened to the cat, and Matt had taken it to the vets. No, his car was still parked outside, at the same awkward angle that he'd left it the night before. She took out her mobile and called Matt's number. Within seconds, Matt's phone started ringing, from somewhere upstairs. Olivia disconnected the call and put the phone down on the kitchen worktop, before walking to the bottom of the stairs.

"Matt? Are you up there? Is everything alright?"

There was no reply. The upper floor of the house remained silent. Olivia put her foot on the first step, wincing as the old wood creaked beneath her weight. Her heart thumped in her chest and beads of sweat broke out on her brow. This was ridiculous. This was her home, and there was no reason for her to feel anything but safe here, yet her every instinct screamed at her to run. Adrenaline surged through her system and an ice chill ran down her spine.

"For fuck's sake, this case has got me jumping at shadows," she said out loud, in an attempt to reassure herself. Pushing through the fear, she started up the stairs, listening for any sound that might be out of place. "Matt? Have you gone back to bed, you lazy tosser?"

She marched to the bedroom and flung open the door. At first, she could not understand what she was seeing. The entire room dripped red. It covered the walls - sprayed crimson patterns in sharp contrast against the flat white paint. Tattered red streamers hung from the lamp shade and curtain rails. The bed was soaked through, their new white duvet set now a deep burgundy. A red mass of mangled meat lay in a heap at its centre, and at the top of the bed, carefully laid on a pillow, was Matt's severed head.

Olivia put her hand to her mouth and backed away from the terrible sight until her back touched the wall. "No. No. Matt...oh God, Matt!"

The wave of grief that welled up inside threatened to drown her. Matt was dead. Not just dead, but butchered in their home. Her safe place. He was gone. He'd never see their baby’s first smile, or take it for walks in the park. He hadn't even known what sex it was, and now he would never know.

The bathroom door creaked open and a naked woman stepped out, covered from head to foot in blood, blocking the corridor. "Ah'm sorry, Olivia. Ah made a wee mess in yer bedroom while Ah was waiting. Ah didn't want to wait until Monday to have a chat with ye. Ah thought it best that we do it now."

Olivia didn't hesitate. She threw herself at Connie Hamilton, putting all of her grief and rage into the punch. The sudden attack seemed to take the other woman by surprise, connecting squarely with Connie's jaw. Blood sprayed from her mouth and she stumbled backwards. Olivia pressed her advantage and kicked out at Connie's stomach, only to feel utter dismay as the blood-soaked woman moved with unbelievable speed and caught her leg.

"Now, Olivia, that wasn't very nice, or smart of ye."

Olivia bent the knee of the trapped leg, closing the distance between them, then sent a savage uppercut up beneath her assailant's chin.

Connie's head snapped back with a sickening crack and she released Olivia's captive leg, which came straight back in a lightning-fast kick, and this time, connected with Connie's stomach. The naked woman stumbled backwards until she was against the banister at the top of the stairs, while Olivia surged forward, launching a fusillade of blows.

Rage welled within her. All she wanted to do was kill this woman who had defiled her home. Murdered her husband. The law be damned. Her blows became more furious and she readied another kick, this time intending to send the bitch over the banister to her death.

Connie lashed out with a vicious back-handed blow that shattered Olivia's nose. Her eyes streamed and she took a step backwards in pain and shock. That second of hesitation was all Connie needed. She stepped forward and grabbed Olivia by the throat, then, impossibly, lifted her off the ground.

Ah, told ye that wasn't very smart. Now yer gonna have tae pay."

Olivia didn't see the punch coming, and cried out in surprise when Connie's fist slammed into her stomach. A warm, wet wave of liquid soaked through her trousers, and she realised in horror that her waters had broken. Connie pulled Olivia close, so that they were face-to-face. Her breath stank of blood and there was something wrong with her eyes.

When she'd spoken to her in the hotel lobby, Connie Hamilton's eyes had been brown. Now they gleamed a feral yellow. These were not the eyes of a human being. The woman's face began to shift and warp. Teeth elongated into fangs and thick russet hair sprouted from her pores. Then the hair receded and those terrible teeth sank back into Connie's gums.

"Ah, ye almost made me lose ma temper. Pull that shit again and Ah'll do a caesarean on ye with ma teeth. Ah think it's time for our wee chat. Ye can start with the names of those coppers that were with ye at the hotel, and the name of that fat, balding tosser."

Connie's grip tightened around Olivia's throat and she kicked out at empty air. Her vision began to fade and she realised that she was about to pass out. Connie's mouth curled into a snarl. "Ah'll not be asking ye again. Give me their fucking names."

Olivia knew that she'd run out of options. She was going to die here, and unless she gave this monstrous woman the information she wanted, then she was going to die right here, right now. Her only chance was to buy more time in the hope that an opportunity for escape would present itself. She barely managed to choke out the words. "Okay...I'll tell you what you want, just please don't hurt my baby."

Connie lowered her to the floor and released her grip. Olivia fell to her knees, sucking air into her lungs. "Ah'm waiting."

"Alright. The boss is called Phil Fletcher. The others were Rick Grey, Mark Briggs and Paul Patterson. Now, please, I've given you what you want. Let me go. I need to get to a hospital."

Connie smiled. "Ah, see, Ah knew ye could be co-operative, given the right incentive."

Olivia crawled back, away from her assailant, towards the bedroom. Connie followed, a smile still on her face. "Where do ye think yer going? Wanna see yer hubby one last time? If it makes ye feel any better, he stayed faithful. I woulda fucked him first, but the soppy twat didn't wanna know." She sniffed. "His loss."

Olivia reached the bedroom door and flung herself inside, slamming the door behind her. She reached up and grabbed the large wooden wardrobe in the corner of the room, using the last of her strength to tip it over. The wardrobe crashed to the ground, wedging itself between the door and bed. Connie pounded against the door, snarling in fury. Olivia stepped around the remains of her husband, to the telephone by the side of the bed. She picked it up and almost cried out with relief when she got a dial tone.

The wooden door began to splinter as Olivia dialled 999. She held the phone in one hand, while she picked up a heavy brass lamp from the side of the bed with the other.

The phone rang and an operator answered on the first ring. "Hello, emergency, which service do you require?"

"Police and ambulance. Please, hurry. My...my husband is dead and I'm being attacked!"

One of the wooden panels of the door split open and Connie's arms tore at the wood, making the hole larger. As she poked her head through the shattered door, Olivia swung the lamp at her, smashing the heavy brass base into her skull. Connie's forehead collapsed under the blow, leaving a spray of blood and bone fragments across the white paint of the doorframe. She slumped back, out of sight.

The operator spoke again. "Ma'am, are you still there? I need you to give me your telephone number and the address that you are calling from. Help is on the way."

Olivia blurted out the details, then held the phone between her shoulder and cheek as she grasped the lamp in a two-handed grip, never taking her eyes from the ruined door.

"Ma'am, can you tell me what's happening?"

"A...a woman. Connie. Connie Hamilton. She broke into my house and murdered my husband, then attacked me. I'm pregnant and she punched me in the stomach and my waters broke and now she's outside and I don't know if I killed her or not. She's not human."

"Ma'am, you need to calm down. Can you get yourself to a safe place?"

"No, I locked myself in the bedroom, but she's broken through the door. I...."

Connie's ruined face appeared in the doorway. As Olivia watched, the terrible wound began to heal. Shattered bone crunched back into place, while torn flesh re-knitted. Connie's mouth curled up into a snarl. "What did Ah tell ye would happen if ye pulled that shite again?"

The blood-soaked woman dropped down, out of sight. A loud ripping sound came from the corridor, as if someone were slowly cracking their knuckles while tearing paper. After a couple of seconds the sound stopped. What replaced it was so much worse. A thick, savage snarl, filled with hatred and fury rang out. Olivia backed away from the door. "No. No, oh God, please, SOMEONE HELP ME!"

The door exploded in a shower of razor-sharp splinters, and something from Olivia's worst nightmares landed on the entrail-covered bed. The creature looked like a wolf on steroids. Corded muscles flowed like liquid beneath layers of thick, red fur.

The monster's ears lay flat against its head and the long, tapered snout wrinkled up into a snarl to reveal rows of razor-sharp fangs. Terrible clawed feet, each toe ending in a black, curved talon, dug into what remained of her husband. It snarled at her, and Olivia knew that it was over. She lashed out with the lamp, throwing every last shred of her strength and desperation into the blow. Connie simply ducked, allowing the lamp to pass over her head. Then the creature leapt.

The impact slammed Olivia back against the far wall, knocking the breath out of her. She struggled to move, to breathe. "Please..." was all that she managed to choke out before Connie's head darted forward. The monster's jaws sank deep into her stomach, then ripped outwards in a single movement. The pain was unimaginable, but it was nothing compared to the anguish Olivia felt as she saw a tiny arm protruding from the werewolf's jaws. The monster bit down, spraying blood from the sides of its mouth, then swallowed.

The terrible emptiness that Olivia felt then eclipsed even the pain. She was hollow. The new life within her torn away and devoured. She couldn't protect it. She couldn't protect any of them. Then Connie darted forward and clamped her jaws around Olivia's throat, and she found that in that last second of her life, she was grateful for the release.

13th December. Catcleugh Reservoir. 10:24.

The twenty-minute drive that Marie had promised turned into an hour-and-a-half of sheer misery for John. His tired muscles cramped up in the confined space, and the fibres from the carpet stuck to his clotting wounds, so that every time he adjusted his position, he tore them open once more. The boot, without the benefit of the car's heater, was freezing cold. His shivering body rubbed itself raw against the coarse man-made fabric.

Every bump or imperfection in the road seemed to be magnified. Eventually, he allowed the steady thrum of the tyres on asphalt to lull him into a half-waking state. He could hear the car's radio, but couldn't make out any of the details. There didn't seem to be any music, only the low murmur of voices. Marie had not spoken a word since they'd left High Moor.

After what seemed like an eternity, the car slowed and turned off the smooth road onto something that felt like a gravel track, complete with some particularly deep pot-holes that compounded his misery. More than once the jolt was so severe that his head banged against the metal boot lid. Eventually, the vehicle came to a halt and Marie opened the boot. She passed him a T-shirt, a pair of jogging bottoms, and a pair of trainers. "Sorry about that, John, but we needed to put a lot of miles between High Moor and ourselves, and I couldn't risk having you visible in case we got pulled over."

John tried to sit up, wincing as another crusted scab ripped away from his skin, and pulled the T-shirt over his head. "I thought you said it was only going to be twenty minutes."

Marie gave John a sheepish grin. "Yeah, I might have been lying about that. "

He pulled on the jogging pants and climbed out from the car boot. "I figured that much out on my own. Where the hell are we, anyway?"

"Catcleugh Reservoir, near the Scottish border. It's isolated enough that we shouldn't be disturbed, and I need some fresh water to clean your wounds up. It's not like we could just take you into a public toilet in the state you're in."

The reservoir certainly was isolated. The area surrounding the vast expanse of water was mostly scrub grassland, with snow-capped pine forests lining the hills in the distance. A steady torrent of water gushed from the sluiceway far beneath them, feeding a stream that meandered through the snow-covered valley floor. The air was bitterly cold, but fresh and invigorating compared to the stale blood-and-body-odour stink of the car boot.

Marie opened the back doors of the car and removed a large bag, then began walking towards a set of stone steps. She motioned for John to follow and the pair made their way down to the edge of the frigid water.

Marie wasted no time. She removed a first-aid kit from the bag and began washing John's injuries with water from the reservoir. Thin rivulets of blood flowed from the open wounds and John winced as she poured the cold water onto him.

"Ah, give over, you big baby. It's only water. It's not going to hurt you."

"You aren't the one freezing to death."

"You think that's bad, then you probably aren't going to enjoy the next bit much."

"What next bit?"

Marie produced a bottle of iodine from the bag, unscrewed the cap, then poured the yellow liquid directly onto the parallel gashes on his chest. John's cry of pain echoed across the water and, off in the distance, a flock of birds took to the sky, startled by the sudden noise.

"Jesus, fuck! God, that hurts."

"Well, if you can try not to scream the place down while I do it, I need to stitch some of these up. I'll be as quick as I can, but it's not going to be pleasant."

It wasn't pleasant at all, but John managed to restrain himself to merely hissing through his teeth as the needle plucked at his torn flesh. Eventually, Marie was satisfied that she'd dealt with the worst of the injuries. "OK, there are some fresh clothes in the bag, along with a toothbrush and a razor. Get yourself cleaned up. I'll be waiting for you, back in the car."

Ten minutes later, John ascended the stairs. His wounds cried out in pain with every step, and he could feel the stitches tugging at his skin as he moved, but he felt better than he had since waking up that morning. The clean clothes - a heavy woollen shirt, jeans and a ski jacket - made all the difference. He still felt frozen through to his bones, but the garments kept the wind chill out, and he was slowly beginning to warm up.

Marie sat on the closed boot of the car, drinking hot coffee from a thermos. She smiled as she saw John, and poured him a fresh cup. "You took your time. I thought you'd got lost or something."

John took the cup, savouring the warmth that seeped through the metal into his numb hands. "Thank you. You have no idea how badly I need this." He took a sip, letting out an involuntary sigh of pleasure as the hot liquid ran down his throat. "So, what's the plan?"

"We're heading north. Right up into the arse end of Scotland. I've booked a holiday cottage for a few weeks, so we can hide out there until you recover and things quieten down a bit. Then we can work out what our next move is."

John took another sip of the coffee, "So, is now a good time for you to tell me how the fuck you're still alive? I saw you gunned down with silver fucking bullets. I mean, Jesus, you were almost cut in half. How the hell do you come back from something like that?"

"You have to understand, John, that what I do...what I did... put me in a hell of a lot of danger. Not just from other werewolves, but from hunters like your good old friend, Steven. Those of us on field teams spend years increasing our tolerance to silver, to the point where it barely affects us." She gave an ironic, bitter chuckle. "At least, that was the theory."

"And Michael? You're telling me that he's still alive?"

Marie nodded. "He's not only alive. He runs The Pack now. He's the alpha wolf. The big boss dog."

John frowned. "Then why are The Pack chasing us? Can't you talk to Michael? Get him to help?"

Marie shook her head. "John, it was Michael who ordered your death. By now, he won't have had any choice but to order mine as well. You have to understand, The Pack will stop at nothing to keep the existence of werewolves a secret. If people knew about us, if there was proof, then they would hunt us down and slaughter us. It almost happened once before, back in 1996. They won't let it happen again."

John finished the last of his coffee and handed the cup back to Marie. "Honestly, I don't understand any of this. I mean, I design bloody websites for a living. I'm way out of my depth here."

Marie put the bag into the boot of the car. "I know. There's a lot that you need to know before you'll be able to understand. Come on, we've still got a long drive ahead of us."

John looked at the boot with a pained expression on his face. "I don't have to go back in there, do I?"

Marie chuckled. "No, I think we can risk you riding up front now. It's time I told you everything, but be warned, you might not like some of what you're about to hear."

CHAPTER 11

13th December. Olivia's House, Bear Park. 09:42.

Phil raced through the traffic, the siren howling on his commandeered squad car. He'd left the headquarters the instant he'd heard that Olivia had been attacked in her home. The first responders would only be arriving at the scene now, and Phil dreaded what they might find. He just prayed that Olivia was alright. Despite her smart, sarcastic mouth, Olivia was one of the most sincere, intelligent, and compassionate people that he'd ever met. If anything had happened to her, then he honestly didn't know how he would react.

The road outside her house was cordoned off, with two uniformed officers turning the complaining motorists away. The ambulance hadn't even arrived yet. The only ones in attendance so far were the armed response vehicle and a traffic car. Phil parked on the pavement just outside the cordon and, ignoring the two traffic officers, marched straight toward the house.

One of the traffic constables stepped into his path. "I'm sorry, sir, but Sergeant Grey and his team have only just gone inside. They need to sweep the property before anyone else goes in."

Phil's face reddened and the vein in his temple began to pulse. "Officer, if you don't get out of my fucking way then I won't be held responsible for my actions. I hear there's a post coming up in the Wildlife Liaison Office."

Phil didn't wait for a response and pushed past the traffic officer. As he approached the front door, Paul Patterson, one of Rick's men, stumbled out of the front door and vomited. He looked up at Phil with wide, staring, tear-filled eyes. "No, Phil. Don't go in there. You don't want to see...to see THAT." Paul's complexion turned from white to a light shade of green, and he doubled over once more. Phil's heart sank as he stepped past Paul into the hallway.

The downstairs appeared normal, with no obvious signs of

disturbance. The living room was littered with empty beer cans and pizza boxes, and Olivia's coat hung over one of the stools in the kitchen. The upstairs floorboards creaked so Phil ascended the staircase, to find Rick Grey and Mark Briggs standing in the corridor. Rick had his arms and forehead pressed against the wall, and both men wept openly, and neither of them so much as looked up when he got to the top of the stairs. "Rick? Mark? What happened? Where's Olivia?"

Rick didn't look up, but motioned towards an open door with one arm. "The...the bedroom. She's in the bedroom."

Phil's stomach flip-flopped as a wave of grief and exhaustion washed over him. The reaction of Rick's team had confirmed the worst. He knew that Olivia had been murdered, and that she'd not died a clean death. He didn't want to see the body. He didn't want his memory of the pretty, funny young woman to be tainted by the manner of her death. Phil didn't want to see, but he knew that he had to. He had to see with his own eyes what had happened to his friend. Have it burned onto his soul like a brand so that he would never relax in his pursuit of her killer. He stepped past Rick, trying hard to conceal his shaking legs that suddenly lacked the strength to walk. His heart pounded in his chest and he paused just outside the room for a moment, to steel his resolve. He took a deep breath, held it, then stepped through the doorway into a slaughterhouse.

The room was covered in blood. Entrails hung from the lampshade, dripping sticky globules of crimson onto the gore-soaked bed. Propped up on the pillow were the severed heads of Olivia and Matt, facing each other as if for one last kiss. The worst horror, however, lay alongside the grotesque tableau. What remained of Olivia's corpse lay slumped against the bedside cabinet. Her slender neck had been reduced to a tattered mess of ragged flesh and shattered bones, while her stomach gaped open, its precious cargo torn out.

It was then that he noticed a tiny, severed hand on the floor beside the corpse and Phil could take no more. He stumbled from the room and bent over, with his hands flat against his legs as he tried to contain the surge of emotions that flooded through him.

The abject horror of the scene in that bedroom, the overwhelming grief at the loss of a close friend, and a small, cold, kernel of rage deep within his chest.

Rick managed to compose himself sufficiently to put a hand on Phil's shoulder and guide him away from the door. Phil shook him off. "No. Not yet. I need to see it one more time. I never want to forget a single detail of what's in that room."

"Phil, when you find the fucker, I want in. The sick fuck that did this isn't going to spend the rest of their lives in a prison cell. Do you understand me?"

Phil moved back into the doorway and looked at the charnel house one more time, letting the details sear themselves onto his mind. Grief crushed his heart, sending sharp flares of anguish through his chest with every laboured beat. Despite the scene before him, it still hadn't sunk in that Olivia was dead. He forced himself to focus on her severed head, mouth and eyes fixed open in a soundless scream. Had she still been alive when her child was ripped from her? Yes, Phil thought that she almost certainly had been. She hadn't just been murdered. She'd been made to suffer in the most appalling manner first. The coal of rage flared brighter. He turned away from the room and looked Rick straight in the eye. "Get in fucking line."

13th December. Nauchnnyy proyezd, Moscow. 13:03.

"Have you lost your fucking mind?"

Michael's hand gripped the telephone so hard that the plastic groaned under the strain.

Connie's indignant voice crackled over the speaker. "What do ye mean? Ah did what ye asked. Ah took care of one copper and got the names of the others. Ah'll take care of them next."

Michael tried to steady his breathing in an attempt to calm himself down. It didn't work. "What I told you to do, was take care of them quickly and quietly. How the fuck does tearing a family apart in their own home, and worse, letting them get a call off to the police, constitute quietly? Do you realise that your name and fucking photograph are plastered all over the internet?"

Connie's tone lost some of its arrogance as the amount of trouble she was in began to register. "Well, what would ye have had me do?"

"For Christ's sake, Connie. You should have made it look like an accident. You've been working on field teams long enough to know that. We leave no fucking trace, not go on a public killing spree in the middle of a crisis." He paused as he considered his next words. "I want you out of the country. Tonight."

The voice on the other end of the phone acquired a whiny edge. "But, the job's not done yet, and there's still that fucker Wilkinson."

"Are you not hearing me? The job's over as far as I'm concerned. The whole point of taking out those police was to prevent exactly this from happening. They're putting as much effort into finding you as they are Simpson. Maybe even more."

"How am Ah supposed to get out of the country? They'll be checking all the ports."

"You know how, Connie. You'll have to do a tunnel-run."

Connie was silent for a moment before responding. "Please, ye can't be serious. The last time anyone tried that they got cut in half by a freight train."

"Do I sound like I'm fucking joking? I'm pulling a team out of Germany to meet you on the other side. They'll escort you back to Moscow."

"But what about Wilkinson? We've been after him for years. We can't just let him get away again, especially now he's turned."

"He's not your problem, Connie. Let me be very clear about this. You will leave the UK tonight. If you do not do this, then I'll have to consider you as having gone rogue, and will take the necessary steps to prevent you causing more harm. Do you fucking understand me?"

"Yes, Michael. Ah understand."

"Good, now get moving. The sound of your voice is getting on my fucking nerves. Gregorz, are you there? What the hell happened with the Simpson hit?"

"We tracked Simpson, but as we moved in, Marie attacked us. It seems she found the tactical kit in Connie's car and made some modifications to the ammunition. By the time we recovered, she'd made it out of the woods, into a public place. It seemed prudent to back off and await a better opportunity."

Michael shook his head, not wanting to believe what he was hearing. "Marie? I...I can't believe she'd do something like that."

"Well, not only did she come looking for Simpson, but she reduced the amount of powder in each cartridge to slow the rounds down. Daniel is still cutting pieces of silver out of himself. She came prepared to take us on, Michael. She knew exactly what she was doing."

"Do you know where they are now?"

"Fortunately, Connie's mobile telephone is still in the car. Daniel was able to track it. They are still moving, heading north. Assuming the battery on the phone lasts, we should be able to find where they go to ground."

"That's something, at least. Find out where they are heading, and keep an eye on them, but from a distance. Don't engage until I give the order."

"Michael, I think it would be a mistake to wait. Marie is resourceful and well trained. It's sheer luck that we were able to track her at all. If she realises they've been found, she'll simply disappear again. Once we find them, we should move immediately."

"No. When you find them, you keep them under observation until I arrive."

"You are coming here? Michael, are you sure that..."

"I don't believe that I asked for your opinion, Gregorz. Now, what about Troy and Gabriela's bodies? Did Oskar at least manage to do what he was supposed to?"

"Yes, he simply walked into the hospital and amended the paperwork to show the bodies as being for disposal. They were incinerated first thing this morning."

"Good. At least something went right. Report back to me when you find where my sister is hiding out. I'll be there with another team in a few days."

Michael didn't wait for Gregorz to respond, and terminated the call. He leaned back in the leather office chair and massaged his temples. "Marie, you stupid fucking cow. What have you done?"

He had no idea how to put this right. Marie had gone too far, and there was nothing he could do to save her. The law was clear. The penalty for harbouring a moonstruck was death. There really wasn't any choice. Even if he ordered her spared, the Council would remove him as alpha, condemn him to the same fate, and then send the death squads after Marie anyway. He groaned. He'd forgotten about the Council. He'd promised a report once he heard from the teams in England. He reached over to the phone and dialled Steffan's number.

"Michael, have you news?"

"Yes, bring the car around to the front. It's time for me to talk to the Council."

***

The ZiL limousine wove its way through the slow-moving traffic, out of the city. The roads in Moscow were hell at the best of times, but the near-blizzard conditions that had set in a few days before made the going even slower than usual. The limo's wipers struggled to clear the windscreen, and a pile of dirty ice had begun to accumulate at the bottom of the windscreen. Michael didn't know whether to be grateful for the delay, or to curse it for dragging out the unpleasant task before him.

The Council had been formed hundreds of years ago, after an

insane alpha wolf declared war on humanity and slaughtered entire villages before the rest of The Pack decided enough was enough. They were elected from pack members and advised the alpha on crucial matters. They also held the power to remove an alpha from his position, should the need arise. In Michael's opinion, they were nothing more than a bunch of squabbling old fools, but at the same time, he would have to watch his tongue and proceed carefully. More than one of them had objected to his appointment, believing that only the moonborn, children born to werewolf parents, should be eligible for alpha. They had nothing but disdain for turned werewolves like himself. Every single one of them was a scheming, devious bastard with their own agendas. Every one of them was also a pitiless killer. Fools they may be, but they were, nevertheless, very dangerous fools.

He looked out of the window, while Steffan drove in silence. The towering concrete blocks of flats were barely visible through the blizzard, but he felt their presence looming through the white blanket. Hundreds of people, crammed into tiny, damp apartments with little in the way of heat or sound insulation. They reminded him of the old prefabricated estate in High Moor, where he'd sometimes played as a child. The stairwells and elevators had stunk of stale urine, and once, he'd spent two hours trapped in a lift with David and John before the fire brigade rescued them.

He shook his head to force the memory from his mind. David was long dead, and John soon would be. There was nothing he could do about that. He had to focus on somehow saving his sister, without condemning himself in the process.

The ZiL turned into an industrial estate in the southern part of the city. Most of the units appeared to be empty, with only the occasional warm glow of artificial light from office windows breaking up the bleak landscape. The limo passed the isolated signs of life and proceeded deeper into the industrial park until it arrived at an empty factory unit. Steffan pulled up outside, getting out of the car to pull open the chain-link gate so he could drive the big vehicle inside. In the car, he turned to face Michael and put a hand on his shoulder. Michael nodded and patted his friend's hand before opening the door and stepping out into the driving snow.

The frigid air made him gasp, so he brought his wolf up to the surface, relishing the warm glow as his body temperature began to rise. The strong wind made it difficult to pick out individual scents, but as far as he could tell, there were only five people in the building. Even with the Council members away on field duty, like Oskar, there should have been more than five of them present. Unless the Council members within wanted to keep the details of what was about to happen hidden from their peers. The thought didn't do much to settle his nerves. He strode to a rusted metal door, pulled it open, and stepped inside.

The office had long since been emptied. Sections of carpet tile had been removed, along with virtually everything else. Even the wooden interior doors had been stolen. Such was life in Moscow these days. He left the office and proceeded down the corridor, enjoying the click of his shoes on the concrete. The others would hear him coming long before he reached the boardroom. It would show them that he was not intimidated by their summons. And if things were to go bad, then he always had the Beretta in his pocket to back him up.

By some miracle, the heavy wooden doors of the boardroom still stood, although the scratches on the walls around the hinges showed that someone had tried to remove them at some point. Without pausing, Michael pushed open the right-hand door and entered the room beyond.

The once-grand room had been stripped bare. The wooden panelling on the walls had been torn off, leaving only cracked plaster behind. The carpet was thin and threadbare, not even worth stealing, apart from the long dark rectangle that showed where the boardroom table had once been. Five men stood in the far corner in conversation. They attempted to look surprised at Michael's entrance and stepped forward to meet him. It was as bad as Michael had feared. The Council members here today were all moonborn.

Krysztof Balazs, a hulking Armenian with grey flecks in his once jet-black hair extended his hand. "Alpha, it is good to see you. What news of the operation in England?"

Michael took Krysztof's hand and suppressed a wince as the huge man tightened his grip. He looked into Krysztof's eyes and smiled. "The news is mixed. We are not in as precarious a position as last night. The moonstruck is no longer in police custody, but he escaped from Oskar's team, and Troy and Gabriela were killed. He's on the move, but Gregorz is tracking him. Once he gets to wherever he's going, we'll set up surveillance on him and then strike when the time is right. He won't get away again."

Lukas Kassik, one of the oldest members of The Pack, and one of the most influential, stepped forward. The old man tilted his head and fixed Michael with his piercing green eyes. "And what of your sister's involvement in Simpson's escape?"

Michael's heart sank. Of course they would know about Marie. Oskar would have made sure of it. "I'm hoping that my sister can be taken alive, so that she can explain her actions before judgement is decided."

Lukas shook his head. "Alpha, you know the law as well as us. From the reports I have received, not only is your sister guilty of harbouring a moonstruck and attacking her pack mates, but it would appear that she's also become human. We have considered the matter, and have decided that the death penalty is the only way to proceed."

"Lukas, I understand what you are saying, but think about this for a moment. If Marie has lost her wolf side, then we need to understand how this happened. It could be something that could be used against us in the future."

The old man huffed. "It is irrelevant. Your sister has broken pack law and must be held accountable. The Council's judgement stands."

Michael raised an eyebrow. "And is this the view of the entire Council, or just its moonborn members?"

Krysztof bristled at this. "And what exactly are you implying, Alpha? We speak for the entire Council. That some of them were unable to attend this meeting is beside the point. Now, how do you intend to resolve the current situation?"

Michael held Krysztof's gaze. "As I said, Gregorz is tracking Simpson and my sister. When they finally go to ground, I will fly over with another team and we will make sure that the job is finished."

Lukas gave Michael a sly smile. "I sincerely hope so, Alpha. For your sake, and ours."

13th December. Naver Cottage, Kinbrace. 21:45.

The snow had started to fall an hour ago. Large white flakes danced in the headlight's beams, obscuring the road ahead, although calling the track a road was, in John's mind, stretching the definition. They'd driven in an uneasy silence after Marie had completed her tale. John felt like he should have said something, but the events of the past twenty-four hours rushed through his mind and he struggled to think of what to say to the woman beside him. He understood the risks she'd taken to save him, but still didn't understand why. Truth be told, based on what Marie had told him, he realised that he didn't know this woman at all, and he found it difficult to relax in her company.

As if sensing his train of thought, Marie turned her head to him. "You've been quiet for a while. Are you okay?"

John nodded. "Yeah, I'm fine. It's just been a hell of a couple of days, you know? I'm just trying to sort it all out in my head."

Marie's eyes searched his face for a moment, as if trying to discern the truth of his statement, then, apparently satisfied, she relaxed and gave a weak smile. "You aren't fucking joking. Well, we're almost there now. Then you can wrap your head around it after a hot shower, some hot food, and more than a few bottles of cheap wine. Sound like a plan?"

John returned her smile, this time with genuine feeling. "At this moment in time, that sounds like my idea of heaven. It feels like we've been in this car forever, although it's a lot better riding up front, instead of in the boot."

"You aren't going to let that go, are you?"

"What? I didn't say a word."

Marie arched an eyebrow, then leaned forward in her seat, as if to get a better view of the road ahead. "Oh, hang on, I think this is it."

John had no idea how she'd even noticed the side track. A small sign stood by the side of the road, its white surface almost invisible against the falling snow. The surface of the road, the lane and the surrounding moorland was covered in an even, flat, icy blanket. Marie seemed to know what she was doing, though, and turned onto the track. They followed the road through a small copse of fir trees and across the open moors until John noticed the dark shadow of a building through the blizzard.

Marie parked the car at the front of the building - an old stone crofter's cottage with glimpses of blue slate tiles just visible beneath the covering of snow on its roof - and got out of the vehicle and lifted the doormat to retrieve a set of keys.

Her face lit up and for a moment, John saw a glimpse of the little girl he used to know, instead of the killer that she'd become. She waved at him, and he followed her out of the car and into the dark cottage, wincing at the stiffness in his sore muscles

The rush of warmth that greeted him as he crossed the threshold was both unexpected and welcome. He'd been convinced that he'd have to spend at least an hour messing about with an antique boiler before they had any heat, but the owner had obviously been round to make sure the cottage was warm for his guests. The oil boiler rumbled away in the kitchen, and the log burner in the living room popped and crackled. The cottage was clean and had been well, if cheaply, renovated. The kitchen looked to be fairly recent, but most of the furniture was made of cheap, varnished pine, which matched the cladding on all of the downstairs walls, and the garish floral pattern on the sofas hurt John's eyes. On the positive side, in what must have been a workshop adjoined to the house before the owner had extended into it, John found a pool table, a table football game, and an Xbox

360, complete with a pile of games.

John stepped back outside to retrieve their bags from the car. He turned to Marie, who'd followed him to the doorstep. "Do you want this metal box bringing in?"

"Yeah, but don't worry. I'll do that."

"It's no trouble, honestly."

"No, I think I should take care of that one. I don't want you dropping it and setting off one of the grenades."

John felt the colour drain from his face. "Grenades? Where the fuck... oh, never mind. I don't want to know. You're right. You handle the explosives. I'll take care of the clothes."

John hefted the two canvas bags containing their supplies and carried them into the house. He strode upstairs to find two bedrooms, one with a double bed and the other with a pair of singles. He deposited the bag containing Marie's things in the double room and put his own bag on one of the single beds. Marie struggled past him with the metal box and put it at the foot of the double bed. She gave him a sideways glance when she saw that he'd taken the other bedroom, but didn't say anything. They both filed downstairs and retrieved the remaining bags containing the food from the car.

Marie rubbed her arms as the door closed, and she applied the deadbolts. "Why don't you go freshen up while I sort us out something to eat?"

John nodded and went upstairs once more, grateful that she didn't seem to have picked up on his discomfort. The bathroom, like the rest of the cottage, was clean and adequately equipped. An electric shower was bolted onto the wall above a white porcelain bath, and John smiled as a stream of scalding hot water burst from the shower head when he turned it on.

John stayed in the shower for longer than he should have. The act of washing was a painstaking process, as he washed around the edges of his wounds. Nevertheless, the water that collected in the bath was stained a light pink by the time he finished, and watery rivulets of blood trickled from in between his stitches. He padded himself dry, reapplied dressings to the worst of his injuries, then got dressed into a loose-fitting T-shirt and pair of jogging bottoms.

He smelled the food as soon as he started down the stairs. The aroma filled the cottage, setting his stomach growling in anticipation. He'd hardly eaten anything that day, just a limp tuna sandwich and a chocolate bar Marie had picked up in a service station, and the smell made him realise just how hungry he was.

Marie beamed at him as he entered the kitchen. "I was starting to think you'd drowned up there. Dinner's not much, I'm afraid. Just some soup and crusty bread. I figured you'd want something quick, instead of fancy."

He pulled a chair out from under the dining room table, and flopped into it. "Soup sounds great. Thank you."

Marie ladled the liquid into two bowls and took a pair of baguettes out of the oven, finally joining John at the table. "Feeling a bit better after your shower?"

John tasted a mouthful of the soup, and despite it being from a tin, couldn't remember anything tasting better. "Yeah, lots. I made a bit of a mess of the bathroom, though. I'll clean the blood up after I finish dinner, so that you can use it."

"Don't worry about it. You just need to unwind a bit. Chill out in front of the TV or something while I sort myself out. Here, this might help." She reached into the bag and produced a bottle of red wine.

John shook his head. "No, not for me, thanks. To tell you the truth, I'm shattered. Once I finish eating, I think I'm just going to have an early night."

She shrugged. "Suit yourself. After the last few days, I'm going to need a bit of sedation before I can relax enough to sleep. Are you sure you won't stay up for a glass? I'd quite like some company tonight."

John finished the last of his soup and mopped up the traces with the bread, then got up and rinsed his bowl under the tap. "No, I'm sorry, but I don't think I'd be very good company. My head’s still spinning from everything that's happened in the last twenty-four hours. I'll see you in the morning. Goodnight, Marie."

Marie's face fell, and John felt a pang of guilt, but steeled his resolve. He glanced backwards as he left the kitchen, to see Marie pouring wine into a mug. She didn't look up.

“Marie. We'll talk in the morning, OK?"

Marie looked up then, but wouldn't meet his gaze. She took a long swig from the porcelain mug, lowered her eyes once more. "Yeah, sure, whatever. See you tomorrow, John."

CHAPTER 12

14th December. Castle Hill, Folkestone. 00:50.

Connie got out of the car and stared across the busy motorway at her destination. The tunnel's entrance was obscured behind rows of chain-link fences, each topped with rolls of razor wire and adorned with warning signs. Floodlights blazed down on the entire area, casting stark shadows across the concrete buildings, while CCTV cameras seemed to cover every square inch of the approach to the tunnel. Getting past that security without being seen was not going to be a simple task. If one of the people monitoring the cameras saw her enter in her wolf form, then there would be an animal control team dispatched to try and catch what they would believe to be a stray dog. Despite her mood, Connie grinned at the thought. The poor bastards would have no idea what hit them.

Another car pulled in beside Connie, and a young couple got out. They paid her no attention, simply heading off to the health club at the far end of the car park, laughing and joking together. It made her sick to her stomach; she considered transforming there and then, if only to remove the smug, self-satisfied expressions from their faces. The couple's happiness only served to remind her that she would never experience anything like that again.

Her capacity for happiness had died with her daughter and, rather than wallow in self-pity, she'd taken that gaping chasm within and filled it with hate. She hated Marie, who should have been watching Megan that night. She hated her alpha, for ordering her back to Russia when her vengeance was so close. And more than anything else, she hated Steven Wilkinson. The bastard who'd looked into the eyes of a crying, eight-year-old girl, and then shot her in the face.

The same thought that had been gnawing on her nerves all day resurfaced. Why was she going back at all? This close to the tunnel, everything became much more real and immediate. Connie realised that she'd never really stopped to consider the consequences of following Michael's order. If she survived the journey through the tunnel, the other team would escort her back to Moscow. That sounded a hell of a lot like being under arrest.

That prick, Michael, would have her put on trial for following orders that he fucking gave her, and then lock her away in some cage, or even have her put to death. Given his insistence that she run through twenty-five miles of railway tunnel, avoiding fucking trains and high voltage lines, it seemed pretty obvious that Michael didn't feel that her life was a priority. And if she were dead, then she'd never have her revenge on Wilkinson. Michael obviously wasn't interested or he'd have sent another team over to deal with him. Hell, he was a werewolf now. Michael might even invite the bastard to join The Pack.

Her lips curled into a snarl, and she felt the first surges of the change begin in her fingers and toes. With effort, she brought herself back under control and considered her options. There was a good chance that she was already marked for death. She might not even make it back to Moscow, especially if the extraction team turned out to be a hit squad. If that was the case, then Michael's threats no longer held any meaning. If she was going to die, then she'd make damn sure she was covered in Steven Wilkinson's blood when it happened.

The weight of her decision pressed down on her. If she did this, then there was no going back to The Pack. They'd hunt her with the same tenacity and determination as a moonstruck - perhaps more. She'd be looking over her shoulder for the rest of her life, and she'd be leaving behind the closest thing to a family that she had left. Her heart ached at the thought, but that pain was a tiny thing compared to her thirst for revenge.

She wiped a tear from the corner of her eye. "Fuck it. If he's gonna make me a rogue, then Ah'll show the bastard what a rogue werewolf is really capable of. Ah'll show all of those fuckers."

Connie took one last look at the chain fences and the CCTV cameras, then snarled her defiance. Getting back into her car, she drove out of the industrial estate onto the slip road for the motorway and headed north.

14th December. Phil's House, Gilesgate. 01:15.

Phil poured himself another whiskey and stared at the wall. Sharon had long since left him to his thoughts, having gone to bed a couple of hours earlier. He'd tried to distract himself by watching television, but he'd been unable to concentrate on any of the programmes. Sharon had tried putting music on and getting him to talk about what had happened, but the emotions were too raw for him to express. He'd spent most of the evening in silence, speaking only to thank his wife when she made him a cup of tea or put a plate of food in front of him, even though he'd only eaten a few mouthfuls.

He'd been sent home from work by Franks as soon as the sanctimonious prick had heard the news. The chief inspector had been uncharacteristically sympathetic, and had insisted that he, along with Rick's team, take a few days off so that they could come to terms with Olivia's death. The man was a fucking idiot, as far as Phil was concerned. There was only one way that he was going to come to terms with Olivia's murder, and that was by getting hold of the bastard who killed her. At work, he would have been able to focus his pain, do something useful with it. Instead, Franks had condemned him to spending the next few days wandering his home like a ghost, agonising over whether he could have done something differently. Whether he could have saved Olivia's life if he'd made a different decision.

His glass was empty again. He hadn't even realised that he'd taken a drink. He picked up the bottle of Jameson's and tipped it up over the empty glass. Only a few drops of liquid dribbled from the empty bottle.

"Bollocks."

He lifted himself from the chair, almost falling back before he steadied himself on the coffee table. He knew that he should really go to bed, but he also knew that he would just lie there, awake, listening to the staccato grunts from his wife until the sun came up. What he needed tonight was oblivion. He remembered a bottle of cheap, supermarket own-brand scotch that Sharon's sister had bought him for Christmas two years ago. He'd banished the bottle to the back of the sideboard and had forgotten all about it until now.

"Fuck it, it's not like I've got work tomorrow."

He stumbled out of the living room and into the kitchen, and then staggered uncertainly into the dining room. He didn't bother turning on the light, instead circumnavigating the dining room chairs until he reached his goal. Steadying himself against the mahogany unit, he reached for the cupboard door, missing at his first attempt. At that moment, he heard the unmistakable click of a pistol hammer being cocked somewhere behind him, and his blood turned to ice.

"Don't do anything stupid. I'm just here to talk. Can we talk, Phil?"

"Please, don't hurt my wife. I couldn't..."

"Relax. Like I said, I'm just here to talk. Now, I'm going to get you to turn around. Do it slowly, then sit down in the chair behind you."

Phil turned to face the intruder, but his face was lost in the shadows and Phil didn't recognise the man's voice. What was recognisable, however, was the 9mm pistol pointed at him. He put up his hands and eased himself into the chair, making sure his hands were visible at all times.

The man nodded at this and took the seat opposite him. As his face drew closer, the shadows receded, bringing his face into focus. Phil felt that he knew this man, that he'd seen him somewhere before. Then it hit him. The man sitting before him was Steven Wilkinson.

Steven smiled. "I see that I don't need to bother with introductions."

"What the fuck? How the..."

"How is a comatose man with a severed spinal cord able to

break into your home and hold you at gunpoint? Come on, Phil. Based on everything that's happened, everything that you've seen, is it really that hard to make the connection?"

"You're telling me that you're a werewolf."

Steven leaned forward in his seat. "You've seen the films. You know the myth. Anyone who survives an attack by a werewolf is cursed to become one on the next full moon. What do you think bit through my spine? A fucking poodle?"

Phil wished that he had another drink. The sudden surge of adrenaline had left him depressingly sober. "OK, let's say for a second that I believe any of this. What the hell are you doing in my house at one o'clock in the morning?"

Steven sat back. "The reason I'm here, Phil, is because you have no fucking clue as to how much shit you're currently in, and there's still enough copper left in me to want to give you a fighting chance. So, here's the summary. John Simpson is a werewolf. He's been one since he was a child, after the attack in '86. He came back to High Moor and managed to infect a local meat-head called Malcolm Harrison. We both went after him when he turned. I got almost bitten in half, and your men arrested Simpson after he'd killed Harrison. You with me so far?"

"I heard more or less the same shite story from Simpson, although he didn't mention your involvement."

Steven reached into his pocket and produced a small flask. "Pass me those glasses behind you, Phil. You're going to want a drink for the next part."

Phil, mindful of the pistol still trained on him, reached over and put two tumblers on the table. Steven poured a liberal amount of the liquor into each, putting the flask back in his pocket afterwards. He pushed a glass over to Phil. "Redbreast Irish single malt. Makes that Jameson's you've been drinking seem like paint stripper."

Phil reached over and took a sip from the amber liquid, savouring the smooth warmth of the spirit. Steven certainly wasn't lying about the whiskey. "OK, so, why don't you enlighten me as to the rest of it. Then, I'm going to have to arrest you for possessing an illegal firearm."

Steven laughed at this. "The problem you have, Phil, is that not all werewolves are poor fuckers that howl at the moon once a month, like Simpson. There are others that can change whenever they like, and seem to retain their intelligence when they do it. They call themselves The Pack, and they'll do anything to keep the existence of their kind a secret. Anything at all."

"And this has what to do with me what, exactly?"

"It wasn't John Simpson that killed your DC this morning. And werewolf or not, John Simpson sure as fuck didn't crash that prison van on his own. There are at least two pack teams operating around here. They are hunting Simpson, but they are also hunting you and me. That's what happened to your friend this morning, and if you don't start accepting what's going on, then you and your wife are going to end up the same."

"What the hell do you mean, hunting us?"

"You're obviously getting too close for them. I'm sorry, I know it's a lot to take in, but you have to realise the danger you're in. These pack teams are trained killers. Assassins. They turn up every time something like this runs the risk of going public, and they erase any and all evidence. Kill anyone who knows, or even suspects what's going on. And then the fuckers vanish. That's what's coming for you."

Phil took another swig of his whiskey, very aware of his heart pounding in his chest. It was ludicrous, but it all made a sort of sense. He'd spent weeks trying to fit the puzzle pieces together around the basic premise that John Simpson's story had been a load of bollocks. Unfortunately, everything that Steven had said rang true. Hell, even his presence here backed him up. He'd been crippled. People didn't just get up and walk away after that. Severed spinal cords didn't heal. He sighed. "So, what exactly am I supposed to do? Get hold of some silver bullets?"

Steven smiled. "It wouldn't hurt. You should have most of my ammunition locked up in evidence. If I were you, I'd send the wife as far away as you can, first thing in the morning. Then I'd borrow a nine millimetre from your friends in armed response and fucking pray."

"So, that's it? That's all you came here to say to me? Steal some ammunition and a weapon, send my wife away and then shoot anything hairy that comes through the door?"

Steven took out his flask and topped up Phil's glass. "There might be something I can do to help you, but I'm going to need some things from you in return."

Phil sighed. There was always something. "And what, exactly, would those things be?"

"I'm going to help you with your little pack problem, but I need you to help me put a mistake right. You have to understand that I've hunted werewolves for decades, ever since that mess in 1986. I've tracked them down and killed them wherever I found them. Men, women, hell, even a child once. If it sprouted hair and fangs on a full moon, I put a silver bullet between the fucking thing's eyes. Every time except one."

"You mean John Simpson?"

Steven nodded, and suddenly looked his age. "Yes. The thing is, I saved John Simpson, when he was a boy. Me and an old Yank called Carl Schneider. Then, when The Pack came to clear up the mess, we fought them again. For the boy. Carl died fighting to save that child. So, when he turned up again in High Moor, what I should have done was blow his head off. I didn't, and everything that's happened since is a direct result of that decision. I need to put things right."

"So, you want me to pass on any information we get about Simpson? In return for what?"

Steven smiled and raised his glass. "I'll help you find and kill those pack fuckers that murdered your friend."

Phil considered this for a moment, then clinked his glass against Steven's. "Then we've got a deal."

14th December. Naver Cottage, Kinbrace. 10:55.

Marie sipped her coffee, trying to ignore the pounding in her head. She'd spent half the night throwing up in the bathroom, and even after taking a handful of painkillers, she still felt like crawling under a rock and dying. She'd never experienced a hangover before. Her heightened metabolism had made getting properly drunk an effort, and by the time she awoke the next morning, she'd always felt fine. That, apparently, was no longer the case. Her tolerance for alcohol seemed to have diminished along with her immunity to the after-effects. She wouldn't have minded, but she'd only drunk one bottle of red wine. It hardly seemed excessive, especially considering the consequences this morning.

She rubbed her hand through her hair, conscious of the fact that it looked as if she'd spent the night sleeping in a hedge. Her fingers caught in the tangles, and when she pulled her hand away, it smelled of stale vomit. "Oh fucking marvellous. In my hair? Really?"

She took another sip of coffee, wincing as the hot liquid aggravated her already upset stomach. She had to have a shower and sort herself out, preferably before John came downstairs and saw her in this state. Not that he'd give a shit, based on his actions last night. She couldn't understand it. She'd turned her back on everyone and everything that she loved. She'd risked her life and shot two people she cared about with an assault rifle, all to save his miserable life. Yet he'd been distant since she let him out of the boot. There was a palatable, uncomfortable tension between them, and for the life of her, she couldn't work out why. Was it something she said? Something she did? Or was the problem something deeper, more fundamental than that? John acted as if he simply didn't like being around her.

Things certainly hadn't gone the way she expected, although, if she was honest, her little romantic fantasy about the two of them against the world seemed childish in the cold light of day. Even so, after everything they'd been through together, and given everything they would face in the coming weeks and months, was it unreasonable for her to expect *something*? For them to be friends at least, if not lovers?

Her stomach burbled again and she forced herself to stand up, steadying herself against the table as the room spun. She needed a long, hot shower and something to eat. Then, perhaps she'd feel less shitty. She fortified herself and began the slow, painful journey upstairs to the bathroom.

***

She emerged from the bathroom almost forty minutes later. The blistering streams of water had left her skin pink; nevertheless, she felt like they'd washed away the worst of her hangover. She was still tired, her head still throbbed, and her stomach continued to do somersaults every once in a while, but she felt better than she had an hour ago. The smell of frying bacon wafted up from the kitchen, and her stomach gurgled, although she couldn't tell if it was in anticipation, or the start of another wave of nausea. She figured that she'd find out soon enough and made her way downstairs.

John looked up and smiled as she entered the room. "Morning. I wasn't sure if you'd eaten or not, so I made you some bacon and eggs anyway. Sorry about last night. I know you wanted to talk, but I was hanging on by a thread. If I'd sat down with you, I'd have fallen asleep in the chair inside of ten minutes."

She gave him a weak smile before shuffling over to the kitchen table and flopping down in a chair. "That's okay, I understand that you were tired. Feeling better today?"

John put a plate of food in front of her, then put his own plate on the table and sat down. "Yeah, lots. I think I must have slept for twelve hours straight, but it did the job. I feel like I could run a marathon today."

She picked at her food without much enthusiasm. "I'm glad at least one of us is feeling alright. Christ almighty, why do people drink when you feel like this the next day?"

John arched an eyebrow. "You have a hangover? Bloody hell, Marie, how much did you have to drink?"

She held up a finger. "One bottle of wine. I am officially a lightweight."

John looked confused. "I don't get it. Shouldn't your...you know, take care of that?"

Marie's stomach flip-flopped again, but this time it had nothing to do with her alcohol consumption. She'd not quite told John everything yesterday, and she'd wanted to keep this from him for as long as possible. "Well, normally it would. Unfortunately, whatever your fucking bastard friend did to me killed my wolf." She realised how bitter that sounded once the words left her mouth, but found that she didn't care. John, on the other hand, looked shocked. Again.

"Wait a minute. You're telling me that you're human? That you're cured?"

Marie's hangover must have been worse than she realised because it was affecting her aim. Instead of hitting John straight between his eyes, her coffee cup sailed harmlessly over his shoulder and shattered against the pine cladding on the far wall. "Cured? I'm not cured. That fucker killed part of me. He crippled me in the worst possible way, and you have the fucking nerve to say that he cured me?"

John raised his hands. "Whoa, hang on a minute. I'm just saying that if it worked for you, then it might work for me. I could be free of this. I could be normal."

She snarled. "Well, I hate to break it to you, John, but your fucking friend's cure involved cutting me in half with a fucking machine gun filled with silver bullets. If I hadn't spent years developing an immunity to silver, then I'd have died. I *should've* died, but I think my wolf sacrificed herself to save me. She burned herself out to heal my wounds, and you have the nerve to talk about her like she was some kind of disease? How fucking dare you!"

John's face paled. "Hang on a second, I didn't mean it like that."

"No, John. That's exactly what you meant. You don't appreciate the fucking gift you've been given, when I'd do anything to get it back. All you do is mope around, feeling sorry for yourself, while everyone around you has to pick up the pieces."

A spark of anger flashed in John's eyes. "Well, I was doing fine until your little plan to lure me out of hiding backfired. I had a house that I loved, a good job, and no-one fucking died because they knew me."

Marie recoiled as if struck. "You...you're saying that this is all *my* fault?"

"Well, isn't it? If you'd left me alone, then none of this would have happened. I'd be at home, working on some project for work, instead of being the most wanted man in the country, hiding out in the arse end of Scotland with a trail of fucking corpses behind me."

Marie took some slim satisfaction that her aim was improving as the porcelain plate struck John on the bridge of his nose. "You want me to leave you alone? Fine. You can fuck off and die, you ungrateful fucking cunt. Let's see how long you last without me."

John seemed to realise that he'd gone too far. He stood up and held out both hands. "Marie, I'm sorry. I shouldn't have said that."

"Yeah, but you meant it. You meant every fucking word. I'm going back to bed to sleep this hangover off, and when I get up I'll grant you your wish. I'll leave and you'll never see me again."

"Marie, I..."

She didn't wait for the rest of his sentence. She stormed upstairs and locked the bedroom door. Then, when she was sure that John hadn't followed her up the stairs, she fell face down on the bed and let the tears come.

CHAPTER 13

14th December. Rick's House, Newton Hall. 11:30.

Phil swore under his breath as the road he'd been following became a cul-de-sac. He'd only been to Rick's house once before, and instead of using his sat-nav, he'd been determined to find it from memory. Unfortunately, the estate was like a rabbit warren. Neat rows of virtually identical houses, laid out in the same manner on each street, meant that he'd been driving around for almost ten minutes, wondering if the red-brick box with the mock Tudor front he was looking at was the one where he was supposed to be, or whether it was just another one of the hundreds of others lining the labyrinthine streets. He realised that he was getting nowhere, and from the sound of Paul's voice when he'd called, the situation could be serious. Defeated, he retrieved the sat-nav from his glove compartment and entered Rick's home address.

"Turn around when possible," said the machine in a helpful, metallic voice.

"I know. I fucking know." Phil put the car into reverse and executed a three-point turn, then drove back the way he'd just come.

"In two hundred yards, turn right, then left, then right, then you have reached your destination."

"About bloody time."

He turned onto Rick's street, stuffing the sat-nav back into the glove compartment without bothering to turn it off.

"You have reached your destination," announced a muffled voice. Phil ignored it and got out of the car.

Paul Patterson and Mark Briggs, the other two members of Rick's team, stood on the block paving drive and nodded a greeting.

Phil lit a cigarette and walked over to the two police officers. "What's going on? It's not like..."

Mark shook his head. "Nothing like that. He's in there by himself as far as I can tell. He told us to fuck off and leave him alone about ten minutes ago, then nothing."

Phil took a deep drag on the cigarette. "Well, he was close to Olivia. They went out for how long? Four years? Five? He's going to be taking this harder than the rest of us."

Paul put his hands against the glass and tried to peer past the impenetrable barrier of the net curtains. "Yeah, but what I'm worried about is how hard he's taking it. Truth be told, Phil, he's been struggling with things ever since that night in High Moor. I think Olivia might have pushed him over the edge. I wouldn't have bothered you otherwise."

"No, I'm glad you called me. I wanted to speak to you all anyway." He strode over to the front door and hammered on it. "Rick? Sergeant Grey? This is DI Fletcher. Open the door."

The house was silent. Phil turned to the other officers. "Have you tried round the back?"

Mark didn't respond, but instead walked over to the ornate metal side-gate and let himself into the back garden, while Phil and Paul followed. Mark walked over to the kitchen window and peered through. "Oh fuck, he's on the floor."

Phil moved to the back door, only to discover it locked. Mark eased him to one side. "I've got this, Phil."

The big man took a step back, aimed a savage side-kick at the lock. The wood splintered with a tortured cracking sound, and the door flew open.

Rick was lying on his back with a yellow crust of dried vomit on his lips and down his chin. Without a word, Paul and Mark crouched down beside him, checking for signs of life. When Paul put his finger against Rick's neck, the seemingly unconscious man sat bolt upright.

Rick looked at them with bleary eyes and his brow creased into a frown. "What the hell are you all doing in my house? And what part of 'fuck off and leave me alone' was unclear?"

Paul reached down to take Rick's hand, but the other man shooed him away. "Rick, we were just worried about you."

Rick tried to get to his feet and stumbled into the dining room table. He steadied himself, then looked at his wrecked door. "Well, you can bloody well pay for that, mate. Look, I'm fine, alright. Just let me sleep it off and I'll be right as rain."

Mark went into the kitchen and put the kettle on. "I'll get some coffee on. You go and have a shower, Rick. You fucking stink and there's puke in your stubble. Phil said that he wanted to talk to us all about something, so we might as well try and sober you up a bit first."

Rick's face took on a pained expression. "No offence, Phil, but can't this wait until later? My head's all over the place at the moment."

Phil shook his head. "No, Rick. I really don't think it can. I think that we're all neck-deep in the shit. Go and get yourself together, and then I'll tell you all about the visitor I had last night."

***

Rick walked back down the stairs ten minutes later. He'd not bothered to shave, but was at least wearing clean clothes, an old T-shirt and a pair of jogging pants. He crossed the kitchen to where the other men sat, gratefully accepting a hot mug of black coffee from Mark.

"Sorry, mate. It's just instant. Couldn't work out how to use your machine."

Rick gave a weak, half-hearted smile. Truth be told, he hadn't fully grasped how to use the complex espresso machine either, not that he'd let his workmates know that. "That's okay. You'd probably have broken it if you'd started pissing about with things." He turned to Phil. "So, what's so important that you come down here on my day off and kick my back door in?"

Phil's expression fell, and the older man looked uncertain of himself, maybe for the first time since Rick had known him. "Okay, what I'm going to tell you is going to sound insane, but bear with me, okay? Like I said earlier, I had a visitor last night - a visitor who bypassed my home security system, got inside without either me or Sharon realising it and then held me at gunpoint. That visitor was Steven Wilkinson."

Mark's head cocked to one side and he stared at Phil with partially squinted eyes. "What? The comatose, crippled gun-nut that went missing from the hospital the other night? That Steven Wilkinson?"

"Yes, that Steven Wilkinson. And if it makes you feel any better, I didn't believe what I was seeing at first either. And I haven't even got to the really insane part yet."

Rick massaged his temples, wishing that he'd been given an Alka-Seltzer instead of coffee. "Let me guess, he says he's a werewolf."

"Yes, that's exactly what he said, and I know what this sounds like, but you don't just get up and walk around after an injury like that. Ever, let alone a month after getting it. That's not the only thing. Bob Adams told me that Wilkinson was a terminal cancer patient, but when he was admitted to hospital there was no sign of it. There's something going on with him that I can't explain."

Rick's stomach burbled, but he fought down the wave of nausea and forced himself to take another sip of his coffee. "Okay, let's say for a second that he's telling you the truth, which, by the way, he isn't, why did he break into your house in the middle of the night? He must have wanted something."

"He wanted to warn us. He said that there is some kind of werewolf assassination squad hunting us. He said that was who killed Olivia, and that we're all next in line."

Rick felt a surge of anger wash over him. "Fucking bullshit. We know who killed Olivia."

"Look, I know how it sounds, but hear me out. We know that Simpson didn't escape on his own, and that the two naked corpses we found probably had a hand in that."

Paul chuckled. "Well, it does explain why they were naked. They just grew their own fur coat as needed."

Mark frowned. "You know those two corpses ended up going in the incinerator? Administrative mistake, apparently. Some sort of mix-up with the labelling at the morgue."

An uncomfortable silence settled over the room. Rick couldn't bring himself to meet Phil's gaze. The pieces all fit, but the picture it formed was impossible. Unbelievable. "Look," he said, his eyes still fixed on the table. "I can see how this looks like it makes sense, but there has to be another explanation. Yes, it looks like someone is doing their best to cover their tracks, but that doesn't automatically make them fucking werewolves."

"The thing is, Rick, if there is even a chance that this could be true, then we are all in a world of shit. You saw what happened to Olivia. You know how tough she was, and you saw the state of the house. Are you really prepared to take the risk that they won't turn up here, looking for you?" He turned to Paul. "Or at your house, when you're in the middle of dinner with your family?"

Rick glanced sideways at Mark and Paul, hoping to see some support, but both men were silent, eyes cast down to the tabletop. He exhaled. "So, what are we supposed to do about it? If what you're telling us is true, then what do we do? Get hold of some silver bullets and crucifixes?"

Mark let out a grim chuckle. "Crucifixes are for vampires, mate. Get your facts right. Didn't your mam let you watch horror films as a bairn?"

Phil took a long drink from his coffee. "Wilkinson said he'd help us deal with them. And yes, he said that we'd need silver bullets. Preferably the ones locked up in evidence."

Rick pushed his chair back and got to his feet. "Oh, for Christ's sake, Phil. Have you heard yourself? You want to work with an escaped suspect, wanted for possession of illegal weapons, who suggests the first thing you do is break the evidence against him out of lock-up? He's playing you. Next time the bastard contacts you, we'll set him up, arrest him, and then find out what he knows down the station. The way that we're supposed to deal with things. Then we can put our efforts into finding that fucking bitch, Connie Hamilton."

A light cough came from the back door. All four men turned around in unison to find themselves looking at a red-haired woman, dressed in a long black overcoat, pointing a pistol at them. A predatory grin played across her lips. "Did someone mention ma name?" She nodded her head at the broken back door. "Ah'd get that fixed if Ah were you. Anyone could walk in. Now, which of ye baw-bags is gonna tell me how to find that bastard, Steven Wilkinson?"

Mark and Paul's reaction was instantaneous. Paul hurled his mug of coffee straight at Connie while Mark got up from the table, grabbed the arm holding the pistol, pushing it away from his friends, and aimed a punch at her face in a single, sinuous movement. Connie Hamilton, however, seemed to have been expecting this. She ducked under the path of the coffee cup, twisted her arm free of Mark's grip, then lashed out at him with a vicious backhand blow that sent him flying across the table to collide with Phil.

"If ye lads want ta play rough, then Ah'm more than happy ta oblige."

Rick had backed away as soon as Connie had appeared. He could barely keep his rage under control. The bitch who had slaughtered Olivia had dared to come here. To break into his home and threaten him. He reached behind him and pulled open one of the kitchen drawers. As the woman advanced on Paul, his hand closed around the familiar grip of a pistol. He thumbed off the safety catch and swung the weapon out from behind him, then put a bullet straight between Connie Hamilton's eyes.

The back of Connie's head exploded in a shower of blood, bone and brains, and she flew backwards, landing in a bloody heap against Rick's dishwasher.

Mark got to his feet and looked at his friend. "What the fuck, Rick? Where the hell did you get that Beretta?"

Rick's sneered. "You going to arrest me, Mark?" He walked around the table and shot the prone body twice more in the head. "In case you hadn't noticed, I just saved our lives."

Paul got to his feet and put his hand on Rick's arm. "No one's disputing that, mate, but you just killed someone in your own kitchen with an illegal firearm. Put the gun down, okay? Then we can work out how the hell we're going to explain this mess."

Rick looked at his friend and felt the rage drain out of him. He felt sick, and he knew that there would be consequences for what he'd just done, but the truth of the matter was that he didn't care. He lowered the pistol, engaging the safety catch. "Fuck it. It'll be worth doing time knowing that bitch is dead."

Phil and Mark disentangled themselves and got to their feet. Mark cast a disdainful look at the remains of Connie Hamilton before turning back to his friend. "No one's going to get sent down, Rick. We just need to get our story straight. We can say that the gun was hers, and that you got it away from her. Right, Phil?"

Phil said nothing at first, then, after a couple of seconds, nodded his head. "Yeah, that's exactly what happened. We'll just make sure that her prints are on the Beretta. But once this mess is cleared up, Rick, you and I are going to have a very long conversation about what you were doing with a cocked and loaded pistol in your kitchen drawer. Okay?"

Rick's hands began to shake, and he put the pistol on the granite worktop. "Okay, Phil. Thanks."

"Well, isn't it nice ta see the police lookin' out for each other an' coverin' up evidence?"

All four men turned to see the corpse of Connie Hamilton get to its feet. The bones in her ruined skull crunched back into place before their eyes, and the three bullet holes in her face closed up. She cricked her neck and smiled at the police officers. "Looks like you lads wanna play rough after all. Now ye fuckers are gonna see ma bad side."

The bones in Connie's face warped and shifted, elongating into a muzzle, while sets of razor-sharp fangs burst through her gums. The raincoat fell to the floor, revealing her naked form beneath. Her skin bulged as the bones beneath shattered and reformed, while thick orange fur burst from her pores, covering her skin like a flowing tide of serpents.

Phil grabbed Rick's shoulder and yelled into his face. "Run."

All four men bolted for the front door, only to find it locked. As Rick fumbled with the key, a deep, guttural growl came from the kitchen.

Mark cast an anxious look over his shoulder. "Any time about now would be good, mate."

The lock opened with a welcome click, and the men tumbled outside. The lights of Mark's Range Rover flashed as he unlocked the doors with his key fob, and they bundled into the vehicle. Mark started the engine, and the car screeched away from Rick's house. Rick, Phil and Paul looked back at the house, expecting something from their worst nightmares to come bursting through the front door and pursue them down the street, but there was no movement from within. Rick tried to calm his breathing; turning to Phil, he said, "So...silver bullets?"

14th December. Naver Cottage, Kinbrace. 12:55.

John crept up the stairs with a steaming mug of tea and a sugar bowl balanced on a wooden tray. He reached the first floor and stopped for a moment, unsure of himself. His dealings with members of the opposite sex had always been limited to work colleagues, and while he'd experienced disagreements on various projects he'd worked on, he'd never been in a situation like this before. He felt as if he were walking through a minefield, where the slightest misstep could cause a catastrophic explosion. The last thing he wanted to do was upset Marie more, but at this point he wasn't sure if that was even possible. He only knew that he had to try. He put the tray down on the floor and knocked twice on the door.

"Marie?"

Marie's disembodied voice floated out from behind the door. "Piss off, John."

He sighed. This was not going to be as easy as he'd hoped. "Look, Marie. I'm really sorry about earlier. Can we talk about it? I made you a cup of tea."

"You do realise that I'm armed?"

Truth be told, John had forgotten about the crate of weaponry in Marie's room, and a momentary flash of fear made his legs go weak. "You're not going to shoot me through the door. You'd lose your deposit on the cottage, for one thing. And you'd have to clean the mess up afterwards."

The door swung open and Marie glared out from the darkened room at him. The skin around her eyes was red and puffy, with dark streaks of mascara running down her cheeks. Her hands were fixed firmly to her hips and she did not look in the least bit pleased to see him. "Here's a little pointer for you, John. You should never piss off an upset woman who has access to firearms." She glanced down at the tray, then back up to John. "No biscuits?"

"Oh, God, I'm sorry. Which ones do you want? I think we have some chocolate ones in the kitchen."

Marie bent over and picked up the tray. "Don't worry about it." She put the tea down on her bedside table, turned back to John, who was still skulking in the corridor. "Okay, say what you have to say, then fuck off. I've got some packing to do."

John's heart sank, but he tried to keep his expression neutral. "Can I come in?"

Marie huffed and rolled her eyes. "I suppose so." She sat on the bed and put two heaped teaspoons of sugar into the tea. John followed, sitting on a chair in the corner.

"Well?"

"Look, Marie. I'm really sorry about earlier. I didn't mean it. You just got me mad and then the words came out. It was a shitty thing to say, and I wish I could take it all back. I'd be dead without you, and if you leave, then I'll either be dead or back in police custody within a week. I need you."

Marie took a sip of her tea, fixing John with a glare that could strip paint. "Do you have any idea how much you hurt me? I risked everything to save you. I gave up everything and everyone that I love, so that I could save your life, and you repay me by acting like an arsehole, and then throwing it all back in my face. How do you think that makes me feel?"

John's face flushed scarlet and, despite the snow falling outside and the chill in the air, he felt uncomfortably warm. He struggled to come up with some answer that would placate the angry woman, but the best he could manage was, "Erm...I...I mean..."

Marie didn't wait for him to finish his reply. "And then, after acting like a first class prick, you think that bringing me a cup of tea will somehow make it all better? Did you really think that was going to help?"

"Look, I know that I've been acting a bit off, but the last month hasn't exactly been easy on me either. My head is all over the place. I mean, this whole thing is just insane and, if I'm honest, you scare the shit out of me sometimes."

Marie couldn't help but laugh at this. "I scare you? I'm not the one who turns into a seven-foot-tall monster. I'm just a normal, boring woman."

"Are you kidding me? You know all this James Bond crap, and you carry a box full of guns and ammo around in the back of your car. You're a trained killer, and I honestly don't know how you're going to react in any given situation. What part of that isn't frightening?"

She shook her head. "That's not everything I am, though. Yes, I've been trained, but really, how different is that to someone who's been in the army or something? That's what I used to do. It's not who I am. Do you understand what I'm saying?"

The guilt that had been building within John threatened to drown him. "I don't know what else to say, Marie. I'm so, so sorry."

She took another sip from her tea. "Yeah, well, it didn't help that you were right. I know that I fucked up, John. I should have just come up to you the second you arrived back in High Moor and explained things. I was just worried that you might not react well, given your last encounter with The Pack, and I wanted to talk to you like a normal person before I brought all of that other stuff up. Maybe I just wanted to feel like a regular girl, having a drink with a boy she liked, for a while. Everything that happened was my fault."

John risked getting up and placed a tentative hand on Marie's shoulder. "No, that's crap. Malcolm got infected before I ran into you, and even if you hadn't tried to flush me out of hiding, it was only going to be a matter of time before I had another episode. That night when you were eating Malcolm's dog, my wolf almost got free. I only just managed to lock myself up in time. I don't blame you for any of this. You've only tried to do what you thought was best for me. Well, apart from that time where you snapped my neck and left me twitching on the basement floor."

"I was wondering how long it was going to take you to bring that up."

"Well, you did break my neck while I was trying to rescue you. Do you have any idea how much that hurts?"

The corner of Marie's mouth twitched into a half-smile. "What are you moaning about? You got better, didn't you?"

John couldn't help but chuckle. "I suppose I did. Are we okay?"

"Yeah, we're okay. I couldn't leave you out here to fend for yourself, could I? Without my 'James Bond crap', you wouldn't last five minutes. Now come here and give me a fucking hug."

John sat next to her and gathered her into his arms, ignoring the pain that flared across his wounds as she pushed against him. The warmth of her body against him was pleasant, and unexpected. He didn't think he'd been this close to another human being in twenty years, and he was beginning to realise what he'd been missing. Then he felt something stir beneath the fabric of his jeans and he broke the embrace, feeling a vague embarrassment. "So, what's our next move? As lovely as this place is, I don't think we can hide out here forever."

"No, we need to get the hell out of the country, but if I'm honest, I haven't decided where yet. We can't stay in Europe, or go to Russia, because it would only be a matter of time before The Pack tracked us down. Unfortunately, most of the other continents are risky as well. America is a possibility, as long as we can keep away from their werewolves. Africa and Asia are complete non-starters."

"How come?"

"Do you really think that werewolves are the only things out there? Every culture on the planet has its own shape-changer myths, and that's before you get started on the demons, vampires, and God knows what else. Supernatural beasties don't tend to play well with others, and are territorial as hell. One sniff of a werewolf and they'd come down on us like a ton of shit."

John exhaled and felt a hard knot of worry form in his stomach. "That doesn't leave us with much. Antarctica, maybe?"

"I was thinking more along the lines of Australia, but we can leave Antarctica on the table if you like the snow that much."

"Australia does sound like a better option. So, they don't have any were-kangaroos or were-koalas that we need to worry about?"

Marie smiled. "Not as far as I know, but we're getting a bit ahead of ourselves. Before we go anywhere, we need to get you sorted out."

"What do you mean?"

Her smile twisted into an evil grin. "Basic training. It's time you learned how to be a proper werewolf."

14th December Edinburgh Airport. 16:05.

Gregorz took a sip of his coffee and picked at the croissant he'd been persuaded to buy. He didn't have much of an appetite, and he was still a little shocked at the price. In Moscow, he could have eaten a three course meal for what the drink and pastry had just cost him. Daniel had not said much since they'd arrived, seemingly content to read his newspaper. His friend's silence was making him uncomfortable.

"Anything interesting happening?"

Daniel looked up and shook his head. "The news is filled with Simpson's escape and Connie's little escapade. They don't have any real leads so far, but that's not stopped the journalists from forming their own assumptions. Most of it is rubbish, but there are one or two articles that are a little too close to the truth for comfort."

"Let them speculate all they want. Once Michael and the others arrive, we can deal with Simpson and get out of here."

"You really think that it's going to be that easy? We've underestimated Simpson before, and now that Marie is with him, there's no telling what little surprises we'll encounter. I don't like this, Gregorz. It feels like we're losing control of things. Michael shouldn't be coming here. He's too emotionally involved to think clearly. And I'm not sure about whether leaving Oskar up there on his own was the best idea either. He's not been the same since Troy and Gabriela's death. I think he's lost his nerve."

Gregorz shook his head. "I agree with you, but Michael's orders were explicit. I have my suspicions that Oskar left the others to die, but there's no way to prove it. Michael should have ordered him back to Russia as soon as the hit went wrong."

"I imagine that the Council had something to say about his inclusion. They want him to keep an eye on things, especially on Michael. Krysztof would love an excuse to depose him as alpha."

"Then let us pray that Michael doesn't do anything to give him a reason."

Daniel got to his feet and nodded over Gregorz' shoulder. "They're here."

Gregorz drained the last dregs of his coffee and followed Daniel out of the crowded coffee shop to the arrivals gate, where Michael had just emerged. Two other pack members, Anya and Leonid, followed their alpha at a discreet distance. Michael made a subtle gesture with his hand and the two assassins strode away towards the car rental desks, while Michael continued on alone.

The pack leader seemed to radiate stress. His face was a creased mask of worry, and his shoulders were hunched. Nevertheless, he smiled at Gregorz and shook both his and Daniel's hands with a firm grip.

"Gregorz, Daniel. Thank you for meeting me here. It's good to see you both again. Has anything happened while I've been in the air?"

"No. Marie and Simpson are hiding out in a holiday cottage north of Inverness. Oskar is maintaining surveillance at a discreet distance, and he'll let me know if anything happens. For the moment, at least, they seem to be settled."

"What's the location like? Any neighbours or other problems that I need to be aware of?"

"The nearest house is a couple of miles away, and the closest village more than ten. The property is in its own grounds, with woodland to the north, but not much cover otherwise. The cottage does have several blind spots that could be used in an assault, but I'm sure that Marie has considered this." He glanced across the airport, to Anya and Leonid. "I'm still not sure why you brought additional resources. Daniel, Oskar and I could have dealt with this situation. All it would take is a single shot from a high-powered rifle and..."

Michael shook his head. "I have my reasons, and I have another assignment for you and Daniel."

Daniel frowned. "Would that other assignment involve Connie, by any chance?"

"Yes. She didn't show up to her rendezvous, so I have to assume that she's gone after Wilkinson. We can't have her running around, causing any more damage."

"So, how do you want us to proceed?"

"She'll most likely go after the rest of those police officers, until she gets a lead on Wilkinson. Track her down, and when you find her, take her out. Quietly."

Daniel shuffled his feet and looked at the floor. Gregorz knew what was going through his mind. Connie had been a loyal member of The Pack for more than two decades, and despite her unpredictable behaviour, had proven herself a worthy asset on many occasions. "Is there no other way? I know that Connie's behaviour has been inexcusable, but her thirst for revenge has blinded her. If we could contain her?"

Michael shook his head. "No, I'm sorry, but you were on that call. I was more than clear about what would happen to her if she ignored my orders. I can't let that go, Gregorz. She brought this on herself."

Gregorz sighed. He felt sick. Hunting moonstruck was one thing, but the thought of going after a fellow pack member left a sour taste in his mouth. "What of Wilkinson, and the police?"

"Don't kill the police unless you have to. If you get a clear shot at Wilkinson then you have my permission to gut the bastard. I don't want you going after him, though. Connie is your target. Once you deal with her, then I want you both out of the country."

"Understood. And what will you do, Michael?"

"I'll take Anya and Leonid, join up with Oskar, and put this matter to rest, once and for all."

"I would tell you that I don't like this, but I doubt that you would listen, so I will simply tell you to be careful. You will be up there, alone with three moonborn, and they will be reporting back to the

Council. They are looking for a reason to depose you, Michael. Please don't give them one."

Michael put his hand on Gregorz' shoulder. "I know what I'm doing, but thank you."

Gregorz gave his alpha a grim smile. "I hope so, Michael. I really do."

CHAPTER 14

14th December. Aykley Heads Police HQ. 18:30.

The Range Rover turned off the main road into the grounds of the police headquarters. Most of the unsightly concrete building lay shrouded in darkness, with only a few isolated office lights shining out into the night. Phil knew that there would be officers inside, of course. The police HQ was never truly empty. However at this time on a Sunday evening, when the shifts were changing, the huge building was as quiet as it was likely to get. A few cars were dotted around the car park, most of them stationed close to the main entrance, so that their owners would not have to brave the freezing conditions any longer than was necessary.

Mark pulled into a vacant space as far away from the main building as he could and stopped the engine. He turned around to face the other occupants of the vehicle. "Here we are, lads. Last stop."

An uneasy silence fell. Phil and Rick exchanged nervous glances, while Paul looked down at his feet. None of them were comfortable with what they were about to do. Paul had been agitated ever since the sun had gone down and wanted to make sure that his family were safe. They only had the one car, however. None of them had wanted to return to Rick's house to retrieve their own vehicles.

Phil arched his back, feeling his spine pop. "Alright, is everyone clear on what we're doing? Rick and I will go inside. I'll get the case-notes while Rick goes down to evidence and grabs the ammo. Then we'll meet up back here."

Paul shuffled in the back seat. "Phil, you don't really need me here. Not right now. I'm going to take a squad car from the pool and make sure that Emma and Sam are alright."

Mark shook his head. "Mate, we really shouldn't be going anywhere by ourselves. I know that you're worried, but once we get the ammo we can go over there together. At least then, if that bitch does show up, we'll be able to do something about it."

"And what if she's there now? Or on the way? I need to get them both out of that house and somewhere safe. Once you finish up here, you can meet me at my place, but I'm not arguing about this. My family's safety comes first. Once they're out of harm's way, then I'm in, but not until."

Rick put his hand on Mark's shoulder. "Paul's right. We don't need him here right now. But, mate, be careful. If something looks off, then you get the fuck out of there and call us, okay?"

Mark let out an exasperated sigh. "Don't you lot ever watch bloody horror films? You never go off alone. Ever."

"Mark, I'll be okay. I won't do anything stupid. If things don't seem right then I'll back off and call in the cavalry."

"Can you at least try to call Emma again?"

Paul pulled his phone out and dialled his wife's number, but the call went straight to answer phone. "Still no reply. She never remembers to charge the fucking thing. Okay, I'm off. I'll see you all soon."

Paul got out of the car without another word and strode across the tarmac towards the main headquarters. Phil turned around to face Rick. "Okay, are you ready? Let's get this over with."

Rick and Phil exited the car and hurried across the frost-covered parking area to the looming building. A welcome rush of heat washed over them as they stepped through the glass doors into the reception. The guard on reception glanced at them, and then, with a nod of recognition, returned his attention to the newspaper he'd been reading. Rick turned left, to where the evidence storage rooms were, while Phil continued past the reception desk to a flight of stairs which he took two-at-a-time.

The intention was to be out as quickly as they could, but Phil needed to be sure that he'd retrieved as many of the case-files as possible. Now that they knew what they were dealing with, there was a chance that he'd overlooked or disregarded some piece of evidence.

He pushed open the door to the open-plan office and groaned when he realised that the room was already occupied. Brian Smith, a long-time colleague and Inspector Frank's chief arse-kisser, looked up from his PC as Phil entered the room. He got to his feet and intercepted Phil before he could make it to his desk. He extended a sweaty hand and grasped Phil's in a warm, flaccid grip. "Phil, I just wanted to say that I'm so sorry about Olivia. We all are. Didn't the inspector send you home for a few days?"

Phil forced a smile and extracted his hand from the other man's, resisting the urge to wipe it on his trousers. "You know how it is, Brian. I can't concentrate on anything at home. I just wanted to go over the case-files again, to keep my mind occupied."

Brian gave Phil a conspiratorial wink. "Don't worry, Phil. I hear what you're saying. I'll keep this between us. Our little secret."

Phil felt his smile starting to slip and forced it back with what felt like a superhuman effort of will. Brian would be straight on the phone to Franks as soon as he left the office. That complicated matters. "Thanks, Brian. I really appreciate it."

"No problemo. If there's anything you need, anything at all..."

"I know. Thank you."

Phil eased past Brian and made his way along the office to his own desk. Olivia's was right next to his, and he felt his throat constrict as his eyes played across the disorganized mess of paperwork, the row of characters from *South Park* lined up on the top of her monitor, and the photograph of her and Matt. He forced his eyes away. He didn't have time to get upset or to dwell on the ragged hole within him that her death had left. He needed to get what he came for and get out of the building before Brian tipped off the Chief Inspector.

He sat down at his desk and turned on his computer. The ancient machine wheezed into life and began the torturous process of booting up. Phil glanced up and discovered that Brian was no longer in the room. Brian could have gone for a coffee, but he doubted it. He had less time than he thought.

He removed a USB drive from his pocket and slotted it into the front of the machine. Then he noticed the manila folder tucked under the keyboard. He pulled the folder free and flicked it open, only to feel his heart lurch again. It was Olivia's report from the night that Simpson escaped. The day that she died. He pushed the feelings down and scanned through the neatly handwritten text. It dealt with her visit to the hotel where she'd tracked Connie Hamilton and he already knew most of the details. Then he stopped as something caught his eye. A name. Gregorz Pawlac. Pawlac had been one of the names given to the assistant pathologist by the bogus police officers when Marie Williams had gone missing. They'd assumed it had been an alias, but if it wasn't...

Phil's computer had finally managed to start up. He entered his login details, drumming his fingers against the table as the decrepit machine tried to process his request, while keeping one eye on the double doors at the end of the office. Once the desktop appeared, he opened his web browser and searched for a list of car rental agents that were located in Newcastle Airport, smiling to himself when a list of only three companies was returned. He dialled the first number, barely daring to hope.

The call was answered on the second ring by a cheerful young woman with a broad Newcastle accent. "How can Ah help ye today?"

"This is Detective Inspector Fletcher of Durham Constabulary. I'm investigating a serious criminal matter, and wondered if you could search your rental records for anything under the name of Pawlac in the last few months?" He spelled out the surname, and waited while the woman keyed the details into the system.

"Yes, I have a rental under that name on 15th November of this year, for an initial two-week period, which was then extended by another month."

Phil felt his stomach flutter, and a smile spread across his face. "Were there any other rentals that day, at around the same time?"

The sounds of frantic tapping came from the telephone. "Only three other vehicles were let that day. To a Mr Daniel Braun, a Mr

Oskar Lassen, and a Miss Connie Hamilton."

If the woman had been standing in front of him, Phil would have planted a kiss square on her lips. There was one more question he needed to ask, but he almost didn't dare. He took a deep breath and held it for a few seconds to calm himself. Then he asked, "I don't suppose your company fits GPS tracking devices to your cars?"

***

Rick forced himself to walk across the car park when all he wanted to do was run. It wasn't just his theft of ammunition from the evidence storage that bothered him. He felt as if predatory eyes watched from behind every tree. A dog barked somewhere in a nearby housing estate, and he was very aware that his home, and the last known location of Connie Hamilton, was less than half a mile away from where he stood. She could be out there right now, and he wouldn't know a thing about it until he felt those awful fangs tear through his flesh.

He pushed the thought from his mind. Connie Hamilton would be long gone by now, and even if she were hunting them, the chances of her turning up here were remote. Nevertheless, he breathed a heavy sigh of relief when he reached the car and slid into the back seat behind Mark.

The other man twisted in his seat so that he was facing Rick. "How did it go?"

"It could have been better. Most of the ammo was 5.56 or 7.62. There were only two boxes of the nines."

Mark considered this, and nodded. "It's still a hundred rounds. As long as we don't start spraying and praying, we should be fine. That's what? Two mags for the MP5s and one each for the Glocks?"

"Yeah, but I'd feel a lot better if we had something with a bit more poke. Like a bazooka or something. Phil's not back yet, then?"

Mark motioned to the building with his head. "This looks like him now."

Phil burst through the glass doors and hurried across the icy tarmac towards them, clutching a manila folder to his chest. He reached them in moments and flung open the passenger door, flopping down in the seat.

Rick put his hand on Phil's shoulder. "Did you get it all? Everything alright?"

Phil shifted in his seat and when he turned to face Rick, his eyes shone. "Oh, it's better than alright. I've found them. I know where the bastards are."

14th December. Paul's House, Durham. 19:00.

Paul hit the siren and accelerated through the red traffic light, barely taking the time to check if the oncoming traffic was making way for him. He played the conversation he was going to have with Emma over and over in his mind. She would be confused and scared, but he needed to make sure there were no questions or arguments. Not something that came easily to his wife at the best of times.

He turned off the light and siren as he entered the outskirts of his home town. The roads were relatively quiet, for which he was grateful. Only a few other vehicles were on the road, mostly churchgoers returning from the evening service or people heading out to the local pubs. He drove as fast as he dared. While the urgent need to get to his family dominated his thoughts, he couldn't forget his training. Having an accident at this point could be disastrous. He reached the junction to the road where he lived and slowed the squad car down. There was no point in arriving home like a lunatic and alerting the neighbours to the potential peril in their midst.

His home, a three bedroom semi-detached house halfway along the street, came into view and he breathed a sigh of relief. The curtains were drawn and lights burned in the living room window. Emma's Volkswagen Golf sat on the driveway, with the first spidery fingers of frost beginning to form across the bonnet and windows.

She couldn't have been home for long. All the other parked cars were covered in a layer of glistening white diamonds that glinted under the beam of his headlights. He parked the car on the road outside his house and rushed inside.

"Emma? Emma, are you here?"

There was no reply. The entire house was silent, with the exception of the noise from the neighbour's television coming through the adjoining wall. He would have expected the TV to be on in the living room, with Sam watching one of her Disney DVD's, while Emma was preparing the evening meal in the kitchen, but the house seemed to be deserted.

Paul's stomach felt like it had fallen into his shoes. He fought to control his rising despair, while his mind frantically tried to come up with an explanation for his wife and daughter's absence that didn't involve werewolves. He walked cautiously down the hallway and pushed open the living room door.

"Emma?"

"She's not here right now. Ah can take a message, if ye'd like?"

Paul felt as if he was about to throw up. He grasped the doorframe and turned to face the owner of the voice. He wanted to scream. To throw himself at the monster that sat in his armchair. To tear her apart with his bare hands until she told him where his family were. Instead, with a wavering voice, he simply asked. "Where are my wife and daughter? What have you done with them?"

A smile played across Connie's lips. "Ah, dinna ye worry. They're fine. For now. And they'll stay that way, as long as ye play nice."

The strength leeched out of his legs and he gripped the door frame harder. "If you've done anything to hurt them..."

The half-smile on Connie's face vanished. "You'll what? Kill me? Avenge them? Well, Paul, it looks like we have something in common after all. Ye see, Ah had a family, once. A husband called Isaac who Ah was devoted to, and a beautiful little girl called

Megan. And when they were murdered, Ah made the same vow that you just made. Ah swore that Ah would stop at nothing to put the evil, murdering cunt that killed them in the ground."

Paul's mind could not process the information. Adrenaline coursed through his system, screaming at him to fight or run, and his panic-stricken brain felt as if it were on the verge of shutting down. "I don't understand. What do you want?"

"Ah don't care about ye, yer mates, or yer family. The only thing that Ah want is the bastard that shot my eight-year-old daughter in the face while Ah watched. Ah want Steven Wilkinson's head. If ye help me, then ye Ah'll let yer wife and little lassie go. Ye fuck me around, or try ta set me up, and they'll die."

"I want to speak to them. I need to know that they're still alive."

Connie shook her head. "Not gonna happen. Ah ken yer pals will be along in a while, so Ah'm gonna make this quick. There's a number on that table. When ye find out where Wilkinson is, ye call and leave a message on the answer phone. When he's dead, then Ah'll let your family go. Understood."

Paul shook his head. "No. I can't trust you. Not after what you did to Olivia."

"Ah was just following orders. The Pack wanted you lot silenced, and the job fell to me. Lucky for ye, Ah've since parted company with ma old friends, or we'd be havin' a very different sort of chat. Besides, it's not like ye have much of a choice. Refuse, and Ah'll rip yer throat out where ye stand, then go and chow down on yer two lovely ladies for dessert. Try an' stitch me up, and Ah'll do the same, only Ah'll make ye watch me eat them before Ah kill ye. The only chance that ye and yer family have of getting out of this alive is ta dae exactly what Ah say."

14th December. Naver Cottage, Kinbrace. 19:12.

"I feel like an idiot."

John sat cross-legged on the floor in the centre of the room with his eyes closed. They'd been doing this for hours, and the only difference he felt so far was a numbness in his buttocks.

Marie's voice had a reproachful tone. "You need to stick with it. I said it wasn't going to be easy, but you need to get yourself under control. In case you hadn't noticed, this place doesn't have anywhere that we can lock you up in come the next full moon. And if The Pack find us, we need you to be able to fight them, because frankly, you can't shoot for shit. Now, let's try it again. We are *going* to bring your wolf up to the surface of your mind and hold off the change. Got it?"

John sighed and shifted position in an attempt to get comfortable. "Okay, I'll give it another go."

"Right, same as last time. Clear your mind, then count, slowly, from one to ten. Feel yourself becoming more relaxed with every breath you take. With every number that you count, you are getting sleepier. You can feel the tension draining out of your body, into the ground. Your mind is quiet, except for the sound of my voice and your slow, even count."

John felt the world fade away, leaving him floating in a dark void. He was not alone. Somewhere, in the darkness, something terrible lurked. John could sense its presence, a hot coal of fury burning in the abyss.

Marie continued to speak in a low monotone. "Are you aware of the other presence?"

"Yes."

"Now, I want you to try and find it. Imagine it as a cosy fire you can't see, but can feel its warmth on your face. Can you feel the warmth, John?"

"Yes, but it scares me."

"There is nothing to be scared of, John. It's a part of you, like your ear, or your foot. It can't hurt you. Now, imagine yourself moving toward it. Feel the warmth filling you up, as if you were lying in a nice, hot bath. The closer you get, the more comfortable you feel."

John drifted through the darkness, guided by the radiant heat that beckoned him. He could feel it now. Its anger and misery gave off palpable waves of aggression, like an abused, chained dog straining to reach its tormentor. Blood-soaked images flashed through his mind. A steel box, filled with the stench of fear. Prey packed in tightly around it, screaming and gibbering, the need to escape fighting with the overwhelming desire to slaughter the creatures trapped in here with it. Then, only blood. John realised that he'd just seen the death of his parents through the creature's eyes and the shock sent him spinning away from the malevolent presence, until Marie's voice broke through his panic and revulsion.

"I want you to slow down, John, and focus on your breathing. Notice how each breath you take is a little deeper and a little slower than the last. After you've taken five more breaths, you will feel calm and relaxed again."

John felt the anxiety drain out of his body. The terrible images still flashed across his mind, but as he reached the fifth breath, they faded into the background.

"Now, start moving towards the warmth again, and remember that nothing here can hurt you. There's nothing to be afraid of. Let it wash over you, fill you up, until it is you, and you are it. Then I want you to bring it up to the surface of your mind. Not all the way. Not yet. We don't want you to change, so just bring it up until it's just below the surface, and then keep it there."

John felt the warmth flare into a supernova. The beast snarled and thrashed against his will, but John held it tight.

"I'm going to count backwards, from five to one. When I reach one, you will wake up, and your wolf side will stay with you. Just under the surface of your mind. Five..."

John moved through the void, towards a glimmer of light far above him, like a drowning man struggling to reach the surface.

"Four."

The light grew brighter. Beckoning him. The wolf snarled, working itself up into a frenzy, but John managed to keep the savage presence under control.

"Three."

The world began to seep into the darkness; myriad strange scents filled his nostrils: the pungent sweat on his own body; the sweeter female scent of Marie, mixed with a faint after-tone of soap; the oily stink from the central heating system; the mingled aromas of food from the dirty plates in the kitchen.

"Two."

Waves of sound flooded John's mind. The low rumble of the oil burner in the kitchen; the soft fluttering of an owl outside, searching the cold night for prey; the thumping heart and rushing of hot blood in the woman beside him.

"One."

John's eyes snapped open, but the world was no longer the same. Everything in the room appeared in an incredibly sharp monochrome, with the smallest detail brought into stark focus. The pounding heartbeat of the female increased in pace. The pungent stench of fear billowed from her, and when she opened her mouth to speak, her voice had a tremble to it that called to ancient, long-buried instincts. Prey.

The woman stumbled to her feet and backed away from him, just as the last vestiges of rational thought were submerged in a tide of glorious agony. His limbs burned with strength and energy, even as his bones flowed like molten lava into a new form. As the change tore through him, John threw back his head and howled.

CHAPTER 15

14th December . Naver Cottage, Kinbrace. 19:27.

"One."

Marie couldn't help but feel a rush of excitement. This time they'd really made progress. God knows, the preceding hours had been painful, but it would have been worthwhile if John managed to pull this off. His eyes snapped open and her heart fluttered at the sense of awe that was ingrained on her friend's face.

"John? How do you feel?"

He didn't reply. His eyes scanned the room, fixating on random objects as if he were seeing them for the first time. Marie remembered the sensation. The utter clarity. The feeling of connection with the world and everything in it. She felt a twinge of loss, but quickly suppressed the emotion. This was not the time to dwell on the past. More important was the here and now.

John cocked his head to one side, sniffing the air. When he turned to face her, his eyes had become flat, green disks, and Marie realised that something had gone terribly wrong.

"John, you're going too far. Push it back down or you'll change."

As the words left her mouth she realised that it was already too late. The beast was too close to the surface and John had lost control. His body seemed to pulse with power and his lips curled up into a bloody half-smile as the change began.

She scrambled to her feet and backed away, not daring to take her eyes from the creature that had been John Simpson. The fabric of his T-shirt stretched, eventually tearing apart. His muscles swelled, his bones shattered and reformed. John's mouth opened as if to scream while his face elongated into a muzzle with razor-sharp fangs tearing through the gums. Thick brown hair raced across his skin while savage claws burst through the flesh of his fingertips in a spray of blood.

Marie realised that she had only seconds left to act and her next choice would dictate whether she lived or died. None of the doors in the cottage would withstand an assault by a werewolf for long. The car was half-buried by the still-falling snow outside, and even if she managed to start it, she'd never be able to pick up enough speed to escape on the icy track. Attempting to escape on foot was likewise futile. The werewolf would be on her before she'd even made it ten feet. That only left her one option. If she wanted to live, she would have to fight.

The beast got to its feet, shaking off the last tattered remnants of the T-shirt, opened its dripping jaws, and howled. Marie's legs almost buckled under her weight as an ice-fist of pure terror grasped her heart. Any hope she had had that John could retain some measure of control of the monster evaporated when it turned its head to face her, wrinkling its snout into a vicious snarl that displayed its bared, blood-soaked fangs, then leaped across the sofa to where she stood.

For the briefest moment, she tried to call on her own wolf, an instinctive reaction to the threat she faced that almost cost her life. Realising her mistake at the last second, she hurled herself into a side roll, feeling the breeze from the werewolf's slashing talons as she passed beneath them. She came out of her roll and regained her footing in a single movement, while the werewolf readied itself for another attack.

"John, please. I know that you're in there. You have to fight it."

Her pleas seemed to have no effect. The beast's muscles tensed, then it hurled itself at her once more. Her body felt as if she were moving underwater. Every action seemed painfully slow, and her once-sharp reflexes were dull. She grabbed a glass pot of steaming coffee from the percolator and smashed it into the werewolf's face. The glass shattered, embedding long shards into the creature's muzzle, while the scalding liquid splashed across its nose and eyes. The werewolf howled in pain and confusion and slashed at itself in an attempt to fight off the burning liquid. She'd bought herself a couple of seconds at most. She pushed through the crippling fear and urged her leaden limbs into action, sprinting for the staircase, taking the old wooden stairs two-at-at-time. A crash from behind her, mingled with the sounds of splintering wood and an enraged snarl, told her that John had shaken off his momentary confusion. Not daring to turn around, she bolted for the bedroom, slamming the door behind her and shoving the double bed against it to form a makeshift barricade.

A shadow blocked out the light filtering through the gaps around the doorframe, while the wooden floor of the landing creaked in protest. Sharp claws clacked against the floorboards. Heavy breathing, with the faintest hints of a snarl, came from the other side of the door, followed by a massive taloned fist bursting through the wood, slashing at the empty air beyond.

She looked around the room, searching for some means of escape, despite knowing that there was none. The window was too small for her to squeeze through, even if it hadn't been frozen shut. Likewise, the interior walls were made of solid stone - too tough even for a werewolf to break through. Then her eyes rested on the metal case containing the weapons.

The wood of the door began to splinter as the werewolf tore at it in a fury. Marie threw open the lid to the weapons crate and began fumbling around inside, unable to take her eyes from the ruined door that stood between her and a brutal death. She looked at the slashing claws and, for a second, considered letting the creature wound her. A small flesh wound. Just enough to re-infect her. She pushed the temptation away. The thought of those vicious talons tearing through her flesh was not something she was keen to experience, and the chances of her coming away from this with only a flesh wound were remote as it was. Plus, there was no guarantee that it would even work.

Her hand closed around the familiar bulk of a pistol handgrip just as the werewolf tore the last remnants of the door from the frame. It stood silhouetted against the stark glare of the hallway light with a glint of triumph in its eyes.

"John, I'm so sorry."

Then she swung the pistol towards the hulking shape and pulled the trigger.

14th December. Steven's House, High Moor. 21:00.

Mark slowed the Range Rover and leaned forward in his seat, trying to peer past the rolling blanket of freezing fog that had sprung up around them. The car's headlights reflected against the swirling white mist, providing only a few feet of visibility before the road vanished into the billowing, opaque cloud. Despite the reduction in speed, he felt the tyres slip on a patch of black ice, so he slowed the car further and engaged the four-wheel drive.

The other occupants had been silent for most of the journey. Paul sat alongside him, lost in thought, while Phil and Rick gazed out of the side windows at the soft, icy cocoon that enveloped them. At least Paul had persuaded Emma and Sam to visit Emma's mother in Whitby for a day or two. Phil had likewise sent Sharon to stay with her sister. That their families were out of danger should have eased some of the tension, but if anything, the mood among the men had deteriorated. The silence had begun to gnaw at Mark's nerves as well. He'd been focusing most of his attention on driving, but at times he felt his attention wandering, dwelling on what they were about to do and what they were going to have to face.

He couldn't stand the silence anymore. He craned his neck around to face the men in the rear seat. "How much further is it, Phil?"

Phil seemed startled by the sudden question, as if he'd been caught sleeping in class. He regained his composure quickly, however. "It should be a little further along this lane. Look for the big metal gates."

"The way this fog is, we could drive past them and not know it. As if shit wasn't creeping me out enough, we have to deal with this. I feel like I'm in a bloody Hammer film or something."

Rick let out a sardonic snort. "The whole fucking situation is like a bad horror film. I wouldn't be surprised if we get a nice thunderstorm in a minute, just to put the icing on the turd."

The fog thinned a little, if only for a moment. The skeletal outlines of trees were just visible through the swirling white tendrils of mist, and a dark shape loomed up on the road before them. Mark stamped on the brakes, a little harder than he'd intended, and the car crunched to a stop on the gravel track, sending clouds of dust up to dance in the twin headlight beams. Before them stood a pair of tall metal gates, topped with spiked railings and adorned with blue-and-white crime scene tape. A heavy steel chain snaked through the railings, holding the gates tight shut.

Mark gave the others a sheepish grin and said, "Looks like this is the place. Come on, let's get this over with."

The four men got out of the car. Phil, Rick, and Paul walked over to the gates, while Mark retrieved a set of bolt cutters from the boot.

Rick grabbed one of the gates and gave it a tug. "Someone really didn't want any unannounced visitors. These things are solid."

Phil nodded his head. "Well, considering the sort of visitors he was expecting, I can't say I blame him."

Mark joined the others and severed the chain, unravelling it from the gates before dumping it on the frost-covered grass verge. "And he said he'd meet us here?"

"Yes. We have to go in and disable the alarm, then wait. Apparently the place is designed to keep werewolves out. He can't get near the place until we turn off the security systems."

The gates slid open on well-oiled runners. Part of Mark was a little disappointed. He'd expected a sinister squeal of metal-on-metal at the very least. The four men climbed back into the car, then drove along the driveway until the dark outline of the farmhouse appeared from the billowing mist.

The farmhouse was mock-Georgian, red brick walls with a slate roof. Ivy sprawled across its façade, its leaves white with frost. Thick metal bars covered all the windows, and the solid oaken doors were plastered with more crime scene tape. Phil walked to one side of the doors and typed a code into a silver keypad. The electronic lock disengaged with a solid click, and a high-pitched whine, just on the edge of Mark's hearing, sounded from within the house. The noise made his fillings vibrate. Phil stepped through the front doors, into the darkness beyond and, a few seconds later, the noise stopped.

The men filed through into the hallway. The farmhouse had been renovated to the highest standard. Expensive oak furniture stood on polished wooden floorboards, while oil paintings depicting a variety of landscapes and pastoral scenes hung on every wall. Everything was covered in a fine layer of white powder. Cupboard doors hung open with their contents scattered across the floor, or left in disorderly piles on top of the furniture. The forensics teams were thorough, but they didn't tend to clean up after themselves. If this had been his house, Mark would have been pretty pissed off at the state it had been left in. He picked up an ornate vase, turning it over in his hands. The craftsmanship was exquisite, and he wondered how much something like this must have cost. He turned to Phil. "So, when is our mystery man coming?"

"He's here," said a voice from the doorway, "and be careful with that vase. It cost me ten grand."

The men spun around in unison to face the newcomer. Steven Wilkinson was not how Mark had imagined him to be. He was not a tall man, or particularly heavy-set. However, he seemed to possess a wiry strength, and when he moved, he did so with a grace that belied his obvious age. The old man seemed to almost glide as he crossed the hallway and gently removed the vase from Mark's hands, before putting it back on the sideboard. He turned to Phil. "Did you get the ammo?"

"Yes, but there were only two boxes of the nine mils. We left the rest. There didn't seem any point, given that we've not got anything to use the higher calibre stuff with."

Steven shook his head and let out an exasperated sigh. "What about the magazines for the Mac-10? Did you at least get those?"

Rick stepped forward. "No, they weren't being stored with the rest of the ammo. Two hundred rounds should be more than enough, though."

Steven brought both hands to his face and massaged his temples. "You don't get it. Silver bullets work on most werewolves, but the ones that we've got hunting us seem to be partially immune. The rounds in those clips were special. Silver particles suspended in mercury. Designed to take those pack fuckers down. Without them, I'm not sure we have much of a chance."

Rick threw his hands up in exasperation. "Well, you could have told us that before I broke into the bloody evidence room. If these silver bullets are no good, what the hell are we supposed to use? Harsh language?"

Steven shook his head. "There's more than one way to skin a wolf. Decapitation works, as long as you can get the head clear of the body before the wound heals. Fire will kill them eventually, but it takes a while because they keep regenerating the burned flesh. Same goes for acid. It's not pretty to watch, but eventually the bastards go down. The trick is to stop them from taking you down with them."

"And I suppose you have a flamethrower or two lying around that the forensics teams missed?"

Steven crossed the room until he stood face-to-face with Rick. "Son, you need to sort your attitude out if you and your friends want to make it through this alive. We are where we are, and you'd better learn to make the best of it. Yes, we're going to have to improvise. No, the situation isn't ideal. But your fucking moaning isn't helping anyone. If you don't have anything constructive to say, do us all a favour and keep your mouth shut."

Rick bristled, and for a moment, Mark thought he was going to swing at the older man. Mark pushed his way between the two men and turned to Steven. "Look, mate, pardon us for struggling with this a bit. We've had a difficult few days, but you getting in our faces won't help either. Besides, it's not all bad news. Tell him, Phil."

Steven's eyes narrowed, and he moved away from Mark and

Rick. "Tell me what?"

"They rented cars at the airport when they arrived in the country last month. And those cars have GPS trackers in them. I know where they are. Or at least, I know where they were a few hours ago."

A smile spread across Steven's face. "Show me."

Steven strode into the living room and removed a rolled-up map from a bookcase before walking over to a large table at the far side of the room. An Ordnance Survey Land-Ranger map of the local area covered the table top. Different coloured pins protruded from it, along with a number of photographs and Post-it notes. Steven removed a handful of pins, then swept the local map off the table and unrolled the other, which showed the entire United Kingdom. He handed the coloured pins to Phil. "On the map. Show me where they are."

Phil's brow furrowed in concentration. "These locations are a few hours old, but I should be able to get an update from the rental company. There was one vehicle up here, in the arse end of Scotland. There was another parked in Thurso, which is about forty minutes' drive away from the first pin. The other two were moving. One was near Edinburgh, heading north, and the last one was about halfway between Edinburgh and Newcastle, on the A1."

Steven put his hands on his hips and studied the map. "Is there any way to get a real-time update on these?"

"Not without having one of us sit in the head office of the car rental place and phone the details through. Still, this should give us a good idea of where they are. What they're doing all the way up there is beyond me, though."

Steven pointed at the first pin. "That'll be where Simpson's gone to ground. It's about as far away from here as you can get in mainland Britain, and it's isolated. It looks like the rest of them are using Thurso as a staging area for their assault. It's the nearest big town. If they were staying in any of the smaller towns, they'd draw unwanted attention to themselves. Thurso is large enough that they'd be able to blend in."

Mark walked forward and peered over Phil's shoulder. "What about the other two?"

"The one going north will be going to join up with their friends in Thurso. The other car is probably coming back here to deal with us."

Mark frowned. "That doesn't make sense. We know that Connie Hamilton was around here this morning, because she came after us at Rick's place. I suppose she could just about have made it to Edinburgh, if she'd left straight after attacking us and floored it the whole way, but if she was doing that, why not wait until she had her mates with her?"

Paul joined them at the table and glared at Steven. "She seemed more interested in you than us. Don't suppose you'd care to enlighten us as to why that might be?"

Steven shrugged. "No idea. I've been hunting them for decades. I suppose they feel like I'm a bigger threat."

"Really? So, you don't think that there might be a more specific reason that she'd want you?"

Steven turned away from the map and took a step forward, so that he was almost nose-to-nose with Paul. "Nothing springs to mind. Unless you've got something you'd like to say on the subject?"

Paul held his gaze for a second, then turned and walked off. Mark started to go after him, but Paul waved his friend away. "I'm fine, mate. I'm just going to phone Emma's sister and make sure they got there OK."

"Don't wander too far. Maybe stick the kettle on if you're anywhere near the kitchen? I could murder a cuppa."

Paul nodded a response and headed towards the kitchen with his mobile phone in his hand.

"So," said Phil, "what's the plan?"

Steven traced the line of the A1 from north to south. "We arm ourselves, then we work out a plan of attack. When we face them, we want it to be at a time and a place of our choosing, not theirs."

Mark narrowed his eyes. "I thought you said that we didn't have any weapons that could hurt them?"

An evil grin spread across Steven's face. "Pay attention, son. That's not what I said. That's not what I said at all."

14th December. Park Hotel, Thurso. 23:40.

The journey north had been slow and tortuous. The snow had begun falling as they'd crossed the Forth Bridge and had grown progressively heavier as the hire car followed the A9 into the Scottish Highlands. By the time they'd passed Perth, the weather had deteriorated into near-blizzard conditions, with the road barely visible through the heavy flakes flaring into a brilliant white as they hit the headlight beams. Michael had found the effect almost hypnotic. It reminded him of the scene from *Star Wars*, when the *Millennium Falcon* enters hyperspace. He didn't say any of this to the vehicle's other occupants, however. Leonid had kept his eyes fixed on the road ahead, the difficult driving conditions requiring his full attention, while Anya had lain down in the rear seat and had almost immediately gone to sleep. Neither of them were comfortable in their pack leader's presence, which put Michael on edge. He'd thought that bringing along a pair of moonborn would placate Krystof, Lukas, and the other Council members, but he found himself regretting his decision to send Gregorz and Daniel after Connie. They would have been much better company for one thing, and at least Michael would have been certain where their loyalties lay.

Despite the atrocious weather, they'd made surprisingly good time. The roads were almost devoid of traffic, with most motorists having more sense than to venture out in such treacherous conditions. For the last hour, the only other vehicle they'd seen had been the snowplough they'd followed into the outskirts of the town.

There was only one other car in the hotel car park, a green Ford

Focus that was barely visible under the thick white blanket. Given that there were no visible tyre tracks, it was clear that the Ford had been there for quite some time. Leonid parked beside the buried vehicle. In the rear seat, Anya sat upright without a word, got out of the car, and made her way across to the hotel entrance. Michael and Leonid left their bags behind and followed her, only to discover that the front doors were locked.

Anya pressed the doorbell and waited. When ten seconds had passed and there was no sign of life from within the hotel, she pushed it again, this time keeping the button depressed until a short, red-haired man appeared from a door behind the reception desk with an irate expression on his face.

"We're closed. Canna ye read tha sign?"

Michael eased past Anya. "We have reservations. Under the name of Johnson."

"Check in closes at eleven. Tha receptionist's gone haem and Ah'm no supposed ta go intae tha office. Can ye no come back in tha mornin?"

"And where the fuck are we supposed to go? It's blowing a blizzard out here, in case you hadn't noticed."

"Tha's not really ma problem, pal. Ah'll get a reet bollockin' off tha boss if Ah start messin' aboot with tha paperwork."

Michael's temper began to fray, and from the look on Anya's and Leonid's faces, they weren't going to put up with this for much longer either. They were both usually quite calm under pressure, but if this went any further, Anya was likely to tear the door off its hinges and feed the man his genitals. "One of our colleagues should have arrived earlier, and he would have checked in on our behalf. Can you at least take a look?"

"Ah told ye. Ah'm no supposed tae touch tha paperwork. Ah'm paid peanuts tae sit here at night, an' take care o' tha place, an tha's it. It's more than ma job's worth."

Michael threw a sideways glance at Anya and was dismayed to

see clouds of condensation billowing from her. The situation was going to go bad very quickly unless he resolved this. "Anya, control yourself," he hissed, then he turned back to the red-haired man and pulled a twenty pound note from his pocket. "I would be very grateful if you could at least let us stand inside while you phone your boss. We've travelled a long way. We're tired and very cold."

The money brought about an instant change in the man's demeanour. He crossed the foyer, unlocked the door, and plucked the twenty-pound note from Michael's hand. He held it up to the light, and when he was satisfied it was real, he stepped aside, making an exaggerated bow as he did so. "Well, Ah suppose there's no harm in ye waitin' in reception while we get all this sorted oot."

Anya pushed her way past the man, her top lip curled into a snarl, while Michael and Leonid retrieved their suitcases from the car. When they got back inside the reception area, the night porter's voice echoed out from the office. His voice had risen several octaves, and most of what he said was unintelligible.

Leonid turned to Michael with a bemused expression on his face. "What does 'Away an boil ye heed, ya Bampot' mean?"

Michael shook his head. "Don't worry about it. It's not worth trying to explain. Where the hell is Oskar? He was supposed to meet us here."

Leonid shrugged his shoulders. "Knowing Oskar, he will have found a nice, comfortable bar to warm himself in. I'm sure he'll be along eventually."

The sound of the phone slamming down came from the office, and the night porter appeared once more, muttering curses under his breath. "Ah've talked ta the boss, an' the daft gowk eventually saw sense. Ah'll give ye yer room keys noo, an ye can sort all tha paperwork-shite oot in tha mornin."

Michael took the keys from the man's outstretched hand, resisting the urge to break the night porter's fingers. "Thank you so much for your help," he said in a voice that dripped venom.

The night porter seemed oblivious to the implied threat in

Michael's tone. "Ah, tha's nee bother, pal. Just doing ma job. If there's anythin' else ya need, dinna hesitate ta fuck off an bother some other poor bastard."

The man walked away without waiting for a response. Once he'd disappeared, Michael turned to the others. "Okay, it's been a long day, and the next few are going to be even worse. Get some rest and we'll meet down here at ten tomorrow morning. With any luck, Oskar will have shown his face and we can work out what our next move is."

Anya and Leonid nodded their assent, took their respective room keys, and headed up to the first floor. Michael walked down a side corridor, unlocked the door to his room, and stepped inside.

He wasted no time. Before the door had clicked shut, he'd already begun to remove his clothes. He unlocked the window to his room, opened it, and climbed out. An icy wind howled down from the mountains to the west, but Michael did not feel the cold. By the time his feet hit the snow, his change was already well underway. He rode the wave of blessed agony as he'd done a thousand times before. The pain was like an old friend, setting his nerve endings alight with sensation.

He knew he wouldn't have much time. The cottage where Marie was hiding lay forty miles away by road, but just over half that in a straight line. Even so, it would be a struggle to cover that distance and get back in a single night, especially in these conditions. He had no other choice. Tomorrow they would descend on the cottage and slaughter everyone inside. He had one chance to make sure that his sister was long gone when the attack came.

Michael crouched low and made his way around the row of conifers until he reached the edge of the hotel car park. Then, with a quick backwards glance, he bounded across the road onto the moorlands beyond.

CHAPTER 16

15th December. Naver Cottage, Kinbrace. 00:04.

John's eyes snapped open. The room lay in darkness and he struggled to remember where he was. His mind was sluggish, unable to concentrate enough to form a coherent train of thought. He rolled onto his side, propping himself up on his elbows as he tried to take in his surroundings. He was lying on the floor amidst shredded fabric and shards of splintered wood. Cold fingers of dread clutched at his heart as his mind began to piece together the series of events.

"Oh God, Marie!"

He forced himself into a crouching position, despite protests from cold stiff limbs. The room had been almost completely destroyed. The last fragments of the door hung on to the twisted hinges, and Marie's double bed was little more than a pile of kindling, foam, and metal springs. He scanned the room, terrified of what he might find, but there was no sign of Marie. John wasn't certain if that was a good thing.

He forced himself to stand, then called out to her. "Marie? Marie, where are you?"

"I'm here. Stop bloody shouting."

Marie stood in the doorway, wearing a pair of pyjamas. She rubbed the sleep from her eyes and scratched at her hair. "You're up, then?"

John stumbled to her and gathered her up into a bear hug. "Oh my God. I'm so sorry. I thought that...I mean, I thought..."

Marie pushed him away. "I'm okay, really. And while I appreciate the hug, do you think you might want to put some clothes on first?"

John's eyes opened in shock as he became aware of his nakedness. His cheeks burned. "Oh shit, I'm really sorry. I didn't mean to... Bollocks."

Marie glanced downwards and grinned. "So it would seem." Trying not to laugh, she stepped out of the doorway so that John could scurry past her into his bedroom.

"You might want to have a shower to get rid of the wet-dog smell. I'll go and make us a cup of tea."

John trudged down the stairs ten minutes later. The destruction of the cottage made him sick to his stomach. The banister on the staircase had been utterly destroyed. Thick gouges scarred the wood-clad walls, and the carpet was covered in shards of broken glass. Marie sat on one of the remaining kitchen chairs, with a steaming cup of tea in her hands. She smiled as John entered the room. "I'd have made coffee, but I sorta broke the machine."

Her joke didn't make John feel any better. "I...I can't believe it. I'm so sorry, Marie. You could have been killed."

"Don't worry about it. The way that I see it is that we made some real progress. Yeah, things got a bit out of hand, but next time we'll be ready for it."

John almost spat his tea out. "Next time? Are you fucking serious?"

"Of course I'm serious. You getting a grip of your wolf isn't something we're doing for a laugh. Both of our lives depend on it. We'll clean this place up in the morning, and then start again. Maybe with a bit less of the changing and attacking, though."

John shook his head. "I don't know, Marie. How the hell did you manage to get away?"

"I got to the weapons crate and shot you with the first thing I got my hands on. Fortunately for you, it was a tranquiliser pistol instead of the .44 Magnum. Next time I'll keep the tranq gun with me and put you out if things start going tits-up again." She winked at him. "Anyway, I'd say that we've pretty much lost our security deposit on this place, so at least we don't have to worry about that."

"I can't believe that you're so calm about this. If you'd been just a little slower..."

"I know. Believe me, it's not the sort of experience I'm keen to repeat. We've got five tranq darts left, so you have exactly that long to beat your puppy into submission. And you shouldn't underestimate what you achieved. I mean, come on, you brought on the change yourself. That's massive. We just need to work on your control a bit, that's all."

John snorted. "Yeah, that's all. I'll sort that out right after breakfast."

Marie put her cup down, got to her feet, and put her hand on John's shoulder. "Don't be too hard on yourself. We made a mistake but we'll be better prepared next time. No one got hurt, so there's no point dwelling on it. Now, I don't know about you, but I'm knackered. I think we should call it a night and sort the mess out in the morning."

John finished his tea. "You're right. I'll take the sofa and you can have my bed. It only seems fair, given that I turned yours into matchsticks."

Marie brought her hands up to John's face, then planted a light kiss on his lips. "That's okay, there's plenty of room for us both in the bed."

"What? You mean...?"

She took his hand in hers and gently pulled him to his feet. "Yes, I do. Now stop talking."

Marie led him through the debris-strewn living area, up the shattered staircase, to the bedroom. She sat down on the single bed and pulled him to her, wrapping her arms around him while her hungry tongue slipped between his lips. John returned the kiss, losing himself in the feeling of the woman in his arms. The warmth of her body. The pounding of her heart as she crushed herself against him. The waves of gooseflesh that sprang up across his back at her caress.

Marie lay down on top of the duvet and removed her pyjama top, then hitched up her legs and slid out of the bottoms. John fumbled with his own clothing, his nervous hands catching on cloth. He tried to remove his jogging bottoms, but got one of his feet caught in the legs, so he had to hop around until he managed to free himself. When he turned back to Marie, she'd already slipped beneath the covers. She turned back a corner of the duvet, beckoning him to her. He was only too eager to comply. He slid in beside Marie, marvelling at the feel of her naked skin against his own. He brought his hands up to her face and kissed her, losing himself to the moment. Right now, nothing else existed but the woman in his arms.

Marie pulled him to her, wrapping her legs around his back, drawing him closer. Her fingernails traced lines across his back, lighting up his nerve endings. He felt the hot, moist core of her push against him. Gently teasing. Then the world seemed to dissolve as a bomb burst of ecstasy tore through him.

John opened his eyes, the realisation of what just happened dawning on him. "Oh. Oh no, I'm so sorry."

Marie seemed to be having trouble keeping a straight face. "Well, that was... brief. Look, don't worry about it. It happens to men all the time. And it's hardly surprising, given that it's, you know, your first time."

John rolled off her. "This is... embarrassing. I can't believe that I..."

Marie stroked the side of his face. "Don't. Worry. We can try again later. Practice makes perfect and all that. Now, would you mind passing me one of those tissues?"

15th December. Naver Cottage, Kinbrace. 03:27.

The dream shocked John awake. He'd been running from something, but as his mind struggled to grasp at the individual threads of consciousness, they became insubstantial, dissipating like breath on a cold winter morning. For the briefest moment, he thought he heard howling outside, and felt a surge of fear that brought him fully awake. Once the last remnants of the dream faded, he recognised the noise as nothing more than the sound of the wind as it whipped around the chimney pot and rattled the windows of the cottage. He relaxed again, enjoying the feeling of Marie beside him, letting the sound of her breathing lull him back to sleep.

It was then that he became aware of his need to go to the toilet. His bladder ached, and, once he had formed the thought, it became the only thing on his mind. He tried to ignore it. He concentrated on the comfortable bed and the woman beside him, but the need was nagging and relentless. Groaning, he removed himself from Marie's arms, doing his best not to wake her, and put a leg out from under the duvet. As he'd expected, the room was freezing cold.

John cursed under his breath, climbed out of the bed, threw on his jogging bottoms and T-shirt. He had every intention of making this excursion as quickly as he could. The cold was already stealing the lingering heat of Marie's body from him, and he longed to be back in her arms.

He staggered into the bathroom, suppressing a sigh of relief as the pressure on his bladder eased. He quickly washed his hands and was about to retreat to the bedroom again when he heard the scratching.

The noise was coming from downstairs. Insistent, like a dog pawing at a locked door. He tried to convince himself that a rat was causing the sound, but he knew from experience that the sounds made by a rodent in the walls or beneath the floorboards would be different than the constant, rhythmic scratching he heard now.

He considered waking Marie, but then thought better of it. She'd had a difficult few days, and the chances were that this was nothing. A fox or badger going through the bins were the most likely candidates. If The Pack werewolves had found them, John doubted they'd be scratching at the door when it was more likely that they'd simply tear the thing off its hinges.

He made his way down the stairs, taking care to avoid the jagged splinters of wood that still covered the floor, and made his way to the front door. Abruptly, the scratching stopped. John smiled. The fox—or whatever it was—must have realised it was not alone. He'd open the door to chase the thing off, then go back and warm his cold body against Marie. He was sure she wouldn't mind.

He undid the latch and unlocked the door, then threw it open, expecting the animal to run away, if it hadn't done so already. The last thing he expected to find was a naked man standing on the doorstep.

The man smiled. "Alright, mate. Long time, no see. Any chance you could let me in? It's a bit nippy out here."

John's mouth fell open. Although he'd not seen Michael in over twenty years, there was no mistaking his childhood friend. The years had taken their toll. Worry lines creased the man's face, and despite the lopsided grin that John remembered so well, Michael's eyes were cold and hard. John registered all of this in a fraction of a second. Then he threw a punch at him.

Michael, however, was ready for the attack. He stepped forward into the punch and brought his left arm up into the crook of John's elbow, blocking the wild haymaker with ease while his right fist slammed into John's solar plexus. John stumbled back, struggling to catch his breath. He felt the beast rise up within him, and this time he welcomed it with open arms. The colour drained from his vision; time seemed to slow to a crawl. He snarled at the intruder and felt a surge of power race through him.

The sharp crack of a pistol being discharged from behind him stopped the transformation dead in its tracks. He turned to find Marie standing on the ruined staircase, holding a .44 Magnum pistol. She did not look happy. "John, back the fuck off. I mean it. Michael, what the hell are you doing here? How did you find us?"

Michael put his hands up, a mocking smile playing across his lips. "The car. You left Connie's phone in the boot and they used it to track you."

"Fuck. I can't believe I missed that." She pointed the pistol at her brother. "Are you here to kill us?"

Michael shook his head. "No, but the others are. Under the Council's orders."

Marie let the gun drop to her side. "Which ones, and where are they now?"

"Oskar, Anya, and Leonid. They're back in the hotel in Thurso, but they're going to move on you first thing in the morning. It would be better if you weren't here when they came."

The strength seemed to drain from her and she held onto the shattered remnants of the banister for support as she made her way down the stairs. She walked over to Michael, handing him a blanket from the back of the sofa. Once he'd covered himself, she embraced him. "I've missed you, big brother." Then she slapped him across the face. "And you're a fucking idiot for coming here. What the fuck were you thinking? If they find out that you warned us..."

Michael put up his arms in a mock defensive pose. "There's no way I was going to let them kill you, Marie." He threw a dirty look in John's direction. "Even if you are harbouring a moonstruck."

"As you saw, he's not a bloody moonstruck. We're working on bringing it under control."

Michael nodded to the devastated remains of the living room. "Yeah, looks like that's going well."

"Michael, we haven't got time to go into this. You need to get back to the others before they realise you're gone. John, clear the snow off the car, and while you're at it, find that fucking phone and smash it. We need to be out of here in five minutes."

John pulled on a coat and opened the front door while Marie turned to go back upstairs. Michael grabbed her wrist.

"Marie, leave him and run. He's the most wanted man in the country. His face is plastered across every newspaper and TV station. You'll stand a better chance without him. Let Oskar and the others have him. Maybe then they won't bother coming after you."

Marie pulled her hand free. "It's not going to happen, Michael. I caused all this. I fucked up his life, and I'll be damned if I'm going to let that prick Oskar get within five miles of him."

"Did you owe him a fuck as well?"

Her lip curled up into a snarl. "I'll screw whoever I want to. It's none of your fucking business. Now, you need to get the hell out of here and stop distracting me."

John pushed the front door wide open. "You heard her, mate. You've outstayed your welcome. High time you fucked off."

Michael walked over to John until he stood nose-to-nose with him. "I'm going. But if anything happens to her because of you, there won't be anywhere you can hide that I won't find you. Remember that, mate."

Just as Michael stepped outside, a long, mournful howl echoed around the cottage. It was joined by another, higher-pitched howl from the open moorlands to the south. The colour drained from Michael's face and he pushed past John to get back inside. He turned his face to his sister, his brow slick with sweat and his eyes devoid of any hope. "They're here. They must have followed me. Oh fuck, Marie. I'm so sorry. I've brought them right to us."

15th December. Steven's House, High Moor. 03:45.

The alarm on Mark's phone brought him awake in an instant. He reached down and turned it off, not wanting to wake Phil and Paul. They'd been given an empty room and some camp beds by Wilkinson, while he slept in his own room down the corridor. None of the spare rooms had beds. They'd been converted into storage rooms and workshops, although the forensics teams had not left much behind. The four police officers and their host had spent two hours gathering everything that could be used as a weapon, but had still come up short. Two Glock pistols with a single magazine each, two H&K MP5's, again with one magazine of silver bullets each, plus Rick's Beretta, loaded with regular ammunition. An ornate, razor-sharp samurai sword had been left behind, the crime scene teams no doubt believing it to be decorative, plus a pressurised weed sprayer that Wilkinson had filled with a mix of acid and silver nitrate. It was hardly an arsenal.

After that, they'd spent most of the evening arguing over strategy. Rick had insisted that they draw the werewolves here, to this house. It made sense. The place was rigged to make it as difficult as possible for the creatures to get inside. The only problem was that they couldn't use any of those defences while Steven was in the house, except for the infra-red detectors that covered the grounds. Steven, understandably, objected to his home being used for the trap. He wanted to go after John Simpson first, and then deal with the assassins in Scotland before finishing up with the ones hunting them.

Rick and Phil hadn't been convinced. They'd argued that the last thing they needed was to get caught between two groups of werewolves, that it was better to deal with one problem at a time. By the time midnight arrived, the situation still hadn't been resolved, so everyone had decided to turn in for the night, then look at things with fresh eyes in the morning.

They'd agreed on taking two-hour watches through the night, and he was due to relieve Rick in fifteen minutes. He eased himself off the wire-frame bed, retrieved his weapon and telephone, and headed downstairs in search of coffee.

Rick sat on the leather sofa, turning his Glock over in his hands. He nodded to Mark as he entered the room and put the pistol down on the coffee table. "Sleep well?"

Mark rubbed his eyes, "Yeah, those camp beds are more comfortable than they look. All quiet, I take it?"

"As the grave. I hate this time of the day. The temperature drops just that little bit, like the night's giving one last 'fuck you' to the morning. My mam used to work in a nursing home, and she said that nine times out of ten, if some old dear died during the night it was between half-three and half-four."

Mark smiled. "Thanks for that, mate. Nice cheery conversation piece for me to mull over while you snore your head off upstairs."

"You're welcome. There's a fresh pot of coffee in the kitchen. I knew you'd want one when you dragged your arse out of bed."

"Cheers, mate. I'll see you in a few hours. Phil's got the last watch, but I'll probably just stay up with him. I'll make sure I get some bacon sarnies on the go before you surface."

"With that bacon in the fridge? You've gotta be kidding? It's gone fucking green."

"Don't worry, mate. I'll pop out to the shops first thing."

Rick nodded in appreciation then left through the hallway door while Mark headed to the kitchen and the tantalising promise of caffeine.

Mark poured a large mug of the steaming liquid, adding several teaspoons of sugar. He hated black coffee, but the milk in the refrigerator was at least a month old, and Wilkinson didn't keep any coffee whitener about the place. With any luck, he'd not notice the bitterness if he piled enough sugar into his mug.

Once he'd sweetened his drink into something tolerable, he walked to the patio doors and peered out into the darkness. This far out into the countryside, the blackness was impenetrable. Not even the comforting orange haze of the streetlights in nearby High Moor were visible. The freezing fog bank had settled over the moors, and if anything, had actually thickened during the night. It swirled like a living thing in the light breeze outside, reducing visibility to no more than ten feet from the window. It made Mark feel safe for some strange reason. Like it was some sort of blanket, come down to hide them from their enemies. Nonsense, of course - what hid them could also hide something with claws and fangs, but he thought he'd rather stay with the positive image. Otherwise he'd be jumping at every shadow, and the paranoia would drive him up the wall. Besides, the alarm system would let them know if something made it onto the grounds. They were as safe as they could be, all things considered. He stepped away from the patio doors and wandered back into the living room.

There were no television sets, anywhere in the house. Not that there would have been anything worth watching at this time of the morning, but Mark was already finding the silence oppressive, so some background noise would have been welcome. He walked across the room to where Wilkinson's sound system sat nestled in an alcove. The stereo was, predictably, top-of-the-line. Mark flicked through the array of compact disks that lined the walls beside it, but found nothing that he felt like listening to. There probably wasn't anything newer than thirty years old in the entire collection. He'd not expected to find any drum-and-bass, but would it have been too much to ask for something recorded after 1979? Instead, he turned the volume down and, after spending a few moments trying to work out the controls, turned on the radio. He was not surprised to find it tuned to *Classic FM*, so he changed stations to *Radio 1*, and settled onto the comfortable sofa with his coffee.

He checked his watch. Yep, his shift had been going for ten whole minutes and he was bored already. He considered field-stripping the H&K again, but he'd already taken the weapon apart to clean it the night before. Then he spotted Phil's cigarettes on the table.

He'd quit smoking ten years ago, back when Julie had got pregnant. When she'd miscarried and the relationship had fallen apart, he'd thought about starting again but had made the decision that he was better off without the ciggies. He'd not even thought about smoking since then, but now, seeing the packet of Marlboro Lights on the table before him, what he wanted more than anything else was a cigarette. Hell, if there was ever a situation that justified a crafty fag, it was this one. He deliberated the for almost an entire second before he picked up the pack, removed one of the white cylinders, walked into the kitchen and out through the patio doors.

The night air was frigid. The tips of his ears and nose tingled, while each breath seemed to freeze his lungs. He thought about going back inside to get his jacket but shook off the temptation. He'd survive the cold for the few minutes it took him to smoke the Marlboro, then he could get some more logs on the fire and warm himself until the others got up.

He took Phil's lighter and lit the cigarette, enjoying the brief flare of warmth from the flame, inhaling the smoke deeply. It was like he'd never given up. The familiar rush of nicotine made him feel slightly dizzy, and he stepped away from the patio doors onto the gravel path that ran around the farmhouse. The last thing he wanted to do was leave a lingering smell of smoke in the house. Wilkinson had been furious when Phil had sparked one up earlier, but given that until recently the bloke had been a terminal cancer patient, Mark could appreciate why he wouldn't want anyone smoking around him.

He took another long drag of the cigarette, noticing that he'd already gone through half of it. He should really have brought the pack. He turned to head back inside when he noticed the alarm panel in the corridor through one of the side windows.

All the security systems were disabled. And the main gates were showing as being wide open.

Suddenly, the blanket of freezing fog did not seem so comforting. Not one little bit. He dropped the still-lit cigarette onto the ground and slowly moved his hands towards the grip of the sub-machine gun that dangled from his neck.

He didn't see the attack coming. Wasn't even sure that he'd been hit at first. A burning flash of pain tore across his abdomen, and when he looked down, he saw his innards unravelling into a steaming pile on the gravel. The pain, while bad, was nothing compared to the feeling of his body emptying out. The impact of every loop of intestine as it hit the floor seemed to dislodge more, at which point gravity took over. Too stunned to scream, he tried to catch his spilling guts, only to feel the slippery organs slide through his fingers and land with a wet splash on the gravel. He tried to pick the glistening organs up. To force them back inside the gaping cavity in his abdomen. Then he heard the growl.

He looked up, mouth wide open in a silent scream, and saw two green eyes staring at him from the billowing mist. The eyes vanished, followed moments later by something hitting him from the side.

Mark fell to the ground amidst his own entrails. A rush of warmth spread across his face and chest. He attempted to speak, but only a strangled, bubbling wheeze escaped his ruined throat. As the last of his life spilled out onto the path and the darkness closed in around him, he saw the huge, russet beast saunter away from him towards the open patio doors.

CHAPTER 17

15th December. Naver Cottage, Kinbrace. 03:50.

Michael strode across the living room to Marie while John slammed the door shut and applied the deadbolt. Michael's face was grim. "What weapons do you have?"

Marie's expression told him everything he needed to know. She shook her head. "Not much. A standard tactical kit. I've modified the ammunition. Cross-hatched the bullets and reduced the charge in each round so that they break apart and stay in the body. I've got an AK-47 with two magazines. A Beretta with two more, plus a few silver knives, a tranq gun and some grenades set around the perimeter on tripwires."

"You set tripwires around the place?"

Despite the situation, Marie gave her brother a knowing smile. "Yeah, you missed them because you walked straight up to the front door. Oskar's too clever for that. He'll want to attack from the cottage's blind spots."

"What about access points? How many ways can they come at us?"

"Three - front door, kitchen door, and the conservatory. That's assuming they don't come through the windows."

Michael mulled this over. The situation was grim, with little chance that any of them would survive. At least he could try to keep Marie safe for a little while longer. "Okay, you go upstairs and use the staircase as a bottle-neck. You should be able to keep them at bay for a while. I'll stay down here and fight them as they come through the door."

Marie grabbed her brother's arm. "You can fuck right off. There's no way I'm leaving you down here alone. You can't take three of them on at once. They'll rip you to pieces."

Michael shook her hand away. "I'll be okay. Oskar won't come at us right away. He'll let the other two come in first." He nodded towards John. "I think his last encounter with your little moonstruck friend here put the fear into him. If I can take Anya out quickly, then I should be able to finish Leonid off without too much trouble."

"Bollocks. You've never been on a field team, Michael. I'm the only one here who's trained to fight and has combat experience. You won't stand a chance without us, and we won't stand a chance without you."

"And you're the only one who's human here, Marie. I can't fight them if I have to worry about you."

John strode over to them both. "Do you two want to postpone your little sibling spat until we've...I don't know, barricaded ourselves in, or something? Michael, give me a hand getting this sofa in front of the door. Marie, see if you can find something to block the door to the dining area."

Marie and Michael exchanged glances, shrugged, then joined John. The sofa was heavier than it looked, and both men had to strain to get it into position. Marie tipped over a large wall unit and shoved it against the other door, after which she began piling armchairs and tables around it. Soon the contents of the room had been stacked against each door. The windows were a problem, but both were small enough that a full-grown werewolf would struggle to squeeze through them before Michael tore their throats out. Even so, no-one seemed confident that the barriers would hold out for long under a sustained assault.

John turned to Marie. "Where did you put those booby traps? In case we need to make a run for it."

As if on cue, the sharp crack of an explosion tore through the silence, followed by a high-pitched howl of agony. Michael's frown deepened. "They're coming. Get upstairs and hold them off from there. I'll do what I can down here." He turned to John. "Can you control it enough to fight?"

John shook his head. "No, I'm sorry. If I change, there's a good chance I'll kill you and Marie as well."

"Then get upstairs, and stay out of the fucking way."

Marie started to walk forward, her chest puffed out. "I'm staying here, with you."

Michael turned to face his sister. Hair was already flowing from the pores on his face, and blood trickled from his gums. "Marie, for once in your fucking life, do as your big brother says. Get upstairs. *Now!*"

15th December. Steven's House, High Moor. 04:04.

It was the smell that woke Steven. The thick metallic stench of blood, mingled with the unmistakable odour of excrement, permeated the air until it seemed to ooze from every surface. The weakened, alien presence of the wolf whined and growled in the deepest recesses of his mind. The silver in his system from the bullet wound may have been keeping it at bay, but it could still sense the blood and was becoming agitated. Steven felt like vomiting, but fought back the urge. His senses were aflame, as if someone had turned them up to eleven. He could hear the soft, rhythmic snores of Phil Fletcher, the troubled murmuring of Paul Patterson, and the shuffling of Rick Grey as he tried to get comfortable on the camp bed down the hallway. Downstairs, the drone of the radio in the living room drowned out any other sound. He shook his head in disgust. Some warbling woman was butchering one of his favourite Leonard Cohen songs, and the noise set his teeth on edge. He pushed his irritation aside and tried to concentrate. There were undertones of other scents, but the hot reek of blood and shit overpowered everything else, driving the wolf within him into a frenzy.

Somehow the monsters had found them, made it past his security systems, and had managed to kill Mark Briggs without making a sound. It was impossible. There was no way The Pack should have tracked them down so quickly, when a few hours ago they'd been in Edinburgh. And there was no way they could have got into the grounds, let alone evade detection from the perimeter security systems. Not without help. Which meant that one of the police officers had betrayed them. There was a good chance that the dead man had been responsible, but there was no guarantee. It meant that he couldn't trust any of them.

He'd let the police officers keep their firearms with the silver bullets. He'd taken the Beretta, despite knowing that it was all but useless without silver ammunition, as well as the silver-edged sword and the weed sprayer. Hardly the weapons he'd have chosen to go into battle with, but unfortunately, they were all he had.

He needed to assess the situation. To find out how many enemies he was facing and where they were. He grabbed the weapons from beside the bed, hastily fastening the straps of the weed sprayer, wedging the scabbard of the sword through them. He drew the blade, took a deep breath, and opened his bedroom door.

The hallway was empty, but far from silent. With his senses enhanced, every creak and groan that the old building made was almost deafening. He tried to filter the noise, to sort through the flood of information and ignore the tortured version of *Hallelujah* coming from the living room: the light breeze outside, rustling the last of autumn's leaves on the trees; the frantic heartbeat of a mouse in the attic as it sensed the predators in its midst; the slight chill in the air that emanated from the open patio doors in the kitchen; the clack of claws on the polished wooden floor.

He gripped the sword with both hands and took light, careful steps along the corridor to where the police officers slept. Each footfall sounded like the first uncertain steps of a baby elephant. The werewolf in the house (because he was pretty sure that there was only one) would know exactly where he was. That it hadn't come tearing up the stairs after him meant that it either didn't care, or was being cautious, stalking its prey like a cat toying with a mouse; assessing the men's ability to fight back. Once it realised they had almost nothing that could hurt it, the situation would change. He reached the door to the spare room and pushed it open, wincing at the amplified squeal of the hinges.

Rick sat upright as he entered, saw the expression on Steven's face, then shook Phil and Paul awake. "Lads, I think we've got trouble."

Phil sat up on the camp bed and rubbed the sleep from his eyes. The rest didn't seem to have done him much good. If anything, he looked even more tired than he had when he'd turned in. The muted light accentuated the lines on his face and the bags under his eyes. He could have been Steven's age instead of twenty years younger. The other one, Paul, looked nervous, although Steven couldn't really blame him. He looked around the room, then turned to Steven. "Where's Mark?"

Steven shook his head. "He's gone. I'm sorry. Somehow they got past the perimeter alarm. There's at least one downstairs."

The colour drained from Paul's face. "Gone? You mean..."

"Do you want me to spell it out for you? I can smell the blood. He's dead, and you need to get your shit together or the rest of us won't be far behind."

Phil picked up his MP5 from the floor, chambered a round, and got to his feet. "So, what do we do now?"

"What do you think? We take the fucker out, and then see if it brought any friends with it. Come on, get your kit and form up."

The police officers gathered their equipment and fell in behind Steven. The stink of fear billowed from the men like a cloud, and the frantic hammering of their heartbeats filled his ears, momentarily masking any sounds from the rest of the house.

My God, how did I ever manage to hunt something with senses this sharp? If I'd had any idea of what I was really facing...

He pushed open the bedroom door and they filed out onto the landing, weapons pointing at the hallway beneath them. Rick opened his mouth to speak but Steven shook his head and put a finger to his lips. The silence would do nothing to conceal them from the monster below, but at least it would be one less distraction for him as he struggled with the influx of sensory data. He cocked his head, trying to find one sound among hundreds, and failing. He couldn't hear the other werewolf. Not its breathing, not its heartbeat. It would have been nice to believe that the creature had retreated, but Steven knew better. The monster was somewhere downstairs, waiting for an opportunity to strike. There was no chance of them digging in and waiting for the dawn because the day wouldn't turn the beast back into a man. This was a cunning, intelligent thing that wouldn't leave until every one of them was dead.

Despite years of experience, Steven had never felt so vulnerable, or so unsure about how to proceed. The staircase was a choke point. It would make sense to try to defend the landing because there was only one way it could come at them. Unfortunately, the beast didn't seem to be inclined to charge in. Which meant it had something else on its mind. Another plan. One that Steven couldn't fathom. There was only one option. They had to draw the werewolf out and pray that they could take it down before too many of them were killed. As plans went, it was shit. Unfortunately, he didn't see too many other options.

He motioned for the others to follow and began the descent with heavy legs. The stairs came down into the centre of the hallway. Five doors led off from there, into the living room, kitchen, dining area, study, and outside. Of the five, only the exterior door remained closed. Not good. Steven reached the bottom of the stairs, ears straining for the slightest sound that could indicate an impending attack, but the radio, now playing "All I Want for Christmas Is You", drowned out everything. Steven felt a surge of fear as he realised that the volume had been turned up several notches. The werewolf was using Mariah Carey to hide itself. That could only mean that an attack was imminent. He moved along the wall, sword held out before him, while the others followed. Phil was directly behind him, followed by Paul and Rick covering the rear.

The predictable thing to do would be to head straight for the radio, turn the fucking thing off, and take away the monster's advantage. The werewolf, of course, would expect him to do that. Which meant that it was probably lurking somewhere in the living room, ready to kill the first thing stupid enough to walk through the door.

But all the rooms of the ground floor were interconnected, so there were two ways to get into the living room. If they split into two pairs, and went through the doors at the same time, then maybe they'd stand a chance. Maybe. He motioned to Rick and Paul, outlining his plan with a series of hand gestures. Fortunately, both men were firearms officers and soon got the gist of what he had in mind. Rick led the way and moved through the open dining room door with his Glock raised, with Paul following. Steven looked at Phil. It was plain from the beads of sweat on Phil's brow, and the sickly shade of white his skin had turned, that the police officer was much more used to paperwork than combat. He'd probably not got his hands dirty in the best part of a decade. Still, the older man held the MP5 like a professional, and in spite of the fear that billowed from him like bad aftershave, he didn't hesitate to follow Steven's lead. They moved to the open living room door, raised their weapons, and got ready to attack whatever was inside.

A scream rang out. The noise was raw: equal parts agony, terror, and despair. Gunshots rang out from the dining room, three thunder-cracks in rapid succession. Steven sprinted into the living room, not bothering to check for ambush, then through the adjoining door into the dining room. The fucking thing had played him, had used the layout of his own home against him. He'd have been impressed if the implications were not so terrible. The werewolf was smarter than he was.

The ornate wooden chairs lay scattered and broken on one side of the large oak table. Rick Grey's twitching legs protruded from underneath, and his flailing arms were just visible. He screamed again, higher-pitched this time, until the sound was cut off with a wet crunch. The fucking thing must have been hiding under the dining room table when Rick and Paul entered the room. Phil appeared beside him, while Paul stood trembling in the corner of the room, pistol raised. No-one moved for a moment, until Phil raised the MP5 and screamed, "Fucking shoot it!"

He opened fire with the sub-machine gun, while Paul began shooting round after round into the top of the table. Steven grabbed Phil's arm. "Stop firing, you fucking idiot. Wait until you have a target."

Steven strode over to the table, grasped its corner with one hand, and flipped it over. He hadn't expected that. He'd only intended to push it out of the way. Apparently, the werewolf hadn't been expecting that, either.

The monster was huge. Thick red fur obscured the musculature of the werewolf, but there was no denying its power. The pulped remains of Rick Grey's head oozed from between its jaws, while the bullet-ridden body twitched. The beast released its hold on Rick's body and glared directly at him. Paul and Phil opened fire, the silver bullets slamming into it. The creature hardly seemed to notice. The physical impact of the rounds made it jerk and twitch, but the wounds healed up almost instantaneously, and its gaze never left Steven's.

After a few moments, Phil's MP5 clicked empty, while Paul's weapon fell silent as well. The werewolf's eyes lit up with a mixture of triumph and absolute hatred. Its black lips curled back to reveal huge, blood-soaked fangs and its growl made Steven's blood run cold. He backed away into the doorway to the living room, then froze as he heard the unmistakable growl of another werewolf behind him.

15th December. Naver Cottage, Kinbrace. 04:19.

John wiped the sweat from his brow and shuffled to get comfortable. It had been almost twenty minutes since the grenade had gone off, but the expected attack had not materialised. Michael prowled the living room, periodically sniffing the air or cocking his head to listen. The presence of the werewolf terrified John. He'd been in proximity to other werewolves in the past, but he'd always been in a fight for his life at the time. Having one just a few feet away, even if Michael was supposedly on their side, was an unnerving experience. The creature was huge, closer in size to a male lion than a wolf. Thick brown hair covered its body, but despite that, the wolf's muscles could be seen moving beneath the fur. Fangs like daggers protruded from the monster's mouth while vicious claws tore strips from the carpet as it paced. The sheer power of the thing was incredible. John could not imagine a more lethal killing machine. And there were three more of them, waiting outside to kill them. The tranquilizer gun in his hands felt like a meagre defence against such things.

Marie sat beside him, her face a mask of tension. Every once in a while, her face would fall for the briefest fraction of a second, her fear, grief, and anger framed in the set of her mouth and the light in her eyes. Then the mask would snap back into place and she'd become focused once more, the flicker of emotion gone. John suspected that in those brief moments, Marie had instinctively tried to reach out with her senses, only to find them muted. He was beginning to understand what she'd lost.

Without realising it, over the last ten minutes or so, John's own senses had come alive. The wolf had slunk from its cave in the deepest recesses of his psyche, waiting just below the surface of his mind. He felt energised, as if he'd taken some sort of powerful drug. His senses gathered information from the surrounding area, processing it until he had an awareness of everything around him for twenty metres. Each fragment of scent or sound added to the constantly updated picture. He felt connected to the world in a way he'd never have thought possible.

There was no fury in the wolf this time, no attempt to break through and initiate the transformation. The beast seemed to be waiting, like a dog lying by its master's feet, tail thumping and ears pricked, eager to go outside, but knowing that it had to wait a little longer. John wasn't sure that he liked this change. He and the wolf had been at odds with each other for decades, and the monster had tried to break free on more than one occasion. The change in its behaviour was suspicious.

He turned to Marie and said a little too loudly, "Why aren't they attacking?"

Michael issued a warning growl from downstairs and Marie put her finger to her lips. When she replied, it was barely above a whisper. "The booby traps have made them rethink their strategy. Unfortunately, Oskar excels at things like that. The best we can hope for is that it was Leonid who found the grenade. He's younger than Anya and Oskar and doesn't have the same level of silver-immunity. If it was him, then there's a decent chance that it fucked him right up. If it was either of the other two, they'll probably have recovered by now."

"So they're just going to let us sit here and stew in our own juices for a while, until they work out a better way to get us?"

Marie gave him a grim smile. "I know. Part of me just wants to get it over with. The rest of me wants to hold off the inevitable for as long as I can."

John reached across and took Marie's hand. He was about to say something reassuring when Michael let out a thick, menacing growl from downstairs. John reached out with his senses, searching for the threat. It wasn't long before he found it. A surge of fear washed over him and he turned to Marie. "I can smell smoke. The bastards have set fire to the cottage."

CHAPTER 18

15th December. Steven's House, High Moor. 04:25.

Phil stepped from the doorway, letting the empty MP5 clatter to the floor. The air stank of gun-smoke and blood, but the combined animal reek of the werewolves overpowered everything else. He found himself beside Paul, in the corner of the room. Paul's eyes were wild, and he held his empty Glock in a double-handed grip so tight that his knuckles had turned white. Steven stood directly opposite the first werewolf, but now two more of the monsters had entered the room, one from the living room and another from the hallway. The massive creatures blocked the exits. There was no hope of escape. Phil realised that he was going to die and felt a sharp stab of pain in his chest. He almost laughed. Having a heart attack right now would be the best thing he could hope for. Better that than be torn apart by those cruel jaws and vicious talons.

The two newcomers snarled and their muscles tensed while the hair rose on the backs of their necks. The first werewolf snapped at the air and crouched as if to pounce. Then, to Phil's astonishment, it began to transform. The creature's bones snapped and twisted, stretching flesh as they shattered then reformed. Thick orange fur retreated into skin, while the bloody fangs sank back into the creature's gums. Within a matter of seconds, the werewolf had been replaced by the naked form of Connie Hamilton.

She picked herself up from the ground, settling into a crouched position that made Phil think of a cat, ready to pounce on its prey. She turned her head to the werewolf that blocked the door to the living room. "Nice ta see ye too, Gregorz. If Ah'm honest, Ah'm a little surprised. Ah thought ye'd have bigger things to worry about than me right now."

The werewolf that she'd called Gregorz snarled and took a step forward, its teeth bared. Connie put up her hands. "Let me have Wilkinson. After that, Ah don't give a shit. Ah'll bare ma throat to ye, if that's what ye want. Just let me have ma revenge."

Phil looked at Steven. The colour had drained from the old man's face and, while he still held the sword out before him, his legs sagged, as if unable to bear his weight. Steven's eyes never left Connie Hamilton, even when Gregorz began to transform beside him. Phil wanted to look away, but couldn't. The change from wolf to man was not as easy for this werewolf as it had been for Connie. It growled in pain at each dislocated joint and shattered bone. The whole thing went on for more than a minute, and when the man got to his feet, his body was covered with a slick sheen of sweat and blood. With some effort, Phil swallowed the vomit that surged up into his mouth and realised that his legs were shaking. That was not something he ever wanted to witness again.

Gregorz looked at Steven, a sneer of contempt on his lips. He turned back to Connie. "We can't let you live, Connie. You went against a direct order from the Alpha, so we have no choice. However, I know what that piece of shit did to you. We won't stand in your way. He's all yours."

Connie's face cracked into a bloody smile. She lifted her head and fixed Steven's gaze. "Do you know me? Do you know who I am?"

Steven straightened himself up, returning the woman's glare. "As far as I'm concerned, you're just another fucking werewolf."

Connie laughed. "An' that's been yer attitude all along, hasn't it? It didn't matter what ye had in yer sights. Moonstruck or Pack, they were all the same. Just another fucking werewolf. Is that what ye thought when ye blew ma little girl's brains out?"

Steven's tough facade fell, and the old man seemed to age visibly. He lowered his eyes to the floor. "Germany, 1996. That was you. The one that got away."

Connie stepped forward and grasped Steven's chin, bringing his eyes back up to hers. "Yes, tha one that got away. Do ye like what ye've made? Ah never used to be a killer. Ah was a wife and a mother before ye took away ma reason to live. Because ye decided that all werewolves needed to die, regardless of whether they were killers or not. Yer a fucking monster and now Ah'm going ta end ye like you ended my Megan."

Steven's shoulders sagged and he closed his eyes, as if he accepted his fate. Then, in the brief moment of silence, the radio's half-hourly news bulletin began.

"Are werewolves real? Astonishing footage has been broadcast online where murder suspect Connie Hamilton states that she is exactly that, before apparently transforming on camera and killing a woman and a young child."

Paul sagged back against the wall, the Glock falling from his hands. A high-pitched, strangled wail escaped from his lips and he covered his face with his hands. Phil realised then who the dead woman and child were. All of the pieces finally fit.

Gregorz' mouth fell open. He looked at Connie with an expression of pure horror. "My God, Connie. What have you done?"

15th December. Naver Cottage, Kinbrace. 04:28.

John and Marie stood in the centre of the living room while Michael continued to pace back and forth. The first tendrils of smoke had begun to seep through the gaps around the kitchen door and John felt the heat against his skin. The crackling flames on the other side of the door had not become the roar of an inferno. Not yet. But it wouldn't be long before the fire caught properly and the wood-framed cottage was consumed. They had to get outside, even if that meant facing the werewolves in the open. They'd die if they stayed here.

John began to clear the front door, throwing furniture aside in a frenzy. Marie grabbed his shoulder. "No, not that way." She nodded toward the other door. "They won't expect us to go through the fire. It might buy us a couple of seconds."

He nodded his agreement, and they both began clearing the door, working frantically as the smoke from the other side began to thicken. Marie coughed, covering her mouth with part of her T-shirt. John's eyes stung, and he had to keep blinking away tears. By the time they pushed aside the heavy wall unit, John felt ready to drop, and Marie looked much worse. Smoke inhalation would kill them as quickly as the claws of a werewolf. They didn't have much time left.

He grabbed Marie's arm and motioned for her to cover the doorway. She nodded her understanding, raising the AK-47 while John grabbed the door handle. His skin sizzled, and the smell of burning flesh filled his nostrils. He ignored the pain, gripped the red-hot handle harder, then threw open the door.

The heat was like a physical wall. John could smell his hair and eyebrows singe. There was no way they could make it through there. It would be like trying to run through a blast furnace. He was about to say this to Marie when a dark shape burst through the conflagration in a shower of sparks. The werewolf ignored the flames springing across its black fur and hurled itself towards the open door with its jaws wide open. John threw himself to the side while Marie raised the AK-47 and stitched the werewolf's flanks with silver bullets. The impact of the rounds knocked the creature aside, slamming it into the doorframe. By the time the creature hit the floor, the bullet wounds had already healed over. It looked at Marie, snarled, then leapt forward with its claws spread wide. She tried to bring the weapon up, but the look in her eyes told John that she knew that she'd be too slow.

Michael flew across the room, a blur of brown fur and flashing talons that intercepted the werewolf in mid-air, sending them both crashing back through the open door into the inferno. Marie raised the AK-47 but was unable to get a clear line of sight on the black-furred monster without hitting her brother. She lowered the weapon, grabbed John's wrist, and said, "Come on, we're going."

They both plunged into the burning room, racing for the conservatory at the far end. The intense heat had already shattered the glass and the freezing winds fanned the flames even higher. The wooden panelling on the walls ignited, while the timbers of the ceiling groaned in protest. A wooden beam crashed down before them, sending a cloud of sparks into the air. Marie leaped around it, narrowly avoiding the thrashing werewolves that fought in their midst.

It was difficult to tell which of them was winning. Both beasts bore terrible wounds, their fur matted with blood where teeth or claws had connected with flesh. The air was filled with the stench of burning hair. Smoke had already begun to curl from the werewolves' fur.

John tried to ignore the searing pain and pushed on after Marie, leaping over obstacles while he held his arms up to try to shield his face from the worst of the heat. They burst from the blazing room and leaped through the shattered windows in unison, relishing the cold night air against their scorched flesh as they landed in the snow.

Marie raised her weapon and turned back to the blazing cottage. "Michael, move your fucking arse."

The brown werewolf bounded away from the black, feigning an attack before changing direction, while Marie opened fire with the AK-47. Silver bullets tore into the enraged black monster, throwing it sideways into a burning table. Marie switched magazines in a single, fluid move and was about to resume firing when something leapt from the cottage roof toward her. She threw herself backwards into the snow, narrowly avoiding the slashing claws of a second werewolf who'd remained hidden until now, waiting for the opportunity to strike. She struggled to scramble to her feet as the new werewolf, a smaller, light-brown creature, landed beside her and advanced, fangs bared. Marie swung her weapon round, but the creature lashed out with its claws and the rifle spun out of her hands, landing in the snow several feet away.

The attack had taken John by surprise, taking a second for him to register what was happening. He remembered the tranquillizer gun in his hands. He had no idea how long it would take for the dart to have an effect, but if he had to, he'd club the fucking thing to death rather than let it hurt Marie. He raised the pistol, took aim, then cried out as the weapon's wooden stock exploded in a shower of splinters. John looked at the ruined weapon in his hands, unable to understand what had happened. Then a gunshot rang out, and the wooden window frame beside him blew apart.

Suddenly, what had happened was all too clear. John dove to his side, behind a low wall as a stream of small explosions burst from the snow where he'd been standing.

John looked up to Michael, hoping to see his childhood friend coming to the rescue. Michael was immune to silver bullets. John, however, was not. His heart sank when he peered into the flames. The creature that Michael was fighting had recovered before he could get clear, and the two werewolves were engaged in battle once more, tearing ragged ribbons of flesh from each other while the building fell apart around them.

Marie screamed his name, and he peered around the wall to see the light-brown werewolf just a few short feet away from her. Then the brick next to his head exploded in a spray of dust and he retreated back under cover. Several more shots slammed into the bricks as he went, as if to emphasise the point. *Stay down, we'll get to you when we've finished with your friends.*

There was nothing else for John to do. He was unarmed, and both Marie and Michael would be dead in seconds if he didn't act. It was his last roll of the dice, the only remaining option. Casting all doubt aside, John threw open the doors of his mind and let the wolf come out.

15th December. Steven's House, High Moor. 04:31.

Steven felt Connie's hand retract and opened his eyes to see a look that could almost be called sheepish on the woman's face. Gregorz looked ill, while the other werewolf snarled in the doorway. "Why, Connie? Why would you condemn us all?"

"Ah was sorta hoping ye'd not hear about that. Ah thought that if I gave ye lot a wee distraction, it'd keep ye off ma back long enough ta take care o' business. Ah wasn't expecting ye to turn up here."

The shock on Gregorz' face was slowly turning to anger. "Do you have any idea what you've done? Of the damage you've caused? They will hunt us down. They'll never stop. You've killed us all."

Connie's lips curled into a sneer. "Why tha fuck should Ah care? Ye bastards were the ones comin' here ta kill me. Fuck the lot of yas."

"We were your family. We cared for you when you lost Isaac and Megan. We gave you a home. A purpose. And you do this? How could you?"

The sheepish look on Connie's face melted into a broad grin, "Oh, it's worse than ye know. Ah've told them the fucking lot. About tha Pack, Simpson, everything. I've sent samples of ma blood to about a dozen different labs, and a list of every pack member living in this country that Ah could think of. Not just tha field teams. I told 'em about tha families as well. Ye shouldn't hae fucked with me, Gregorz. If ye and that prick Michael had just let me finish Wilkinson off, then none o' this woulda happened. If yer looking for someone to blame, try looking at yerself for a change."

Gregorz' face turned scarlet. He rushed forwards, his hands grasping for Connie's neck. The man's face was twisted into a mask of rage. Veins bulged at his temple and his eyes turned into luminous green disks as the change began. Connie ducked under his outstretched hands and delivered a slashing blow to his throat before skipping off to his side. Gregorz fell to the floor in a spray of blood, grasping at the bubbling wound in his throat. Connie took a step back from the dying man and brought her clawed hand up to her mouth, where she licked the blood from her talons. Her body was already covered with fine orange stubble, and the tips of her ears elongated before Steven's eyes.

"Now, lads. Where were we?"

CHAPTER 19

15th December. Steven's House, High Moor. 04:40.

Steven looked on in shock at the spreading pool of blood beneath the old werewolf, then back up to Connie Hamilton. The change was sweeping through her, transforming her flesh, apparently with as little effort as changing clothes. Already the thin covering of fur had thickened into a coarse, red carpet. Muscles swelled and stretched, while Connie fixed him with a flat green stare and grinned with rows of glistening fangs.

The other werewolf, a muscular, silver-furred creature, leaped to attack, snarling in utter rage. It crashed into the half-transformed Connie, and they flew across the room into a glass wall unit in a flurry of teeth and claws.

Steven grabbed Phil's arm. The police officer's eyes were glazed, and for a moment he didn't seem to register him at all. Paul still had his hands over his eyes, as if to deny the horror unfolding before him. Steven leaned into his face and yelled. "Fucking run, you idiots."

That broke the spell. Phil and Paul lurched for the doorway and out into the corridor. Steven reached the door close behind them, risking a look over his shoulder. The two werewolves tore into each other with a fury he could not believe. Their attacks were blurs, so fast that his eyes hardly registered the movements. Claws sliced through flesh, while teeth tore away chunks of muscle. Both beasts were terribly wounded, but their savagery remained undiminished. The silver wolf launched itself into the air, diving forward and lashing out with its claws across the flank of its opponent, sending a spray of blood and fur into the air. The orange monster twisted at the last moment, taking the hit, but putting its jaws in range of the silver beast's neck. It bit down with a sickening crunch of bone, and the silver monster went limp. Then it turned its head to Steven and howled.

Steven glanced over his shoulder. Phil and Paul had already

reached the front door. Phil was fumbling with the lock, while Paul's face was blank, devoid of anything approaching emotion or reason. Steven knew then who'd betrayed them. He'd sacrificed his friends to save his family and had ended up losing everything. Steven realised that he didn't blame him. He would probably have done the same thing in his position, but it wouldn't make it any easier to live with the consequences. Not that it would matter when Connie Hamilton finished with them. They were defenceless against her. All he had was the sword and the weed-sprayer filled with the acid and silver nitrate mix he'd taken from...

Of course. He could have slapped himself for not thinking of it sooner.

Phil managed to get the door open. He turned back to Steven. Steven nodded. "I've got this, Phil. You two get the fuck out of here."

Phil didn't say anything. He led Paul through the door and out into the night, letting the door click closed behind them. Steven shifted the grip on his sword, and turned around to face his death.

Connie stood in the doorway, less than ten feet away. She'd sustained terrible injuries. One of her front legs was broken, with white shards of bone protruding from the blood-stained fur. Chunks of muscle had been torn away from her shoulders, and the blue bulge of internal organs was visible through the ragged tears on her abdomen. Steven wasn't even sure how she was still standing until he realised that it was hate. Connie Hamilton's hatred for him had kept her going long beyond where she should have lain down and died. She would spend her last breath tearing out his throat.

She glared at him, wrinkled her snout, and snarled. Steven looked into her eyes and let the world fade around him. All that mattered was the monster. Time stretched out. The scent of blood washed over him, energising him. The werewolf's eyes twitched, a tiny movement that lasted for a fraction of a second and betrayed the creature’s intentions.

It sprang forward and Steven rushed to meet it, driving the sword before him. The blade sank into her chest up to the hilt and

Steven drove Connie backward, pushing steel through the wall to impale the monster. The beast howled in agony as the blade sliced through internal organs, its attempts to escape inflicting more damage than the initial wound. Her claws lashed out, tearing through Steven's flesh, and her head darted forward. Steven felt her jaws close around his collarbone, shattering it in a single bite.

The pain was unbelievable. Steven had suffered some grievous wounds in his life, but nothing like this. He reached up with his uninjured arm while his shoulders exploded in a white bomb-burst of pain. Connie ripped her head back and forth, rending his body into tattered strips of meat. Despite the pain, he managed to gasp. "For what it's worth, I'm sorry about your daughter."

The werewolf's eyes flared with fury and it plunged its head forward again, this time aiming for Steven's heart. As the fangs punctured his skin and cleaved through his sternum, his hand found what it had been looking for: the activation panel for the house security systems. He jabbed at the buttons frantically while Connie chewed her way into his chest.

The world dissolved into a red cloud of agony. The security system had registered werewolves inside the property and took appropriate measures. The ultrasonic siren dropped him to his knees, while Connie thrashed on the sword, howling in anguish at the all-consuming shriek of the alarm. Steven felt a warm trickle of blood run down his face as his ear-drums burst. He knew what was coming next.

Rough hands grabbed him under his arms, pulling him away from the screaming figure of Connie Hamilton, who tore herself apart on a samurai sword. He looked up and saw Phil and Paul drag him towards the open door, at which point, the sprayers burst into life, filling the air with a grey mist that burned everything it touched, a mixture of sulphuric acid and silver nitrate, concentrated enough to eat through flesh in seconds. Phil and Paul both cried out in pain as the acid began to dissolve their skin. Steven wouldn't have blamed them if they'd dropped him and run. Instead, the two police officers redoubled their efforts, dragging him outside into the cold night air.

Once outside, the howl of the ultrasonic siren lessened to the extent that Steven was able to think. The pain from the wounds Connie had inflicted were agonising, and he was dizzy from blood loss, but he didn't think she'd disrupted anything vital. The alarm had stopped her attack before she'd finished chewing through his ribcage. The acid, however, was another story. The pain was worse than anything Steven had ever experienced. The corrosive chemicals ate into his flesh as his wolf tried to heal the damage. Unfortunately, the silver nitrate weakened the monster further, making its regenerative abilities less and less effective while the acid seemed to burn hotter with every passing second.

How much worse then, for Connie? Steven looked back through the door to her screaming form, pinned to the wall like a bug, caught halfway between human and wolf states. The acid melted her skin faster than it could regenerate, but not by much. Her face trickled down her mangled chest, washed away by the constant stream of fresh sulphuric acid, while the burn marks grew gradually larger. Connie Hamilton was dissolving before his eyes. After long minutes, her screaming stopped and she slid off the sword, crumbling into a smoking pile of ruined flesh on the floor just as the acidic deluge stopped.

Phil grabbed two bottles of water from Mark's Range Rover, splashing the liquid over his own injuries before passing the other bottle to Paul. Phil reached his side and poured the rest of the water across the worst of his burns. Steven grabbed Phil's wrist. "Thanks, you didn't have to do that."

Phil nodded. "No problem."

He looked up past Steven, to where rows of headlights could be seen through the thinning mist. "Looks like the cavalry's turned up, then. Late as usual."

Steven coughed and looked again at the headlights. Too big for a squad car or ambulance. Even with the shriek of the ultrasonic alarm reverberating through his skull, he could still make out the heavy diesel growl of the vehicles' engines. The same sound that military transports made. He shook his head. "Phil, something tells me that's not the cavalry."

15th December. Naver Cottage, Kinbrace. 04:40.

Marie scrambled back, trying to put some distance between herself and the werewolf in front of her. During her time with The Pack, she'd known Anya, but they'd kept a respectful distance from each other. She'd always had a typical moonborn stick-up-her-arse attitude, however they'd tolerated one another and had even worked together on occasion. 'Friends' would have been pushing it, but they'd certainly respected the other as a colleague. One look at the elation in the werewolf's eyes told Marie that none of that counted for a damn thing anymore. Anya was enjoying this. She knew Marie was defenceless and was savouring her prey's fear before moving in for the kill.

Another gunshot rang out, blowing a chunk from the wall that John was hiding behind. Marie couldn't help but feel a surge of contempt for Oskar. It was just like him to stay back and not get his hands dirty. The Norwegian rarely transformed on an operation, claiming that he was more effective as a strategist in his human form, orchestrating the assault like a conductor. Marie knew the truth, however. Oskar had not responded well to the silver immunisation process. His wolf form was small, stunted in comparison to the other wolves on field teams. He was still a formidable killer in human terms, but in reality, little more than the poisoned runt of the litter.

Anya's eyes blazed and she snapped at the air by Marie's feet, sending her scurrying back until she hit the low wall separating the gardens from the woods beyond. She had nowhere else to go. Anya's lips curled into what could almost have been considered a smile. For a second, neither of them moved. Then Anya surged forward and sank her fangs into Marie's side.

The pain was nothing compared to the horror she felt when she realised that Anya was eating her. The werewolf tore its head back, ripping away a bloody scrap of her abdomen in the process. It tilted its head down so that it fixed Marie's gaze, then slowly chewed and swallowed the chunk of flesh. It darted forward again, but despite the pain and terror, this time Marie was ready for her. As Anya's muzzle snapped at the wound in her side, Marie's right arm flashed out, driving a silver knife through the bottom of Anya's jaw into her brain.

The monster let out a high-pitched squeal of agony and fell to the side, its claws leaving deep gashes across Marie's thighs as it twitched and thrashed on the ground.

Marie started to crawl away from the wounded creature, not daring to look at the wound. She felt nauseous and weak. Her vision began to darken around the edges, but she fought against it. If she passed out now, she was dead. Her hands closed around the stock of her assault rifle. She brought it up to her shoulder, then looked through the conservatory into the blazing house.

Michael and Leonid's combat had slowed in pace, the heat, smoke, and combined injuries taking an obvious toll on both of them. Part of Leonid's fur was on fire, but the black werewolf ignored the flames and circled its opponent, searching for an opportunity to strike. Michael bled from dozens of dreadful wounds. One of his eyes was little more than a pulped, bloody mess, and white bone gleamed from beneath the tears across his ribcage. Another part of the ceiling crashed down into the room, sending the flames higher. Marie didn't hesitate. She opened up with the assault rifle. Bullets punched into Leonid, the wounds erupting in flowers of blood across his side, throwing him backwards, away from Michael.

Michael surged forward, using the distraction to his advantage. He slammed into Leonid before the black wolf was able to recover, clamping his jaws around the other beast's neck. Leonid howled in fury and lashed out with his lethal claws, opening more gaping wounds across Michael's chest. Michael ignored the fresh injuries and bit down. Blood sprayed from Leonid's throat, and his howl of pain turned into a bubbling cry of anguish. Then Michael's jaws closed. Leonid's head rolled from his body. Michael turned to face his sister, hardly able to stand. Then the roof of the cottage collapsed.

Marie dropped the assault rifle and brought her hands up to her face. "Michael!" The grief hit her like a punch in the stomach, driving the air from her lungs, constricting her throat until drawing breath was painful. Her brother was dead. There was no way he he could have survived that. The loss threatened to overwhelm her, when, from behind her, came a savage growl. Her heart froze in her chest. She turned her head, knowing what she'd find. Anya had managed to dislodge the blade and stood four feet away from her, with bloody saliva dripping from her open jaws. She reached around for her only remaining weapon, the Beretta tucked into the waistband of her jeans, knowing that she might as well throw snowballs at Anya for all the good it would do.

A furious roar split the night, freezing Anya in her tracks. The werewolf turned away from Marie to the source of the noise as John burst from cover.

Marie's heart sank. John had not fully transformed into a wolf, as she'd hoped. Instead a hulking, seven-foot-tall moonstruck werewolf hurtled towards her and Anya. The beast's eyes shone with a feral rage. There was no reason behind them, only fury. John would probably kill Anya, but then she would be next.

A gunshot rang out, and the snow beside her erupted into a white cloud. She'd almost forgotten about Oskar, hidden in the trees with a high powered rifle. There was nothing she could do about John. When the time came, she'd go without a fight and hope that eventually, John would be able to come to terms with it. Oskar, on the other hand, was a problem she felt able to handle, comparatively speaking. First, however, she needed to get something. Clutching her wounded side, Marie threw herself over the low wall, then staggered away into the trees.

***

Oskar wiped the sweat from his eyes and tried to get the moonstruck in his sights. John Simpson's transformation was an unfortunate turn of events, even if not wholly unexpected. That was part of the reason Oskar had stayed back, letting Leonid and Anya assault the cottage while he provided cover. He had no intention of getting into close proximity with that monstrosity. Just seeing it through a telescopic sight had made his heart pound and his palms ooze perspiration.

He'd set up his sniper's nest almost twelve hours before and had simply sat back and waited. Leonid and Anya had been under instructions to follow Michael if he attempted to leave the hotel, and the former alpha had played right into their hands. Krystof would be overjoyed when he found out, although he had indicated that Michael be taken alive if possible. It was unfortunate that he'd perished in the burning cottage along with Leonid.

He huffed in frustration as another round failed to find its target. Anya was among the fastest wolves in The Pack, and the moonstruck was having difficulty in landing a blow. The combat was so fast and fluid that the damn thing didn't stay in one place long enough for him to blow a hole through it. Anya snapped at its legs, darting it to swipe gouges in the beast's legs or sink fangs into exposed flesh, before leaping back. She was working the beast, tiring it before she moved in for the kill. Still, Oskar remembered what it had done to Troy and Gabriela. Anya would not stand a chance if the raging moonstruck managed to grab her. And once it had finished with her, Oskar had no doubt as to where it would turn its attention.

He fired again, splintering the truck of a pine tree where Simpson's head had been a second before. The moonstruck turned its head toward him and snarled before renewing its attack on Anya. Oskar tried to aim the rifle again, but his hands trembled, unable to keep the weapon steady. He reached a decision. The Council needed to know about Michael's treachery. That was more important than Simpson at this point. There was no sense in his dying here.

"Fuck this."

He slung the rifle over his back, drew a Beretta, and climbed out of the tree. His car was down a small lane, almost quarter of a mile to the west. With luck, he would be able to reach it before the moonstruck finished Anya off and then come after him. If he was really lucky, the beast would go after Marie Williams first, drawn by the scent of blood from her stomach injury. He really just needed to be further away from it than she was.

He reached the ground, only to freeze in his tracks at the sound of a pistol being cocked. He turned his head and almost laughed. Marie Williams stood twenty yards away from him, along the trail leading to his car. She was bloodied, seemed on the verge of collapse, and yet she faced him down with a Beretta in her hands. The absurdity of it was ridiculous.

A tortured howl ripped through the night air, turning into a scream of absolute agony before cutting off in a strangled wheeze. It seemed that Anya's luck had run out. Oskar strode towards Marie, not even bothering to raise his weapon. "You are in my way, Marie. I suggest you get out of it. Nothing you can do will hurt me."

Her lips curled into a sneer. "I'd like to see you try it, you fucking runt. Even in this state, I'm more than a match for a pathetic coward like you. I'll make you beg before I finish you off."

Oskar's cheeks burned, and an old, familiar rage bubbled up from deep within his chest. "You...dare?" Thoughts of the moonstruck at his rear vanished in a cloud of red rage. This woman, this *human* dared to stand in his way? He'd tear her apart for her arrogance.

He quickened his pace, feeling the power of his beast surge through him, driven on by Marie's mocking smile. His fingertips itched, then burned as sharp black claws burst from under his fingernails. Fangs burst through his gums, spraying blood and spittle across his face. It had been too long since he'd killed a human in his wolf form. Already he could imagine the taste of her hot blood as it gushed from her twitching corpse. He was going to enjoy this.

Something snagged on his leg, and two light, metallic tinkles whispered to his side, sounding almost like a bell.

Or the pins falling from grenades.

He looked up to Marie, who said, "Surprise, motherfucker!", blew him a kiss, then threw herself behind a fallen log.

Twin explosions tore through the night, savage thunderclaps that burst his eardrums and threw him back onto the trail. The pain was unbelievable. He'd been wounded before, on many occasions, but had never felt anything this intense. His entire lower body felt like it was on fire. He tried to push himself into a sitting position, but the waves of pure anguish that wracked his body were more than he could bear. Oskar looked down to the tattered ruins of his legs. His right leg had been blown off at the knee, while his left was little more than a mass of splintered bone adorned with smoking scraps of red meat. His body was already trying to heal the damage, but it was catastrophic. He'd never re-grow the severed limb, and it would take hours for the other leg to heal enough to support his weight.

Marie slowly got to her feet, a grim smile fixed on her face. She let the pistol drop to the ground and her shoulders seemed to sag. Oskar realised then that she wasn't looking at him. She was looking at something on the trail behind him. Oskar turned his head and came face-to-face with his worst nightmare.

John Simpson's body bled from dozens of wounds. To her credit, Anya had managed to inflict a significant amount of damage to the monster before she'd met her end. None of this seemed to matter to Simpson, however. His feral, green eyes regarded Oskar with a hunger and fury that turned the Norwegian's blood to ice. It curled back its lips into a snarl.

"Please. Don't. I'm begging you."

The beast either didn't understand the plea, or simply didn't care. It plunged its talons into Oskar's chest until they burst from his back, then lifted him from the ground until they were face-to-face.

Oskar felt his consciousness fading. The last thing he felt was the moonstruck's hot, charnel-house breath against his face. Then John Simpson tore him in half.

CHAPTER 20

15th December. Naver Cottage, Kinbrace. 04:53.

Marie watched the two halves of Oskar's body slip from John's grasp, landing with a wet splat on the frozen ground. The great werewolf's breath billowed into clouds of condensation as it threw back its head and howled in triumph. It looked at the eviscerated corpse at its feet, then turned its head to Marie.

The fear she felt in this thing's presence was almost overpowering, but Marie knew that there was nowhere to run to, no possible way to fight, and no will to, in any case. She was tired. Drained. She took a deep breath then stepped forward towards John's looming form.

The creature watched her approach, blowing puffs of steam into the frigid air. She reached out a trembling hand, towards the side of the werewolf's muzzle. "John? Do you know me?"

The wolf rubbed its head against her hand, and when she looked into the creature's eyes, she saw her friend looking back at her. "Oh thank fuck for that," she said, and threw her arms around John's huge, hairy body. "You could have fucking said something, you prick. I was shitting myself."

John pushed her away as gently as he could, then cocked his head to one side. He snarled, turned away from her, and leapt into the undergrowth. Marie couldn't understand what he was doing at first. Were there more enemies, hiding in the darkness, waiting to attack? Then she understood. Michael. John was going after her brother.

She stumbled through the undergrowth, ignoring the pain from her wounds, guided by the flickering glow of the fire through the snow-covered trees. When she emerged from the woods, her hand flew to her mouth. There was very little left of the building. The fire had almost completely gutted the place. The roof had long since collapsed, leaving only the exterior walls standing. Smoke billowed from the empty windows, while the U-PVC of the conservatory had burned away leaving only a twisted metal skeleton behind. There was no sign of John. No sound but the crackle of the fire as it consumed the last remnants of the cottage.

One of the outer walls finally succumbed to the inferno, collapsing into a blazing pile of wood and stone. The flames flared brighter as the clouds of dust thrown into the air were incinerated. Marie gazed into the blazing building, hoping to see some sign of life or movement, but the smoke was too thick and obscured her view.

"John! Michael!"

Her voice echoed off the last remaining walls, and faded into silence. She thought that she heard a roar of pain and rage from within the building, but it could as easily have been the arctic wind that howled through the shattered windows, coaxing the blaze to further heights. Her heart sank, unwilling to even consider the possibility that John had gone in there for Michael. She couldn't lose both of them, not to something as ridiculous as a fire. Not after all they'd faced together.

The smoke billowed up into a thick black cloud before her, almost seeming to form a shape. A familiar shape. Marie couldn’t believe her eyes and cried out in joy as John burst from the blazing cottage with Michael's burned body in his muscular arms.

John's fur was ablaze and Michael's body was little more than a blackened piece of meat. John lowered Michael to the ground, then, as if becoming conscious of the flames consuming his body, he leaped into a snow drift, rolling around until the fire had gone out.

Marie crouched beside her brother, hardly daring to touch the scorched remains of his flesh. He was back in human form and was unmoving. Smoke curled from his burned body, and the snow around him began to melt.

Marie began shovelling handfuls of the white powder onto her brother's body. Weren't you supposed to put cold on a burn? Did that even apply when every part of someone's body was a charred mass of ruined flesh?

"Come on, Michael. Wake the hell up. Get your arse up, you lazy shit."

John put his hand on her shoulder. She'd not noticed him transforming back to his human form. His body bled from dozens of wounds. Not only the ones inflicted during tonight's confrontation, but the ones from his earlier battle with The Pack, and which had reopened. Rivulets of blood ran across his chest and legs, yet he didn't seem to care. His eyes held a strength that Marie had never seen in him before.

"I can't hear him, John. I can't fucking tell if he's alive or not. It's like being underwater or something. I should be able to hear his heartbeat, or the air being sucked into his lungs, but I fucking can't."

"It's okay, Marie. I can. He's still alive." He pointed to an area of pink skin amidst the cracked black flesh. "See, he's already started to heal. He's going to be fine."

Michael's remaining eye flickered open. He tried to speak, but the only sound that escaped his lips was a wheeze of agony.

Marie piled more snow around her brother. "You just lie still, okay? You'll heal up in no time, then we can all go and find a bar."

Michael's eyes fogged over and he coughed bloody phlegm across his lips in a series of wracking spasms that made Marie wince. By the time the coughing fit ended, almost a quarter of his face had regenerated. Despite the pain, he gave Marie a lop-sided grin. "For future reference, next time let's *not* go out through the fire, okay?"

Marie let out a sharp laugh, born more from nervous energy than genuine humour. "Alright, next time we can charge out of the front door if you want."

Michael turned his head to John. "Listen, I know things haven't been great between us today, but thanks for coming in there for me. I'd have been dead before much longer. What happened to Anya and Oskar? Did you..."

"I took care of it. Don't worry. Just hurry up and heal your arse up so we can get the fuck out of here and find some clothes. I'm freezing my bollocks off." John turned to Marie. "I don't suppose you've..."

He stopped mid-sentence and cocked his head to one side. Marie put her hand on his arm. "What?"

John waved her into silence, his brow furrowed in concentration. "Shit. Michael, can you walk?"

He shook his head. "No, I'm a fucking mess. It's going to be at least ten, maybe fifteen minutes before I'll heal enough to move. Why?"

John tilted his head to the east. "We've got company coming. Helicopters. Four of them, plus I can hear trucks on the road maybe half a mile out."

Marie grabbed her brother's arm in an attempt to pull his charred body into a standing position. Michael screamed as her hands sank into the oozing blisters and burned muscle. He pushed her away. "Marie, will you fuck off. I'm not going anywhere." He turned to John. "Mate, you two have got to get the fuck out of here. I'll play dead then get away when I've healed. You two need to go. Now."

Marie kicked snow onto her brother's face. "Didn't we go through this shit once already today? There's no way we're leaving you here to get caught by whoever-the-fuck that is. Now stop being a baby, grit your teeth, and get on your bloody feet."

She reached for him again, but Michael swatted her hand away. "Marie, I fucking can't. And if you stay here, they'll get you as well. Oskar's car should be close. You need to get out of here. I'll join you as soon as I'm able." He turned to John. "Get her out of here. Carry her if she won't go on her own."

"Michael, go fuck yourself. If you think..."

John stepped over to Marie's side. "He's right, Marie. Those choppers will be here in less than a minute. We'd not get a hundred yards carrying Michael. We need to go."

Marie looked from Michael to John, praying that one of them would relent, but their expressions were set in stone. She could hear the *whump* of the helicopters now, even with her own limited hearing. Four of them. Dual blades. Chinooks. Which meant they were military.

She slammed her hands against her thighs. "Fuck. Fucking bastard bunch of fucking cunts." The landing lights of the helicopters were visible now through the heavy, snow-laden clouds. Getting closer by the second. She looked down at her brother again.

"Will you go, for fuck's sake? There's no point in us all getting caught. Besides, who'll come and bust me out if you're locked up as well? Go. Now."

Marie bit back the tears as John took her arm. She glanced back at her brother, lying in the snow as his flesh reformed. Then she shook off John's hand and they both disappeared into the woods as the helicopters drew closer.

17th December. Underhill Military Base. 14:27.

Steven's eyes flickered open and he winced at the harsh fluorescent light above him. His body ached in ways he'd not thought possible. The wounds on his shoulder and chest burned with a searing pain that licked at the edges of his awareness, while the acid burns across his back itched. He tried to sit up, only to find his wrists and ankles restrained. He craned his neck, trying to focus through the thick fog clouding his mind.

He was strapped to a plain hospital bed with steel manacles. IV drips pumped a clear liquid into the veins of his right arm, while an array of expensive-looking machines sat beside the bed, monitoring his vital signs. A catheter ran down the inside of his thigh to a half-full bag of dark-brown piss suspended from the bed.

Other than that, the room was bare. Walls made of concrete

block-work, painted a glaring flat white, surrounded him. There were no windows in this room, only a large green reinforced door, which took up half a wall. Above the door, a state-of-the-art video camera whined as its lens refocused. A single green LED pulsed from behind the camera's dark eye.

Steven tried to reach out with his senses, but the drugs made it difficult for him to form a coherent thought. The scent of cheap floral disinfectant mingled with bleach overpowered his sense of smell, and no sounds reached him from the other side of the door. The room had been soundproofed to a very high standard.

"Hey, any chance of some breakfast? Or a pot to piss in?"

There was no response, but then, Steven hadn't been expecting one. Letting your prisoner be alone with their thoughts until their nerves started to get the better of them was standard interrogation procedure. Now that he was awake, they'd be along in their own time, and there wasn't a damn thing he could do about it.

He angled his head down and saw the criss-cross pattern of sutures on his chest. Connie Hamilton had really done a job on him. He marvelled that they'd managed to find enough to sew together. He'd heal himself, of course, eventually. Assuming that his captors didn't cut him apart and put him under a microscope before then.

There it was. The first sliver of doubt creeping unbidden into his mind. He chided himself for allowing the circumstances to dictate his emotions. If they wanted him dead, then they wouldn't have bothered sewing him up. Which meant they wanted something else.

He settled back down on the bed and closed his eyes. The effect of the drugs was not unpleasant, and if he was going to have to wait a while, he might as well enjoy the trip.

He could have been lying there for five minutes or five hours when the door to the cell opened. Time had lost all meaning within the comfortable warm haze of the opiates. He didn't bother to open his eyes. Two men had entered the room. One of them smelled of harsh soap and gun oil. He didn't need an enhanced sense of smell to pick out the other man. The stink of his expensive aftershave burned Steven's nostrils, almost obscuring the distinctive smell of his Italian leather shoes.

"Mr Wilkinson? Are you awake?"

Steven didn't open his eyes. "Yes. Did you bring my breakfast? I like my coffee black and my bacon well-done."

"Erm...I'm afraid I...could we get Mr Wilkinson some breakfast? Well, you heard the man. Black coffee and bacon."

"Well-done bacon. I don't like the fat unless it's crispy."

"Yes, erm...well-done. Now, how are you feeling, Steven? Can I call you Steven?"

Steven opened his eyes and stared at the man. He wore an expensive, tailor-made suit with a blue tie. His face seemed too smooth, like a wax figurine that had just begun to melt. Nervous, greedy eyes flickered across Steven's face, never once meeting his gaze. A few droplets of sweat broke out on the man's forehead. Steven gave the man his best, insincere smile. "I'm about as well as can be expected for a man tied to a hospital bed, being pumped full of drugs. How about you? Having a nice day?"

The man seemed to relax a little. "Yes, Steven, I'm having a very nice day. Tell me, do you know who I am?"

"Of course. I've seen your shiny fucking forehead plastered over every bus and billboard for months. What I'm not entirely sure about, though, is what the leader of the opposition is doing here, making idle chit-chat."

The man's face broke into a grin. "Well, I was hoping that we could have a little talk. I'd like you to tell me everything you know about werewolves."

18th December. Ashton Court Estate, Bristol. 14:27.

Daniel adjusted his binoculars, bringing the tree into sharp focus. He smiled and removed a battered notebook from his pocket, hastily making some notes before bringing the binoculars up once more. The waxwing flew from the tree, landing on a hawthorn bush to feast on its red berries. There had been flocks of waxwings during the autumn when he was a boy in Germany. He'd loved to watch the birds, trying to count the numbers in a flock as they swirled in the sky outside his bedroom window.

He didn't often think of his human life. How he'd been before the night he'd become infected by a rampaging moonstruck, two weeks after his sixteenth birthday. Yet over the past few days he found himself thinking back to that other Daniel Braun. The sickly, nervous, but intelligent child. What would he have become if he'd not been turned? What kind of a life might he have lived?

A light cough came from behind him, and a woman's voice said, "I hope I'm not interrupting anything?"

"No, it's just a pleasant way to pass some time in beautiful surroundings. Plus it looks less suspicious than a man sitting alone in some woodlands. Especially now. How are you, Marie? I admit, I was surprised to get your call."

He turned to face her. She was dressed in a Lycra crop-top and baggy tracksuit bottoms. Tendrils of steam rose from her body in the freezing December air, and she wiped sweat from her forehead. "Thank you for coming, Daniel. And for what it's worth, I'm sorry about Gregorz. He was like a father to me as well."

"Gregorz talked too much. If he'd just torn Connie's throat out as soon as we found her, or let me do it, then he'd still be alive."

Marie took his hand. "He did what he thought was right. He had a good heart. That was why we loved him."

Daniel nodded through the thinning woods, towards the sprawling city beyond. "It's getting bad out there. I was hoping that Connie's message might have been passed off as a hoax, but no such luck. The media are in a frenzy and the public are demanding action. Did you hear that they'd installed infra-red scanners at the airports and docks already?"

"I know. Fuck knows how they knew to do that. Why haven't you gotten out of the country? I was surprised to find you still here."

"And go where? It's the same all over the planet, sheep panicking because they've found a wolf in their midst. The Pack is in disarray. Krystof and Lukas are making a play for power, but the non-moonborn are still loyal to Michael. All the while, the Russian authorities are raiding Mafia properties armed with flamethrowers and silver bullets, looking for werewolves. It's all falling apart, Marie. Connie fucked us."

"Listen, I came to you because I need your help. They've got Michael. He's under guard, but I know where they're keeping him."

Daniel raised an eyebrow. "And what, you and I are going to charge in there, guns blazing, and get him back?"

"Not just you and I."

Daniel let out a bitter laugh. "Oh yes, I forgot about Simpson. Where is your little moonstruck friend?"

"Keeping his head down. He's still pretty messed up from the fight, and then there's the whole 'world's most wanted' thing. He'll be ready when we need him."

"Marie, you have lost your mind. I'm sorry about Michael, but there is no way you can get to your brother, even with me and the moonstruck. Get out of the country while you still can and take Simpson with you."

Marie shook her head. Her mouth curled into a smile and, for a moment, her eyes flashed green. "Oh, ye of little faith. Trust me, I have a plan."

TO BE CONCLUDED

ABOUT THE AUTHOR

Graeme Reynolds has been called many things over the years, many of which are unprintable. He breaks computers for a living by day, but at night he hunches over a laptop and dreams up new ways to upset people with delicate sensibilities. Graeme is the author of the best-selling High Moor series and owner of Horrific Tales Publishing.

Graeme lives somewhere in South West England with his wife, step-children, two cats and a giant German Shepherd that thinks he's still a lap-dog.

ALSO FROM HORRIFIC TALES PUBLISHING

High Moor by Graeme Reynolds

High Moor 2: Moonstruck by Graeme Reynolds

High Moor 3: Blood Moon by Graeme Reynolds

Of A Feather by Ken Goldman

Angel Manor by Chantal Noordeloos

Doll Manor by Chantal Noordeloos

Bottled Abyss by Benjamin Kane Ethridge

Wasteland Gods by Jonathan Woodrow

Dead Shift by John Llewellyn Probert

The Grieving Stones by Gary McMahon

The Rot by Paul Kane

Deadside Revolution by Terry Grimwood

High Cross by Paul Melhuish

Rage of Cthulhu by Gary Fry

The House of Frozen Screams by Thana Niveau

The Cold by Rich Hawkins

Scavenger Summer by Steven Savile

And Cannot Come Again by Simon Bestwick

A Song for the End by Kit Power

Wild Hunters by Stuart R Brogan

When the Cicadas Stop Singing by Zachary Ashford

http://www.horrifictales.co.uk

www.ingramcontent.com/pod-product-compliance
Lightning Source LLC
Chambersburg PA
CBHW030339310726
48979CB00001B/105

* 9 7 8 1 9 1 0 2 8 3 3 5 6 *